LORD JAMES HARRINGTON AND THE SOLSTICE MYSTERY

James and Beth happen upon an accident where the driver, Bernard Potter, is seriously injured. While receiving first aid, Potter mumbles concerns about his daughter which James takes as the ramblings of a dying man. But when visiting Mrs Potter, they realise that Bernard, a police constable, was secretly investigating the goings-on at a local commune where his daughter lived. Meanwhile, James's cousin Herbie is helping Scotland Yard with an art fraud ring — and when a villager is approached to be a part of the enterprise, James is drawn into both investigations.

LYNN FLORKIEWICZ

◆

LORD JAMES HARRINGTON AND THE SOLSTICE MYSTERY

Complete and Unabridged

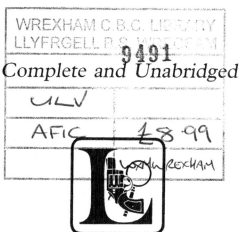

LINFORD
Leicester

First published in Great Britain

First Linford Edition
published 2020

A catalogue record for this book is available
from the British Library.

ISBN 978–1–4448–4444–3

Published by
Ulverscroft Limited
Anstey, Leicestershire

Set by Words & Graphics Ltd.
Anstey, Leicestershire
Printed and bound in Great Britain by
T. J. International Ltd., Padstow, Cornwall

This book is printed on acid-free paper

1

'Do you ever wonder about how insignificant we all are?' James said as he steered the Austin Healey through the country lanes.

He and his Boston-born wife, Beth, had spent a pleasant couple of hours hiking along the South Downs. It had been the perfect summer's day and they'd parked the car at Ditchling Beacon, a position that afforded, to the south, views across the English Channel and, in the opposite direction, the North Downs. The wide valley between the two formed an area called the Weald and went on as far as the eye could see.

They'd walked among grazing sheep, watched skylarks flutter from their nests, heard horses neighing in the distance, waved to farmers, chatted with fellow walkers and completed four miles of rambling, interrupted by a pause for a flask of tea and a sandwich. James was pleased to be getting out and about. This last month, he'd become used to smaller portions and had reluctantly declined some refreshments that inevitably came his way. As a result, he'd shed the excess pounds and vowed to stay in shape from now on.

Before journeying home, they'd popped into Lewes Police Station to sign prepared statements relating to Theodore and Maximillian Livingstone, a father and son who had tormented many an individual with their criminal activities over the previous few months.

Beth nudged her sunglasses up the bridge of her nose and echoed his question. 'How insignificant we all are? That's an interesting statement.' She shielded her eyes from the sun flickering through the trees.

'It's just that when you get out into nature and all that sort of thing, you realise how small you are. I mean, when we gazed across the Weald, you could see twenty miles in the distance and it looked absolutely vast. But, when you see it on a map, it's tiny.' He slowed down to take a sharp bend. 'If we ever get a man into space, can you imagine how small the earth would appear to him? The universe is beyond comprehension and we're smaller than the tiniest mote of dust.' He straightened the wheel and put his foot down. 'Makes you think, doesn't it?'

'Putting it like that, yes, it does. And when you think of those awful Livingstone men and how horrible they were to people, well, then you begin to think, why can't we all be civil and respectful to one another? We're on this earth for such a short time.'

'Exactly.' He reached across and held her hand. 'Sorry, darling, this is a little philosophical for a pleasant drive home.'

'But thought-provoking too. Sometimes it's good to step back and look at things like that. God knows those Livingstone men could have done with a lesson in humility.'

He turned the radio on where Buddy Holly was singing his latest hit, 'It Doesn't Matter Anymore'. They listened, neither feeling the need to speak. Beth closed her eyes and rested her head back.

3

After a couple of minutes, she said, 'Now that all this business with the Livingstone has been sorted, we can get back to normal. It's coming up to a busy time for Cavendish with the midsummer celebrations. Has Dorothy started organising? We've been so engrossed in other things, I didn't even think about it. And that steam rally was a much larger function than I thought it would be.'

The previous month, James and Beth had loaned out a couple of fields at Harrington's, their country hotel, for a week-long steam rally. The Sussex Steam Guild normally held it further east on the Sussex/Kent border but because their usual field was waterlogged, James had come to the rescue. It had proved to be an enjoyable and successful event and a few of the residents had suggested replicating it but on a smaller scale, perhaps over a weekend. It was something else to add to the already-packed village agenda.

Dorothy Forbes, self-appointed director of the Cavendish Players, was the main organiser of events and, although somewhat pompous at times, they had to admit that she was the best person for planning and delegation.

James turned left where a wooden signpost stated that Cavendish was four miles away. 'She's arranged a meeting tonight at the Half Moon and rehearsals are under way for the next Cavendish Players production. We missed the first two.'

He grinned as Beth clapped her hands together. 'Oh, I'm so looking forward to this one. An old-time music hall event. We'll have to make sure we do a performance at the old folks' home.'

'Mmm, perhaps we should ask Mr Irwin. He'd enjoy that, I'm sure.'

'Fluff' Irwin, a World War One casualty, was a permanent resident in a nursing home on the south coast. They'd met him over the previous Christmas after an unpleasant death had occurred at Harrington's. Irwin had suffered with severe shell-shock and now had the mental capacity of an eight-year old. His was a sad story but, James had commented at the time, how fascinating it was to see the way he reacted to the world, as if everything was exciting and new.

'It's a shame he wasn't able to go his way in the world but how lovely to have that childlike wonder and enthusiasm.'

'It'll be good to see him again,' she replied. 'I have a real soft spot for him.'

James went down the gears to take a sharp bend, then slammed his foot on the brake. The Austin skidded to an abrupt halt.

'Oh, my,' Beth said with a hand to her mouth.

They leapt from the car.

Ahead of them, the front end of a beige Austin A40 was scrunched against a tree. The radiator dripped water and the bulbous bonnet was squashed to half its length. James ran over to the driver's side and yanked the handle. It had jammed and it took some effort to release it. As the door creaked open, James swallowed back his horror. The driver had clearly hit the windscreen. A gash had opened up on his forehead but it was the man's right leg that worried him. Blood had soaked through the driver's trousers and his ankle was set at an alarming angle.

'I'll get our first aid kit,' Beth said, running to their car. She returned seconds later.

'Darling, how far is the nearest telephone box?' James asked.

Beth took James' keys from him. 'There's one just up the road. I'll drive up and call an ambulance.'

James turned his attention to the driver, a man in his early fifties, slightly greying at the temples. His breathing was shallow and his complexion pallid. He detected the distinct metallic smell of blood. James didn't like the look of him at all.

He squatted down. 'My name's James. James Harrington. What's yours?'

'Potter,' the man replied wearily. 'Bernard Potter.'

'Right, Bernard Potter, I'm going to ruin your trousers, I'm afraid, but I need to see that wound and patch it up. My wife's gone to call for an ambulance. We'll have you out of here in no time and off to hospital.'

Potter groaned and winced. 'My leg

. . . I think it's broken.'

James retrieved some scissors from the first aid kit and cut along the length of the trouser leg. Peeling the material back, he did his best to hide his shock.

'Is it bad?' Potter asked, his eyelids drooping.

'Nothing we can't sort out,' James said cheerily as he discarded his jacket and tore the sleeve off his shirt. He twisted it into a tourniquet and positioned it just above Potter's knee. When he pulled it tightly, Potter yelled in pain. Keen to keep the man talking, James studied the first aid box for items that might be of use while convincing himself this was simply a scratch, not the bleeding wound he was staring at. The man had lost a lot of blood and he wondered how long he'd remain conscious.

'Are you married, Bernard?' He grabbed a bottle of antiseptic and proceeded to clean the wound to get a better idea of what he was dealing with.

The man bobbed his head and flinched.

'And what's the lady's name?' Blood

continued welling up at an alarming rate. He pulled the tourniquet tighter.

Another cry of anguish. 'Dora.'

'Dora, eh. Married long?' He rummaged around the kit for a bandage and, using his teeth, tore open the wrapping.

'Thirty years.'

'How lovely. Any children?'

He started as the man gripped his arm. 'Wendy . . . she shouldn't be there . . . it's too late. We've lost her.'

James studied him. The man was drifting in and out of consciousness. And that gash on his head wasn't good. He must be concussed. He hoped there wasn't any internal bleeding.

'Don't let her stay there,' the man murmured as he began to drowse.

Doing his best to remain calm, James returned to bandaging the leg as tightly as he could. 'And that's your daughter's name, is it, Wendy?'

'Wendy. You have to get her out.'

Beth pulled up in the car and rushed toward him. 'The ambulance is on its way. How is he?'

James attached a safety pin to the

bandage to secure it. He'd stemmed the flow of blood slightly but already he could see spotting on the bandage. He got up, rubbed his chin, then wiped his bloodied hands down his shirt.

He whispered to her. 'Could you check the other side of the car? I think he thinks his daughter's with him.'

Beth did so and, looking through the passenger side, she shrugged. Potter's head dipped.

James sat on the door frame and gently slapped Potter's cheek. 'Bernard, come on, stay awake for me. You're going to be fine but I need you to speak to me, all right?'

Potter gave a weary nod.

'Everything is fine, Wendy's not in the car with you, you have no need to worry about her.'

A shake of the head. 'You don't ... under ... stand. It's not what you think it is. It's not what you think it is.'

Over the next few minutes they did their best to make him comfortable but struggled to keep him conscious. They heard the shrilling of the ambulance bell and James couldn't be more pleased to see the vehicle pull up. 'Ambulance is here, Bernard, they'll get you to hospital and you'll see Wendy and Dora very soon.'

Two ambulance men sprinted to the car. While one assessed Potter, the other asked James for an update.

'He's drifting in and out. I'm not sure if that's blood loss or the knock on the head.'

Beth asked if the man would be all right. The ambulance man said it was too soon to say, but he thanked them for their help and asked if he could have their details.

'Of course,' said James, picking up his jacket and bringing out a card. 'By the way, his name's Bernard Potter. His wife is Dora and he has a daughter, Wendy.

'Thanks, we'll take over now.'

'Please,' said Beth, 'let us know where you take him, we'd like to visit.'

'I will.' The man's colleague called out for him. 'I'd best get on.'

At their own car, James opened the boot and brought out a bottle of water which he promptly poured over his hands. He shrugged his jacket back on. 'I don't think he's out of the woods. That injury to his leg was serious and he'd lost a lot of blood.'

He checked the section of road along which Bernard had driven. The tyres had left a swirling set of black skid marks as the car headed toward the tree. 'He must have been going at some speed, Beth.'

'There are a lot of sharp bends in this road. Perhaps he lost control.'

James decided to change from his jacket and shredded shirt. He threw them in the boot and slipped on a jumper he'd put there in case it turned cold. He reached into the picnic basket and brought out a small hip flask but found his hand shaking as he took a swig.

Beth rested a hand on his arm. 'I'll drive. You're suffering from shock. Are you still all right to pop in to see Stephen and Anne?'

Their local vicar and his wife, Stephen and Anne Merryweather, had asked them to call in after their walk and they'd happily agreed to.

'Yes, it'll be nice to sit with them and calm down a bit.'

Settled in the passenger seat. Beth was about to pull away when the ambulance man they'd spoken to, still in attendance by Potter's car, held a hand up. He came over and ducked to peer into their vehicle.

'I'm sorry,' he said, 'Mr Potter's died.'

'Oh dear.'

James leant across. 'I did wonder whether he'd make it or not. He seemed to have lost a lot of blood. Someone will need to get in touch with his wife and daughter. I suppose you have all of that in hand.'

'We'll sort that out.' He held up a wallet. 'We've got his driving licence here and a warrant card. He's a policeman.' He read the name on the card. 'PC Bernard John Potter, stationed at Hayward Heath. I'll get on to them.' He went to go then turned. 'By the way, thanks for what you did. If you'd have stumbled across him earlier, you might well have been able to save him.'

As they drove away James saw Potter's

body being manoeuvred out of the car. His heart went out to the man's family. He didn't envy the person who had to break the news.

2

The vicarage in Cavendish stood alongside the old Saxon church of St Nicholas. It was a beautiful cottage that overlooked the village green. The Merryweathers were a couple in their early thirties with two boys, Mark and Luke, who were eleven and nine respectively. Their arrival in Cavendish had been a welcome one as the previous vicar had become, in the opinion of many villagers, old and cantankerous. Before they came, attendance at church had slowly diminished and James had wondered whether the parishioners would ever return.

Stephen, a tall, angular man, had come in with fresh ideas and, more importantly, a sense of fun. At his very first service, he'd spoken to a full house. It seemed as if the whole village had jostled for position in the pews because firstly, everyone wanted to scrutinise the new vicar and secondly, an unusual death had taken place and villagers wondered whether their new vicar would mention it. Stephen had certainly taken the congregation by surprise. His humour, anecdotes and the way he delivered a sermon ensured that subsequent Sunday gatherings were as popular as the first.

Anne Merryweather, a homely lady with a ready smile, opened the front door and wiped her hands on her apron. The smell of baking drifted out to meet them. Before she could welcome them properly, Radley, their springer spaniel, raced into the hall and went to leap up. She grabbed his collar in the nick of time and, after a bit of fuss from James and Beth, led him into the kitchen. On returning, her welcome changed to a frown.

'What happened? Are you hurt?'

James looked in the hall mirror and noticed a smear of blood on his chin. 'Not me, no. We happened upon an accident on the back road toward Loxfield and lent a hand. Do you mind if I use your bathroom to clean up?'

'Go on up, you know where it is. Use

the flannel and towel by the sink.' She untied her apron. 'I'll get the tea on.'

A few minutes later, they were ensconced in the front room, relaying the details of the accident.

Stephen, in light flannels and open-necked shirt, suggested they hold Mr Potter in their thoughts. 'I'll be sure t-to pray for him. And his family,' he said with his endearing stammer.

Anne, who had opened the windows wide to let some air in, lifted the lid on the Brown Betty teapot and stirred the contents. 'Hot, sweet tea. That's what you're supposed to have for shock, isn't it?'

Beth let out a tut. 'Not if you're James. A swig from the hip flask is his settler.'

James accepted the cup from Anne. 'Our flask of tea was empty.' He gave Beth a 'so there' nod.

'Y-you say this man was a p-policeman?'

'Mmm. PC Bernard Potter of the Sussex Constabulary. Stationed in Haywards Heath, apparently.'

'Would George know him?' asked

Anne, handing round a plate of chocolate bourbon biscuits.

Detective Chief Inspector George Lane was one of James' oldest friends and the pair of them had investigated a number of mysteries together. As much as George was frustrated by James' interfering, he had to admit that James had been a tremendous help on many of those cases. So much so that the Sussex force had recently awarded him a commendation.

'I'll have to ask him,' James said taking a biscuit. 'I don't see a reason why he should do but I'll give him a call. If he does know him, he'll want to hear the news.'

'His poor wife and daughter,' Anne said.

James sipped his tea. The shock of dealing with the accident had subsided and he was beginning to think more clearly. 'Odd about the daughter, though. Wendy, he said her name was. Kept insisting that it was too late, that he'd lost her and that she wasn't to stay there.'

Stephen admitted that sounded

18

strange. 'Perhaps she left h-home or something.'

'Perhaps. He did say something peculiar: 'It's not what you think it is.''

'Don't forget that he was in and out of consciousness,' said Beth. 'He could have simply been rambling, talking nonsense.'

James agreed. 'He'd certainly had a bash to the head. He must have hit that windscreen with some force. I'm surprised he didn't go flying through it.'

Stephen topped their cups up. 'Well, it c-certainly puts my worries into context.'

'Oh?' said James. 'What are you worried about?'

His friend reached across to the sideboard and picked up a leaflet. He handed it to James who read the details aloud:

''Celestial Faith Commune

Connect with the Universe

Speak with the Galaxy

Ground yourself with Mother Earth

The sun nourishes you; the earth feeds you

Worship them, they are your power, your celestial soul.'' He stared at

Stephen. 'What on earth is all that about?'

'Look here,' said Beth. ' "Contact Father Sun at The Celestial Abbey." There's a telephone number.'

James was almost lost for words. 'The Celestial A — '

Anne burst out laughing. 'Your face is a picture.'

'Anne, th-this is no laughing m-matter.'

'Oh, Stephen, it's just a fad. You know these things pop up every now and again. In a few months' time, it'll shut down.'

'But two of my c-congregation have gone there.'

James perched on the edge of the sofa. 'But what is it, exactly? I mean, have you spoken to this . . . ' he checked the leaflet, 'Father Sun chap?'

'Not yet, no.'

'But you're saying it's some sort of religion.'

Stephen tugged at his cuffs. 'It is m-most certainly *not* a religion.'

'Well, if two of your congregation have swapped allegiance, what exactly is it?'

His friend got up and paced the floor.

'From what I understand, they worship the sun and the moon and all that s-sort of thing. They get up to w-welcome the sunrise and send prayers up to the stars. It all sounds complete nonsense.'

James encouraged him to sit back down. 'But you clearly don't think it's nonsense, otherwise you wouldn't be getting in such a stew about it. Do you consider them threatening?'

'Not in a physical sense, no, but they're handing these leaflets out left, right and centre and enticing people to ch-change their beliefs. They prey on the v-vulnerable, James. The two who have left me are women who are easily led.'

'This sounds a little like the Druids, don't you think? Don't they worship Mother Earth and the seasons and all that nature business?'

Beth said they did. 'I remember speaking with Professor Wilkins about it, just recently actually. Weren't they here before Christianity? And I don't think it's a religion.' They waited for her to continue. 'I think they just celebrate the cycles of nature and, of course, the summer and winter solstice. I don't think there's anything harmful about them.'

'The solstice thing is well-known,' James continued. 'The Druids gather down at Stonehenge to welcome in the summer solstice, don't they?'

The ancient stone-circle of Stonehenge had been a gathering place for the Druids for centuries and it was believed the circle itself had been built to line up with the rising and setting of the sun, stars and constellations.

'But,' said Anne, 'I don't think the Druids worship specific stars and planets, do they?'

James said that he didn't think so but that he wasn't a great authority on the matter.

'Stephen heard that the crowd at the commune don't go by their real names. Father Sun and Mother Moon are the leaders and we've heard there's Sister Jupiter and Brother Neptune.'

'Oh, for heaven's sake,' James mumbled. 'Are you serious?'

'She i-is, James. That's why I'm w-worried.'

'What about Native American beliefs?' said Beth.

Again, they all turned to her.

'I don't profess to know much about them but I remember, when I was at school in Boston, we had a history teacher who told us about their belief system. Many of the tribes there believe they come from the stars and worship the galaxy as well as the earth.'

This didn't appease Stephen one iota. 'But that's a different c-culture, a different history. We're not from that culture. We're in the middle of the Sussex countryside, not the Badlands.'

'Stephen,' said James, 'I think you're getting unnecessarily worked up about this. You wouldn't be cursing someone if they decided to convert to Hinduism, would you? I mean, I know you wouldn't be overly happy but . . . we hear about people marrying into other faiths and having to take up that faith, like Catholicism, Judaism, that sort of thing.'

'They are still following the path of God.'

James sat back and wondered if he was

being too blasé about the whole thing. If people wanted to go off and worship Neptune, it didn't bother him, providing they weren't harming anyone else. 'I respect your anger, my friend, but I'm presuming the people who are joining the commune have gone of their own free will. No one has kidnapped them.'

Stephen conceded that nothing underhand had gone on. 'I'm c-concerned that they are preying on the vulnerable. And,' he added, 'they are insisting on m-membership fees.'

'Well, now you're making it sound more like a club than a religion.'

Stephen let out a frustrated moan. 'Oh, I don't know what it is.'

Anne comforted her husband and suggested that perhaps it was more of a get-together of like-minded people rather than any particular faith.

'Look,' said James, 'why don't we all toddle off down there tomorrow and take a look around? The fact that you haven't even spoken to this Father Sun chap means you're feeding your imagination with all sorts of notions. I'm sure a chat and a scout about will settle you down. Where is this Celestial Abbey anyway?'

Anne explained it was the old farm on the road to Loxfield. 'I think it was called Burdock Farm.'

'Good grief, I thought the place had fallen down. No one's lived there for years.'

'We heard that someone purchased it and they'd done the place up. That must be these people.'

The slam of the front door made them all jump. Luke and Mark burst into the room with their school satchels dragging behind them. Their shirt tails hung out, their shoes were muddy and their socks had fallen to their ankles. Fresh-faced with freckles and button noses, they were wide-eyed with excitement.

Mark, his hands smeared with mud, declared that he and Luke had found a frog.

Luke held the poor thing up. 'Look, it's huge.'

Beth instinctively drew back and pulled a face.

Anne leapt up. 'Really, boys. I'm sure

Uncle James and Auntie Beth don't need to have a frog paraded in front of them. And look at the state of you? You were lovely and tidy when you went to school this morning and you're traipsing mud through the house. Where have you been?'

'We went past the pond,' said Mark oblivious to the telling-off. 'The tadpoles have grown and there's loads going on.'

'I — I think you'd best return the frog,' said Stephen.

'But I wanted to take it to school,' said Luke.

'And I want you to return the poor thing to its home. I'm sure its family w-will be missing him.'

With some reluctance, Luke said that he would. The boys dumped their satchels in the middle of the floor.

'Before y-you go back out, grab Radley and t-take him with you.'

The boys raced out. They heard Radley's excited barking and footsteps running down the hall before the front door slammed shut. Peace was restored.

Anne gathered the satchels and flopped

down. 'Honestly, it's like a whirlwind the moment they open the door.'

James chuckled and confirmed that their boys were exactly the same at that age. 'Are you coming to the Half Moon tonight? You know Dorothy is gathering us to sort out the forthcoming events.'

Both said they were coming.

It suddenly dawned on James that a particular celebration was taking place. 'You know, Stephen, Jonty's birthday parade is all about worshipping the sun. D'you think he was a Druid?'

Jonty's parade had begun back in the 1930s when a rather bohemian visitor by the name of Jonty Reece had wanted to celebrate his birthday which fell on the 14 June. He had, at the time, lamented the fact that it was not the 21 June, the summer solstice. On his birthday, Jonty had dressed in a long velvet gown and a floppy black hat and, during the evening, he had danced and sung mesmeric songs in what was thought to be a Celtic language. Those songs, he'd said, were to do with the summer solstice, something he appeared obsessed with. His personality and character had woven its way into everyone's hearts and the villagers all thought that he would remain there permanently. But then, one day, he packed his things and left. He never returned, having been in the village for less than three months.

The villagers at the time were both intrigued and enthralled by Jonty and, although he'd only been in Cavendish a short time, everyone was sad to see him go. The following year, on Jonty's birthday, one resident had suggested they celebrate the fact that this peculiar man had come into their lives. And from that suggestion, Jonty's Birthday Parade was born.

James grinned. 'I wonder if Father Sun would be interested in joining us?'

Stephen gave him an old-fashioned look. It was clear this commune was going to be an annoyance for him. It would be interesting to hear what some of the other residents had to say about the Celestial Faith Commune. He made a mental note to bring the subject up later at the pub.

3

'Emergency. Which service do you require?'

Mrs Millerson, a plump lady in her late seventies, gripped the telephone receiver with both hands. 'Oh, yes, yes, my dear, I think I've been burgled.'

'I'll put you through to the police. Hold the line.'

A few clicks and she heard the voice of a young man. 'Lewes Police.'

'Ah, yes, young man, something is missing in my hall.'

'Can I take your name please?'

'Yes, dear, it's Mrs Millerson. I'm calling from a phone box in Charnley.'

'I see, Madam, and you think something is missing.'

'Yes.'

'When you say missing, Mrs Millerson, do you mean mislaid or stolen?'

'Well, stolen of course. I wouldn't dream of telephoning you if I'd simply mislaid it. I may be old but I'm not a ditherer. The trouble is, I don't know *when* it went missing. I get so used to it being there, I rarely take much notice.'

She received an apology down the line with the explanation that she would be surprised at the reasons people gave for calling the police.

'I'm sure you're correct,' she said, 'but I am not one of those people. Now, come along, are you going to send someone round to me?'

'I'll be delighted to, Mrs Millerson. Could I ask what it is that's gone missing?'

'A sketch of the Eiffel Tower.' She caught the hint of frustration. 'Before you admonish me, constable, the sketch is a rare commondity; a rough drawing by Cézanne. My father knew him for a short time and he kindly gave this to him as a gift.'

'Sorry, Mrs Millerson, I'm not that well up on the arts. Could you spell that for me please?'

After doing so, she gave her address and told the constable that it would take her about half an hour to return home. The constable went through the details again and assured her that someone would be with her shortly.

She thanked the young man and made her way through Charnley, her heart heavy at the loss of a piece of such sentimental significance.

4

James couldn't hear himself think. The summer evening was a balmy one and it appeared that the world and his wife had descended on the village green and, in particular, the bar at the Half Moon. But he loved the hustle and bustle of the old inn which had been an ale house since the late 1600s and, although it had gone through several transformations, the sense of its history was still evident.

The ancient oak beams, part of the structure of the building, had sepia photographs of farmers and plough boys from earlier times pinned to them. A large image of the Pals regiment from the Great War took pride of place over the inglenook fireplace and horse brasses were placed wherever space allowed. Behind the bar on a high shelf above the optics were numerous Toby jugs and pewter tankards. The ever-present smell of hops and tobacco hung in the air.

Beth made her way to the far corner where Dorothy Forbes had taken up residence. James leant on the dented, polished bar and surveyed the ales on tap.

The landlord, Donovan Delaney, a Dubliner who had settled in the village several years ago, was heaving a barrel into place. His sleeves were rolled up and after connecting the keg he swept an arm across his forehead and let out a satisfied sigh. His wife, Kate, a petite woman who hailed from Brighton, entered with a tray of clean glasses.

She caught his eye. 'I didn't see you come in. Are you being served?'

'Not yet, you finish what you're doing.'

'Ah, yer man, James,' Donovan said in a soft Irish lilt. 'I've a barrel of Solstice Gold delivered. It's a new beer from Harveys; will you be wanting some?'

The label advertising the ale showed a golden sun about to dissolve into a dark blue sea.

'I'm always keen to try whatever's new. I'll have a half. Beth want a gin and tonic.'

'I'll do them,' said Kate. 'I'll bring

them over, you can settle up later. Looks like you've quite a crowd on your table.'

James manoeuvred his way through the crowd, greeting people and exchanging pleasantries as he did so. In the corner booth, which had a view of the green, were Stephen and Anne with Radley sprawled across them, Dorothy Forbes, George Lane and his childhood friend, Bert Briggs. They shuffled around to make room.

He sat back as Kate delivered the drinks. 'Shame we couldn't get one of the benches outside. It's sweltering in here.'

'We shouldn't be too long,' said Dorothy.

Dorothy had her clipboard close to hand. He couldn't say anything but she had overdone the Tweed perfume and the aroma stuck in his throat. He could almost taste it. She was a spritely woman who had dreamed of becoming an actress but, unfortunately, that path had not been successful for her. She'd spent some time with a costumier in the West End of London and helped dress some of the notable thespians of the time but then decided that life wasn't for her.

Instead, she chose to settle down and get involved in amateur dramatics. She'd been in charge of the Players now for several years and her organisational skills were second to none. So much so that she now helped with the other events in the village. James didn't know what they'd do without her. Although things were eventually completed, it was Dorothy who ensured tasks were carried out in a timely manner.

'And what are we discussing tonight?' asked James, sipping his beer and feeling that he'd lost track of events since the Livingstone business.

'At the moment, two things. We have ongoing rehearsals for the Music Hall. We're staging it for three nights from the 18th of June. It won't take too much organising because there's no actual stage direction or lines to learn as such. I mean it's not as if it's a play.'

Beth asked who would be compèring.

'Mr Bateson,' Dorothy replied and murmurs of approval went around the table.

'Splendid,' said James who always felt their solicitor was entertaining even when he wasn't supposed to be. 'He'll do an admirable job and I'll bet he has some wonderful songs to sing himself.'

'H-how many acts will there be?' asked Stephen, fondling Radley's ears.

'We have around a dozen who have put themselves forward at the moment.' Dorothy sipped her sherry. 'The thing is, I don't want it all to be songs. During our first rehearsal, that's all we had.'

James turned to Bert. 'This is your area, isn't it? Music hall. What sort of things do you normally get there?'

He'd known Bert since they were children and had met during a chance meeting at the Natural History Museum where their respective schools had arranged a trip. An unlikely friendship had arisen between the pair of them and James couldn't imagine life without the man being around. Although from the poorest of backgrounds, Bert was knowledgeable and well-read and, considering the advantages of James' private education, still managed to cause him embarrassment when discussing various topics. The man was a walking encyclopaedia.

'Yeah, it is, Jimmy boy,' said Bert, his flat cap pushed back. He turned to Dorothy. 'There was a lot of singing, a few monologues, some dancing, maybe a group of people acting something out. A lot of audience participation and a lot of saucy, close-to-the-mark songs. You can put me down for one of them.'

Everyone laughed, even Dorothy. She jotted his name down adding that he would be perfect for the evening.

James and Beth exchanged a surprised look. It wasn't often that Dorothy accepted advice or help from Bert, let alone praise him.

George lit his pipe. 'James, what about that song we used to mess about with? We always liked it. That was a music hall song.'

'You're talking about the cup of coffee song.'

'That's the one. How about we do that one together.'

'Mmm, put us down for that, Dorothy.

It's a bit of a tongue-twister. Bert, what're you going to do?'

'I've got something planned, a comedy monologue.' He asked Beth and Anne what they would be performing.

'Costumes,' they chorused and then laughed.

'You know that Anne and I don't do front of house,' said Beth. 'We'll stay in the background and make you look good.'

'Oi, Dorothy' said Bert, 'you need something for the end. It's as well to get a good act, someone who knows what they're doing.'

The group were noncommittal. They didn't really have a stand-out star and no names sprang to mind.

Dorothy broke the silence. 'We're having rehearsals so perhaps someone will show themselves to be the show-stopper. I'm fitting in a rehearsal of sorts on Monday evening. Can you make yourselves available?'

They said they would.

Anne suggested that Rose and Lilac Crumb might want to sing. James' own title for them was 'the Snoop Sisters'. He had taken a dislike to them when they'd moved to Cavendish because of their nosiness and love of idle gossip but his disdain had slowly turned to admiration.

They'd gone through quite a bit over the last couple of months and, after all that business with the Livingstones, had proved themselves to be brave and determined women. Now, as they became more involved in the community, residents were seeing a different side to them. They'd be a good addition to the music hall production. He'd heard them sing the previous summer at the folk festival and had been bowled over by their delicate harmonies.

He checked his watch. 'Anything else on the agenda?'

'J-Jonty's Parade,' said Stephen.

'Oh, I love this,' said Beth.

Anne agreed. 'It's an unusual thing to celebrate but such a unique one too.'

George simply harrumphed. 'You don't know when to stop with all of these events. Celebrating a man who lived here for a couple of months is ridiculous. And don't you have the Midsummer Ball at

Harrington's too?'

'Yes, we do,' said James, reminding Dorothy that he and Beth wouldn't be available for the last night of the music hall because of it. He turned his attention back to George. 'You'll have to do the song as a solo that night.'

The Midsummer Ball was a tradition at Harrington's country hotel and attracted a good many regular guests. It was a black-tie affair with a mouth-watering buffet, along with dancing until midnight. James always did his best to secure the services of a well-known band and he and Beth had discussed the menu options with their chef, Didier, well in advance. Indeed, they were due to get together the following day to finalise the menu.

George got up. 'Right, I'm off.'

James asked him to wait. He slid out of the bench seat and steered his friend outside. The sun was still warm and would keep the evening light for at least another two hours. On the green, some of the children had set up a spontaneous game of football with jumpers for goalposts. Luke and Mark were sitting cross-legged on the cobbles, reading their comics.

'I wanted to ask, George, did you hear about the fatality on the Loxfield road?'

'Nasty business. Potter only had about four years to go until retirement.'

'Did you know him?'

'He was stationed at Lewes for a while and then asked for a transfer to Haywards Heath. I think it was good for him being on the main line up to Clapham. That's where his parents used to live.'

'Are you calling in to visit his wife?'

'I am as a matter of fact. I didn't know him that well but well enough to pay my respects. I thought I'd pop down there tomorrow. Sounds like you did what you could, James. I heard good reports about your first aid skills.'

'Shame we didn't come across him sooner. I say, did he have a problem with his daughter, Wendy?'

His friend shrugged. 'I hadn't seen him in a while. Why d'you ask?'

'He seemed quite fraught about her. Be a sport and make sure she's all right, will you?'

'I will. See you at the rehearsals, if not before.' As he marched across the green, he turned. 'Get hold of Charlie and see if he's got a copy of that song in the library. I can remember the chorus but not all the verses.'

On returning to their table, he found that Dorothy had disappeared and the group were discussing the Celestial Faith Commune.

'It's all well and g-good you telling me n-not to fret,' Stephen said to Bert, 'but I have two of my congregation who have moved in with them.'

'It's a free world, vicar,' Bert replied. 'You can't save everyone. These things pop up all over the place. It don't mean anything, does it? I think it's quite nice to worship the earth. I mean, if it weren't for the earth and the sun and all of that, we wouldn't be 'ere would we?'

'You can't argue with that,' said Beth.

Anne linked an arm through Stephen's. 'You are getting in a tizz about this. Let the two members of your congregation find their own way. They may decide that the commune isn't for them and come back to the flock.'

'Like lost sheep,' James added as he sat next to Beth. 'And Bert's right. You can't force people to stay with you if they want to try something else. Just make sure you're there for those people who do need you.'

Appeased by the show of support, the Merry weathers decided it was too hot for Radley and that they really should take him for a walk. James settled his bill with Kate and he, Beth and Bert wandered out on to the green.

'Are you off to see the love of your life?' asked James.

Bert had recently announced his engagement to Gladys Smith and, as he flung his jacket over his shoulder, his delight was plain to see. 'I am, Jimmy-boy. The bus is due in ten minutes. Change at Crawley and get up to London in time for a nightcap.' He executed a mock bow to the pair of them. 'See you at re'earsals.'

'Give our love to Gladys,' Beth called out. She turned to James. 'Are we going home?'

'Give me ten minutes. Let's pop in to Charlie's. I want to see if I can track down our music hall song.'

5

Charlie Hawkins had lost his wife to illness several years before and had impressed James with the way he was raising his two children while holding down his position in the library. Fortunately, the library was next door in a converted cottage but, even so, the way he struggled through the grief caused by his loss was nothing short of admirable. During those first few months after her death, the whole village had come together to ensure the family were eating properly and many had taken it in turns to sit with his children or simply had them spend the day with their own families while Charlie worked.

James and Beth still had the children spend the odd afternoon with them, especially now they were at an interesting and enquiring age. Tommy was ten and Susan just a year younger although James felt she was the more mature of the two.

James was teaching Tommy how to fish and Beth and Anne were showing Susan dressmaking, knitting and cookery skills.

Charlie was an open, honest man whom everyone was proud to consider their neighbour and friend. His temperament was calm and patient. James didn't think he'd once seen the man lose his temper and, like Bert, he was well-read. He thought his job as a librarian was more of a hobby than a chore because he loved to read. If you raised any topic, he would know a little about the subject simply from the books he'd read.

Dressed in flannels and a short-sleeved shirt, he swung the door open. The smell of cooked beef reached them. 'James, Beth, lovely to see you. Is it me you've come to see or the library? I can open it up for you if you need something.'

James said that he was trying to track down a music hall song.

The young man gave a knowing nod. 'Ah, this is for the Cavendish Players' production. I've got a few books here that may suit. Come on through for a minute, Dulcie's here.'

Dulcie Faye, a young actress who had been touted as Britain's version of Doris Day, had moved to the village several months ago and become inadvertently mixed up with the Livingstones. Her acting ambitions had faded after a couple of films and she'd decided that once her current play in the West End had finished, she would retire. Show business, she said, was not for her and she yearned for normality, even if it meant returning to being a shop-girl at the Co-operative.

They followed Charlie into the back room which had a sofa and two mismatched armchairs. Tommy and Susan were in the garden with trowels.

'The kids are planting sunflower seeds,' said Charlie. 'I think they may be putting 'em in too late but they don't care.'

Dulcie came through from the kitchen. She beamed. 'Lord Harrington, Lady Harrington, how lovely.'

James couldn't help but be surprised. The lovely Dulcie, a stunning girl of around twenty, had an apron on. In one hand was a soapy dish and, in the other, a tea towel.

'I was just washing up after dinner. We don't have a rehearsal so I've had a relaxing day.'

Beth gave Charlie a mock look of reproach. 'And you have her cooking?'

Charlie grinned. 'I don't, actually, Dulcie volunteered. She did a really nice mince and vegetables.'

As everyone sat down, Dulcie perched on the arm of the sofa. 'It's a bit of a winter dish, I know, but it's an easy dinner to throw together.'

'When does your play begin?' asked Beth.

'August. It's a short run, only six weeks. I wish I hadn't agreed to it. Now I've put my mind to retiring, I just want to get on with it.'

'Are you sure that's what you want?' said James. 'You have an opportunity to become a big film star. A lot of women would jump at the chance.'

'Let them jump,' said Dulcie. 'It wasn't what I thought it would be. Oh, the glamour side of things is nice and, of course, the pay is beyond what I ever thought I'd earn but I just don't enjoy it.

And money isn't everything; well, not for me anyway. I've decided I'm a home bird. Going on location doesn't suit me at all.'

'I think that's a good enough reason. But what will you do?'

The look between Dulcie and Charlie was not lost on James. There was certainly a chemistry there. Was this really a blossoming romance? The pair of them got on remarkably well and Dulcie was wonderful with the children. He hoped it would turn into something good. Charlie deserved a woman in his life and Dulcie, although significantly younger, suited him well.

Dulcie stressed that she didn't have expensive tastes. The salary from her two films had been invested and the cottage that Theodore Livingstone had purchased in Cavendish, to her surprise, had been offered to her by his daughter, Felicity. Felicity had discovered how her father had manipulated the young actress and said she could stay in it, rent-free.

'It can't remain like that,' she continued. 'I mean, it's very kind of her to help me but she should either sell the property or let me pay rent.'

'She's selling the bigger house that Theodore Livingstone had just down the road,' said Charlie.

'Felicity's an intelligent woman,' said James. 'She runs a business and appears to be shrewd and intelligent. She won't beat around the bush about the cottage when she's ready to do something with it. At the moment, I believe she feels dreadful about the way her father treated you and this is her way of saying sorry.'

Dulcie had accepted the decision. 'Anyway, that's not your worry. Do you want tea?'

Beth answered. 'We were just going home. James wanted to see what you had in the library for the music hall songs.'

'I've got some books here,' Charlie said, leaping up from his chair.

The room appeared to be an extension of the library, with floor to ceiling shelves full of paperbacks and reference books. They spilled out onto the surfaces of tables and chair arms. He slipped a large hardback book out.

'Here you are: one hundred popular music hall songs.' He handed it to James.

'Did you know,' said Dulcie, 'that I'm going to start giving acting and make-up lessons to the Cavendish Players?'

Beth exclaimed, 'How wonderful! You can count me and Anne in. One of the reasons we stay in the background is because the thought of getting on stage terrifies us. We mainly do the costumes and improvise with make-up. Having a professional teaching us would be marvellous.'

'I'm learning a considerable amount during these rehearsals so I'm going to pass on what I know. Hopefully, I can help you with the confidence thing too.'

'It's strange that you can be so confident on stage but felt so intimidated by meeting new people here in Cavendish.'

When they'd first met Dulcie, she had been terrified of meeting strangers and it had taken some persuasion to introduce her to the villagers.

'Most actors are shy. I'm normally fine when I'm acting because I'm not being me. When I have to be myself, I shrink into my shell.'

'Here it is,' James said slapping a page in the book. ''All I want is a proper cup of coffee made in a proper copper coffee pot.'' He closed the book. 'Do you mind if I borrow this and jot down the words?'

'Go ahead,' said Charlie.

They rose from their seats.

'I heard you came across a nasty accident earlier,' Charlie observed.

James winced. 'Yes, not a nice way to end what has been a pleasant day. Poor chap must have been there a while. Lost quite a bit of blood. Shame.' A leaflet on the sideboard caught his eye. He picked it up. 'Ah, the Celestial Faith Commune.' He turned to Charlie and Dulcie. 'Have you been over there?'

'Not me,' said Charlie pulling a face. 'Not my thing, all sounds a bit weird.'

Dulcie, who wore a pretty turquoise dress under her apron, tucked her hair behind her ears. 'I saw one of the commune people put it up on the notice board by the green. Stephen came haring out of the vicarage, yelling at the man.

They had a bit of an argument and then the man marched off laughing. Stephen ripped the poster down and threw it in the bin but it fell on the ground. He didn't notice because he was more or less back in the house. I wondered what on earth would make Stephen so annoyed. I don't know him that well yet but I've never seen him like that so I went over and picked this up. Do you know what it is?'

Beth did her best to explain. 'We thought it sounded a bit like the Druids with some native American beliefs thrown in. Stephen does seem to have let this get under his skin though.'

James put the book under his arm. 'Only because a couple of his parishioners have strayed over there. We're going to pop over with the Merryweathers tomorrow and see what all the fuss is about. Hopefully, that'll settle Stephen's mind a little.' He opened the front door. 'Lovely to see you.'

Beth thanked them both and skipped along the garden path to join James. 'Charlie and Dulcie would make a handsome couple, don't you think?'

'You are incorrigible, Lady Harrington. But, yes, I have to agree, they would make a delightful twosome. Let's go home and put our feet up.'

6

Father Sun's tall, lean frame seemed to float across his office floor. He wore an ankle-length, pale blue gown with an image of the blazing sun embroidered on it; the sun's flames lapped around the garment. His thick brown hair was combed back off his face but an unruly lock flopped over his forehead. He knew he bore a resemblance to Richard Todd and chose to take advantage of that by copying the way the film star looked and walked. He'd studied interviews with prominent men who exuded charm and, over the last decade, had honed his own personality to match. Anyone meeting him today would assume he hailed from a well-to-do background, not a poor suburb on the outskirts of industrial Birmingham.

He sat at his desk. It was a light, airy room with a few photographs on the wall, a couple of filing cabinets and a large walnut desk. He opened the top drawer and brought out some paperwork. There was a knock on the door. A woman entered.

He beamed. 'Ah, I thought you were out in the grounds.'

Mother Moon made her way across to him. She also wore a long pale blue gown but this one was embroidered with an ivory moon.

He pushed his seat back.

She gently sat on his thighs and wrapped an arm around his neck. 'Paperwork?'

His shoulders fell. 'I'm hopeless at bookkeeping. Isn't there one member here who can do figures?'

She pouted. 'No, darling.' She sighed. Her voice was quiet and educated. 'Isn't this the most perfect place?'

They kissed. He drew back and raked his fingers through her shoulder-length hair. He gazed into her piercing green eyes. 'It covers what we need it for. The members are happy and they have more space.' He manoeuvred her off his lap and went to the windows which opened out to a recently-mowed lawn. 'It's ideal. No shadows. No noise. No interruptions. We should make a sundial and place it in the centre, don't you think?'

She joined him and slipped her hand in the crook of his arm. 'I think this will be your most successful enterprise. The other building simply didn't have the privacy that this one affords. We've already enrolled a dozen more into the fold and they've all paid their fees.'

'That'll help with the bills we do have. The allotments are beginning to provide fruit and vegetables that we can sell locally. We could do with a few more of our members working those plots.'

'Already in hand. Brother Mars has mapped out more land for winter root vegetables and he brought in half a dozen chickens today.'

'That's good. Make sure they're secure though. We don't want the foxes getting in. We need to expand that enterprise. It'll be nice to have eggs but even better to have the odd roast chicken. Does Brother Mars have any way of getting some cattle?'

'He's working on it. It's nearly midday. Are you coming out for the noon sun-worship?'

'I'll be along in a moment.' He returned to the desk and gathered his papers.

When she got to the door, she turned. 'Did you hear about the car accident?'

Father Sun stopped what he was doing. 'Car accident? No, is someone hurt?'

'Mr Potter.'

He paled. 'Oh, how dreadful.'

'He drove into a tree.'

He pushed the paperwork back in the drawer and turned the key. 'What? Drove into a tree! Is he all right?'

'He died at the scene.'

His throat tightened at the news. 'What about Sister Bellatrix?'

Mother Moon darted across and hugged him. 'You've no need to fret. Don't let your nerves get the better of you. I'll sit with Sister Bellatrix. It's all in hand. No one else was on the road, he must have lost control. This is no one's fault.'

Feeling his anxiety bubbling under the

surface, he was loath to release her. 'You'll handle it all, won't you? I can't deal with news like this.'

She reassured him and, pulling herself away, reminded him that he was due on the lawn. 'Don't keep your followers waiting. Let me deal with real life, you get on with fulfilling your dream.'

Feeling calmer, he followed her out and locked the door behind him.

On the lawn at the front of the Celestial Faith Commune, approximately twenty commune members had gathered. Each wore a navy blue, ankle-length gown bearing a symbol they'd chosen. Some had opted for the name of a planet, others had chosen star systems and many were drawn to the astrological signs. A handful wore simple brown robes, indicating they had yet to join the commune permanently.

They were a mixed bunch, young and old, and they stood patiently until Father Sun and Mother Moon appeared, at which their anticipation rose. The couple glided across the lawn and stopped by a heavy wooden table, constructed by the members and carved with images of shooting stars and planets. Mother Moon joined the commune members to await Father Sun's blessing. A blackbird chirped on the nearby bench.

Father Sun spread his arms wide. 'Welcome, brothers and sisters. Welcome to a glorious day and what a beautiful day our universe has sent us. Our sun warms us from the clearest of skies, our moon guides our seas and moods and our galaxy spins its way, watching over us and surrounding us with love and peace. Let us reach out and ground ourselves with Mother Earth.'

The members slipped their sandals off. Father Sun felt the cool grass beneath his feet. 'Mother Earth feeds us, waters us, provides us with the air we breathe. Let us stand in silence to treasure this moment and give thanks to her.'

The members closed their eyes and retreated into silence. The only sounds were the chirp of birdsong, the leaves rustling in the breeze and the distant rumble of a tractor. Father Sun checked his watch. This contemplation would last exactly five minutes and then the members would return to the allotments and their various chores.

Warmth radiated through him. He mentally revisited the hurdles he'd had to jump to get here. A nervous breakdown, a new identity, a change of character, a new vision in life, a woman he adored who prevented any stress from reaching him, a move to the countryside. He'd left his past behind. Now he could make something of himself.

When the allotted time had passed, Father Sun spoke to each commune member individually. He made a point of doing so. He wanted them to feel special and loved. He spent far longer with his two potential members. They were, he knew, part of the traditional congregation at Cavendish; two vulnerable widows. They'd been drawn to the commune after he'd spoken with them in the village and they, in turn, had visited several times. Father Sun permitted this for a few weeks, after which he asked guests to make a sacrifice to join the commune permanently. It was getting close to that time.

The two women were dressed in plain brown robes and holding their handbags.

He rubbed his hands together. 'Ladies, from your expression and demeanour, I take it that you're still enjoying the life of our Celestial Commune.'

'Oh yes,' Mrs Long gushed, her eyes bright. 'To be out in the open with the gardening and being completely self-reliant — it really suits me to the ground.'

'And you, Mrs Fellowes?'

Equally enthusiastic, she said: 'The same, Father Sun. I still find it a little odd. I'm afraid I find it peculiar to be speaking to everyone as if they're a planet. Do you understand?'

'Of course. But if you join us, you know that this will all become second nature and you'll think nothing of it. Have you thought about your own names? If you join us you'll relinquish your given name and take one from the universe.'

'I rather fancy Halley,' said Mrs Long, 'as in the comet. Is that allowed?'

'It is. It's the first time someone has mentioned a comet.' He turned to Mrs

Fellowes. 'And you?'

'Io, one of the moons of Jupiter. I've always loved the sound.'

They walked toward the allotments. 'And have you given some thought to joining us? The day visits are an opportunity for you to find out about us; but, to truly be part of the Celestial Faith Commune, you will need to give up your life outside and join us here.'

The two women faltered.

'It's a big step,' said Mrs Long. 'I've been in that cottage for forty years. Will I have to sell it?'

'It is a big decision to make. Remember that the commune needs funding. You could perhaps offer it for rent. A percentage of that would come to us.'

Mrs Fellowes hesitated. 'I rent from the council. I don't have much money. Just my state pension.'

'You wouldn't need money in here but we don't ask you for a large contribution, just a percentage. Why don't you come along to the office and I can discuss everything with you? If I lay all the facts out for you, you can take the information away and give yourself time to consider it.' He held their hands. 'Remember that you are loved here. Our members have grown fond of you and often say how lovely it would be to have you with us permanently; to sit down and eat with us and worship with us full-time.'

They thanked him and said they would, most definitely, meet with him and suggested the following day. For the next hour, they wanted to meditate in the gardens.

Father Sun again beamed and bade them adieu.

His expression faltered when he spotted four people standing by the entrance. He recognised Stephen Merryweather straight away. Biting back his annoyance, he strode toward them and forced the smile back on his face.

7

The brief sign of irritation was not lost on James. The man approaching them was over six-foot-tall, with an elegant gait and, James had to admit, a charming air about him. Father Sun opened the cast-iron gate. His voice was soft and gentle.

'Welcome to the Celestial Faith Commune.' He turned to Stephen. 'We meet again.'

Stephen gave a curt nod in return.

James, not wanting any aggravation, took up the conversation. 'We noticed some of your leaflets and thought we'd drop by. We're Lord and Lady Harrington and I believe you know the Reverend Stephen and Anne Merryweather.'

Father Sun led them to the gardens. 'It's a beautiful day for basking in the warmth of our glorious sun.'

The four of them exchanged wary looks. James pulled Stephen back. 'I say, I know you're not his greatest advocate but please humour me. You're coming across as very hostile.'

'I-I will give you that courtesy, James, but I cannot say I'm happy about being here.'

Beth whispered. 'Sometimes ignorance of a subject makes us suspicious. This could all be above board.'

Father Sun led them to a glade where several benches were dotted around. 'Please, join me. Many of our commune come here for quiet contemplation.' He lifted a finger. 'You'll see Mrs Long and Mrs Fellowes in the shade there. They enjoy meditating in this particular area.'

Stephen bristled, but then, looking at James, forced a smile. 'Am I-I permitted to speak with them?'

'We prefer that our members be given their time and space. If they wish to speak with you, they'll come over; or perhaps it would be easier for you to call in on them in the village.'

James noted Stephen's pursed lips. He'd never seen his friend so annoyed.

'How many commune members do you have?' asked Anne.

'Twenty-three. We also have half a dozen day visitors who have yet to make their minds up about whether to commit themselves to us or not. They are the ones in the plain brown robes with no design on them.'

'Commit?' queried Beth.

'We allow those interested to visit and they worship and pray with us. It gives them an opportunity to see what we do. They get to see most things but we don't allow involvement in everything until they join us on a permanent basis.'

'By everything,' said James, 'what do you mean?'

'We have communal dinners, a small-holding, a large allotment. We are basically self-sufficient to keep our costs down. The building here can house up to twelve members. The old cowshed has been converted for accommodation. Once we've filled those beds we may look to renovating that heap of a thing behind the house.'

If James' memory served him right, the building had been used by the military during the war and there was a smaller building behind. The corner of it was visible but from what he could see, it appeared poorly maintained.

Father Sun explained that there were quite a few 'Do Not Enter' notices on the ruined property at the back and the entrances and windows had been boarded up. 'I think it's past renovating. The council has told us it needs to be knocked down and we'll build an accommodation wing from scratch.'

'You say you have allotments?' said Beth.

'We grow fruit and vegetables. One of our members, Brother Mars, is a superb gardener, self-taught. He's teaching everyone what he's learned. Everything from sowing seeds to harvesting. He's gleaned a lot over the last two or three years.'

James couldn't help but be impressed but something the man had said a while back nagged at him. 'When new members decide to commit themselves, does that mean a financial outlay too? You say you need to keep costs down.'

'I see where you're going with this,

Lord Harrington,' he said with a sardonic curl of the lip.

James insisted he meant nothing by it. 'I'm interested, that's all.'

'We're not one of these underhand religions that insist you donate all of your money. We're not a church. We're not a religion. I know the Reverend here detests what we're doing. But we simply offer something different. We don't dictate to people about what deity they worship. If they want to continue to pray to God, Jesus, Buddha or whoever, they are free to do so. The Celestial Faith Commune is simply a way of living with our creator. We give thanks to the universe. Mother Earth is just that. Our mother. She feeds us, she provides water and shelter. Without her we would not exist.'

'That's true to some extent.'

Stephen straightened up. 'God created us. God created this. To prioritise the galaxy is inappropriate.'

'It's not my place to say,' said Father Sun. 'I told you that everyone can worship their God. We have no problem with that. But don't you think it's good to worship the very things that your God created?'

James could see slight discomfort in Stephen.

'A-And what is this commitment, financially?' he said.

'We ask for a percentage toward utilities and necessities. We go through what people can and can't afford. If you own your own home, you sell it — '

'Sell it!' said Anne.

'The person with their own home either sells it or rents it out. They have no need for the property if they are joining us here.'

'But what if they decide they want to go back?' asked Beth.

'Then they may do so.'

'But if they've s-sold their house, what do they go back to?' Stephen said with some alarm. 'You can't throw p-people out on the street?'

'Nor would we,' Father Sun replied calmly. 'We ask that they give us notice, as if you were in employment. We then help that person settle back into their old life. But so far we haven't come across such a problem.'

'Can we possibly speak with a few of your commune members?' James asked.

He was met with a blunt refusal. 'The members are busy. We cannot have people in and out of here without an appointment. The gates are locked to keep non-believers out.'

'You do realise that you are slowly getting a reputation for being a secret society,' said James, knowing that he had probably exaggerated things slightly.

Father Sun rose from his seat and indicated that it was time to leave. 'That's not my problem, Lord Harrington. If people want to make assumptions about us,' he made eye contact with Stephen, 'then I can't stop them. Ask Mrs Long and Mrs Fellowes. They've been coming for three weeks now and are, at this moment, contemplating on whether to make a full commitment or not.' He steered them toward the gates. 'We're not doing anything wrong here. There is nothing underhand going on; no secret society or brainwashing. Everything is entirely legal and our finances will show

71

that.' He mumbled, 'If I can figure out how to do the accounts,' under his breath. 'I appreciate that it's not for everyone but, for those people who wish it, we have a belief that runs alongside those conventional religions. We are a peaceful and loving community. We want nothing more than to be left alone to pursue those beliefs.'

'Why do people have to commit themselves permanently? Why can't they simply visit?'

'Because it disrupts the flow of things. If you have dedicated people, the group works together. If we had a handful of members who came and went as they pleased, it would have a negative effect on what we do here.'

He swung the gate open.

'Thank you for coming by. If you feel the need to visit again, please let me know and I'll schedule some time in to show you around.'

The gate was locked behind them and they watched as Father Sun ambled into the distance, the embroidered sun on his robes glinting.

James turned to Stephen. 'What do you think?'

'I-I don't like the man. He seems smarmy and over-confident.'

'Beth?'

'I don't know. He was exceptionally charming and if I were a vulnerable person I could quite easily be swayed by him.'

He turned to Anne.

'Beth's said what I was thinking. I'm sure everything is above board. If you're running something like this you'd still run it as a business. He says his finances are good and it's all legal but he seems very keen to keep people like us out. Mrs Long and Mrs Fellowes don't have access to everything. Who knows what happens when you commit yourself and you're locked up in here.'

'Maybe they are being brainwashed,' said Beth. 'We only have his word for what happens once you sign up permanently.'

James pulled out his cigarettes. 'Well, unless something crops up that calls for another visit, I don't think we can do anything.'

'Can't George do something?' asked Stephen as they approached their respective cars.

'Not unless there's some proven criminal activity. He'd have my guts for garters if I made him go in there for no reason. Not to mention what old Father Sun would say.' James opened his car door. 'No. I'm afraid the Celestial Faith Commune is here to stay. For the time-being anyway.'

They said their goodbyes to the Merryweathers and James swung his car on to the road. Although there didn't appear to be anything underhand going on, he'd felt the same as the others. Something lurked beneath the surface of the charming Father Sun and his Celestial Faith Commune. He wondered whether to have a natter with George just to see if there had been any complaints about their activities.

8

Simon Drake, a man in his mid-thirties with an olive complexion, removed his eyepiece and looked at the gentleman in front of him. 'This is good. To have access to a working drawing, well, it's incredible.' He cleared the small desk in front of him and placed the drawing on the flat surface. Using a camera, he positioned it over the artwork and took a number of images. 'That'll do it.'

He wound the film on, opened the back of the camera and took the roll out. 'I'll get that developed. And,' he popped the artwork back into its frame, 'make sure there's a provenance that goes with it. Get on to the old man, he's working on that. I'd like that back in its rightful place as soon as possible.'

His messenger turned to go but Simon summoned him back and handed over another framed drawing. 'This one's done. Return that tomorrow night.'

'What, the original?'

Simon handed over a key. 'Yes, here's the front door key. She's in bed by ten o'clock. Go back in the middle of the night and you can simply slip in there and hang it on the wall.'

He watched the man disappear. It had been a long day. He'd been up all night overseeing the work. He should get some rest but the jobs were coming in. And he had his own gallery to run. He needed more people, more experts with an eye for detail but he had to be careful. He'd half a dozen men and women at his disposal but the more people involved, the more precarious his situation could become.

He'd be working again tonight. He turned the desk lamp out, opened the door and squinted as he walked into the dawn.

9

James and Beth had spent an evening at the cinema enjoying the antics of the latest Carry On film, *Carry On Nurse*. As always, it had provided laughs and a smattering of innuendos that sent theatre-goers on their way with a smile.

Arriving home, he opened the drinks cabinet and reached in. 'Do you fancy a small brandy and an early night? I have a good book on the go.'

'Mm, that would lovely.'

The doorbell rang. He left the drinks and opened the front door to find George Lane on the doorstep. A police car was parked on the drive.

'You're a bit late, aren't you? It's nearly half past ten.'

Beth joined him at the door.

'I'm not stopping,' said George, declining James' invitation to come inside. 'PC Fulton's driving me back to Lewes but I asked him to make a detour. Saves me telephoning.'

James leant on the door-frame and waited.

'I popped in to give my condolences to Mrs Potter.'

'Oh George,' said Beth, 'how is she?'

'Distraught, as you can imagine and completely flummoxed by the whole thing.'

'Flummoxed?' queried James.

'Bernard Potter was nearing retirement and a stickler for detail in anything he did. He used to go around the schools teaching road safety and cycling proficiency to the children. Always checked his car once a month for brake fluid, oil, water, that sort of thing. What I'm saying is that he was a careful driver.'

'And she doesn't understand how he came off the road?'

Beth frowned. 'Do you think someone else caused the accident and drove off?'

George made a yes or no movement with his hand. 'Hard to say. I saw the crash site earlier and there's only one set of tyre marks. Perhaps he didn't know that part of the road well and took the bend too fast.'

'Easily done,' said James recalling an accident a few months ago near the same spot. 'That bend does come up quickly and it's always sharper than you think it's going to be. Have you checked the car?'

'It's with our mechanics at the moment so we'll see if they can shed any light.'

'Perhaps a fault he hadn't seen. Car engines and brake pads are not always reliable, no matter how much you check them.'

George felt in his pocket and brought out a slip of paper. He handed it to James. 'Mrs Potter wanted you both to call in. She said she'd like to thank you in person for all the help you gave.'

'We'll be sure to,' said James.

Beth asked if Mrs Potter had stipulated a time.

'She mentioned being in tomorrow.'

'I say, George, was the daughter there? Wendy?'

George shook his head. 'I asked if she was there but Mrs Potter seemed too upset so . . . '

James thanked him for the message. 'We'll be sure to call in.'

Closing the door, James slid the address in his wallet. 'Poor Mrs Potter. Let's make that our first call after church tomorrow.'

They knew it would be a difficult visit. James hoped that Wendy would be there, not only to ensure that her mother had company but to establish that all was well. Bernard Potter's anxiety over his daughter had dominated his conversation with James. He hoped the pair hadn't fallen out. Wendy would never forgive herself. Only calling in at the family home would answer that question.

10

The following morning, James and Beth emerged from the Sunday service and spoke with Stephen and Anne at the entrance of the church.

'Lovely service, Stephen,' said James.

'You always manage to put so much humour and enthusiasm into what you speak about,' added Beth. 'You're more like an entertainer.'

'Th-that's what keeps the congregation coming back for more. I'm aware that church sermons can be as boring as watching grass grow. The Bible is f-full of wonderful parables and lessons to learn. They just need to be brought to life.'

'And,' said Anne, 'no one likes being preached to these days, especially some of the younger members of our congregation.'

James squeezed Stephen's shoulder. 'Well you certainly have people eating out of your hand here. We'll see you soon.

We're calling in on Mrs Potter. She's asked to see us.'

A look of sympathy crossed Anne's face. 'That poor woman.'

'Do l-let me know if she needs Anne and me to visit, for spiritual c-comfort.'

'Of course.'

Beth turned to Anne. 'Changing the topic completely, did you decide on what you're doing about the Midsummer Ball? We forgot to ask you last night.'

'Oh yes, we're definitely coming. My parents have offered to stay and look after the children and Radley. I've found some lovely material so I'm making a dress especially for that evening.'

'Wonderful.'

They left the Merryweathers chatting with their parishioners.

James brought out his car keys. 'Right, come along, darling. Let's visit Mrs Potter.'

*   *   *

After driving through Loxfield to the outskirts of Haywards Heath, they pulled up outside a modern terraced house. Built by the council just a few years before, the estate was pleasing on the eye and not dissimilar to those James had visited in Crawley over Easter. All the houses had a front and rear garden, either two or three bedrooms and an area along the road for garages.

Within a minute of James' rap at the door knocker, Mrs Potter answered it. She was a plump woman, her eyes tearful and complexion blotchy from crying. Realisation dawned.

'Lord and Lady Harrington. I'm so pleased you were able to come.' She ushered them through to the lounge which afforded views to the front and rear. It was neat and tidy, with several photographs on the walls. A vase of colourful flowers stood on the dining table, along with a handful of bereavement cards.

As she stood a little over five feet tall, James towered over her. She wore tartan slippers, a cotton skirt and blouse with a cardigan draped over her shoulders.

She patted the sofa. 'Please make

yourself comfortable. Can I offer you a drink or something?'

James said there was no need. 'Unless, of course, you're making yourself one. I'd hate to stop you.'

She linked her fingers. 'I asked the police inspector, Mr Lane, to get you to come over. I just wanted to thank you for helping Bernard. The doctors said you did all the right things. It's such a shame you didn't come across him earl . . . ' She sniffed and felt for a handkerchief.

Beth moved forward in her seat. 'Oh, Mrs Potter, we really are so sorry this has happened to you.'

James spotted a bottle of sherry on the sideboard and asked if she'd like a glass. A nod answered his question. 'We made him comfortable and, when the ambulance arrived, the medical team helped him as best they could.'

She accepted the glass of sherry but seemed dazed. 'I just don't know what happened. He was such a careful driver. Never went over the speed limit; always hooted the horn if he was coming to a sharp bend. He knows that road . . . I can't comprehend it.' She came out of her musing. 'Do the police think there was another vehicle? Mr Lane didn't seem to think so but he must have swerved to avoid something.'

'That road is out in the country, Mrs Potter. You can be the most careful driver but if a deer or fox runs out, it can take you by surprise.'

She accepted the explanation. James studied the room. It was light and airy but with very little on show. Mrs Potter, he decided, was in her mid-fifties so the daughter would surely be a grown woman by now, perhaps married with children of her own. There didn't seem to be any magazines or items that would belong to a younger woman. Two or three photographs he noticed had a woman in her twenties in them. Was that Wendy?

'Mrs Potter, I'm sure the police have already asked but is there anyone you'd like us to contact? Your husband talked about Wendy when I was with him. Is she nearby?'

To his horror, the lady burst into floods of tears. He gave Beth a helpless shrug as she moved from the sofa to the arm of Mrs Potter's chair.

'Oh, Mrs Potter, would you like us to speak with Wendy? Does she know about her father?'

'They wouldn't let me in.'

Beth's gaze sought James; her confusion mirrored his own. James took the sherry glass from Mrs Potter and set it down on the table.

'Who wouldn't let you in? And let you in where?'

The sobbing eventually reduced to sniffles and finally Mrs Potter simply wrung her handkerchief. 'I didn't tell the Inspector yesterday. I was all over the place but it really upset me. It's been upsetting Bernard too.'

'What has?'

'That Celestial Faith place. Do you know it?'

James could almost feel the jolt in his chest. 'Are you saying that Wendy is part of that commune?'

Mrs Potter reached for another handkerchief. She seemed to be pondering something.

Beth, too, had picked up on her hesitation. It was she who spoke next. 'Are you saying that they refused to let you see her? Your own daughter?'

Her posture sagged. 'I can't honestly remember. I wanted to break the news but the police had already done that. I just wanted to see her.'

James watched her as she blew her nose. The poor woman was distraught. He asked her to think back. 'Did they suggest you return at another time or say they'd bring Wendy out?'

She struggled to think.

Beth hinted that the shock was probably muddling her memory. 'I can't believe they would deliberately stop you from seeing her; not at such a sad time.'

'Your husband spoke about Wendy as if it caused him some concern. He said something about it being too late now. Does that mean something to you?'

She rose from her chair and retrieved several more handkerchiefs from the drawer in the sideboard. Returning to her seat, she leafed through some magazines and newspapers on the table and plucked out a leaflet which she handed to him. It was the same flyer that the commune had put up outside the vicarage; the one that had incensed Stephen so much.

'Did Wendy attend church?'

'All the while she was growing up we attended church. The little one in Loxfield. She went to Sunday School and always enjoyed it but you know what it's like. Once they get older they don't go so much. Well, she's twenty-five now, a grown woman, so she can do what she wants.'

'She doesn't live at home?'

'Oh yes, she lived here until . . . ' She faltered then jutted her chin at the leaflet. 'She got chatting to one of their members in the village who was handing those out. It's not that she lost her faith but she said the vicar at Loxfield was boring.' She bristled. 'I told her the vicar's not there for entertainment. He's there for spiritual guidance and makes sure we behave as we're supposed to.'

James couldn't help but recall their chat with Stephen earlier. He delivered superb sermons but had made his appearances as entertaining as possible. By doing so, he had doubled the congregation and even the young people were happy to come along without being cajoled by their parents. Why vicars had to be serious and lack humour he didn't know. This exchange made him all the more grateful that the Merryweathers had landed on their doorstep and not anyone else's.

He resumed the dialogue. 'And the person she met in the village swayed her to go along and see what this was all about?'

She stood to rearrange the flowers. 'Me and Bernard said that it all sounded very airy-fairy; not a religion. You can't pray to the earth, can you? But it fell on deaf ears. She started going straight from work every day. She tried to get us to go along with her. Kept going on about the man that led this commune place. I said to Bernard, she's too easily led. That's what I said. She insisted that it wasn't a religion but more a way of life and that everyone should worship the earth. It all sounded strange to me.

But that wasn't the end of it.'

They waited as she returned to her seat.

'Because she was a day visitor, she wasn't included in everything. She wanted to be there all the time. Of course, if you want to do that, you have to give up your job, give that commune some money.' She drew herself up. 'I said to her, what are you going to do for money? How are you going to live? How are you going to afford to eat?' Pursing her lips, her frustration turned to anger. 'The commune will look after us — that's what she said. As if there's a money pit somewhere that'll keep giving. Bernard told her, you can't live on fresh air. They had a big argument and she stormed out.' Her voice broke. 'That's what Bernard probably meant about it being too late.'

'I think that not allowing you to see Wendy at such an upsetting time is inexcusable,' said Beth, locking eyes with him.

He knew, from her expression, that she wanted him to intervene. But he wasn't sure what he could do. The only thing that sprang to mind was to try and talk some sense into that Father Sun chap. He must have parents or certainly people that he cared for. How would he feel if he were denied access to those he loved and forced to grieve on his own? He voiced his thoughts. 'Perhaps we could go to the commune and insist on some common sense.'

Mrs Potter thanked them and muttered something about Bernard not being able to finish what he'd started.

James asked what she meant. 'Is it something we can help with?'

It was some time before he received an answer. 'Can I show you something?'

Mrs Potter asked them to follow her upstairs. It was a narrow staircase with a worn, patterned carpet that led onto a tiny landing with four doors leading off. James surmised that this was a three-bedroomed house with a bathroom.

Mrs Potter's hand hovered over the door handle. 'Bernard had started looking into something. Not officially. You know he was a policeman, don't you?'

'Yes,' they said.
She opened the door.

11

They entered what was the spare bedroom, a small room with a single bed in the corner. The wallpaper was a pattern of small daffodils and on a bookshelf were a number of paperbacks, photograph albums and annuals. On the bed lay spare linen, towels and pillow-cases. The window was open and a gentle breeze made the curtains billow.

Mrs Potter squatted down and pulled out a large cork board from under the mattress. She placed it on the bed. It was about a yard square and pinned to it were photographs, notes and several arrows linking the various items.

James moved forward to get a better idea of what he was looking at. The centre of the board had a copy of the Celestial Faith Commune flyer. Arrows pointed to several photographs with their titles underneath. He recognised Father Sun walking across the grounds. Going in a clockwise direction, the next was a lady in her mid-thirties named Mother Moon, then Sister Venus, Sister Saturn, Brother Neptune, Brother Mars and Sister Jupiter.

A family photograph was pinned to the side of these. No gowns or celestial motifs. The name underneath: Wendy Potter and, in brackets, Sister Bellatrix. A second photograph, taken from a distance, showed Wendy walking through the commune grounds in her blue gown.

Surrounding the photographs were newspaper clippings concerning cults and the conduct of cult leaders. There was a list of characteristics observed by various psychologists: egotistical, vain, selfish, lustful, secretive, self-admiring. To one side was a rough drawing of the area and where things were; the house, the disused building to the rear, the allotments, garage and meditation area.

A piece of paper to the side of the board bore the name Father Sun. Underneath this were a few notes: 'real name Johnny Barton', 'cannot go through official channels', 'no authority to enquire further'.

He examined a piece of thick paper with italics on. They showed the end of one word and the beginning of another. He read it aloud. '-oric Pi.' He then turned to Mrs Potter with what he knew was a look of complete bewilderment.

'Bernard was convinced there was something dodgy about that commune so he started looking into it in his spare time.'

'By dodgy,' said Beth, 'what did he mean?'

'He wouldn't tell me. He kept calling it his copper's instinct, if there is such a thing. Something not right, he said, so he started going up there, taking photographs and asking questions.' She jabbed the picture of Father Sun. 'That man there eventually told him he was upsetting the members and asked that he didn't come back. Told him the gates would be locked because they were fed up with people prying.'

'And your husband didn't elaborate on

anything? There must have been something that caused him to start an investigation. Or was it simply that he was worried about Wendy?'

'He always worried about Wendy. If I'm truthful, our Wendy's a bit naïve, easily taken in, so it didn't surprise us that she thought this commune thing was so wonderful. But Bernard couldn't understand how they were making ends meet. That house they've got, that old farmhouse, it's huge and it wasn't for rent. They bought it. You don't buy houses like that by starting up a commune.'

James had to agree. 'Did your husband speak to his colleagues about this?'

'He spoke to his sergeant but there wasn't enough to even ask questions and, Bernard admitted himself, if someone had brought those concerns to him, he would have said the same thing.'

He returned his attention to the piece of paper. 'And what's this?'

She shrugged. 'I don't know. Bernard didn't know either but he pinned it up there. 'You never know when something may fit the puzzle,' he said.'

Beth asked what she was going to do with it.

Another shrug. 'I don't want it. The police aren't interested. I'll probably throw it away. Wendy might decide to come home and I don't want her seeing this. She'd be mortified to think her dad had been spying on her.'

'I say, Mrs Potter, would you mind if I took these things with me. I rather like a puzzle and I wouldn't mind having a look to see if I can make out what your husband was doing.'

'You'd be doing me a favour. Bernard got too obsessed about it over these last couple of weeks.'

They collected the photographs, maps and notes and returned to the hall where Mrs Potter opened the door. 'Thank you, again, for doing what you could for Bernard. I'm glad he wasn't on his own . . . you know . . . when he went.'

Just before she closed the door, James spun round. 'One thing, Mrs Potter. Your husband's car was coming from the direction of Loxfield. Do you know where he'd been?'

'Oh yes. He'd been to that commune.'

* * *

Later that morning, James and Beth had commandeered a table on the terrace at Harrington's with their chef, Didier. Alongside them were their head waiter, Adam, and Paul, their *maître d'*. Wisps of cloud drifted lazily across the sky and the warm sunshine was doing its best to burn them off. James had chosen a table at the very end of the terrace that gave a view across the grounds and down to the river. Beyond that, some way in the distance, they glimpsed the sparkling English Channel.

To the left were the converted stables where GJ and his wife, Catherine, were holding a painting workshop. James couldn't believe how popular this particular pastime had become with their guests.

GJ, a handsome, blond-haired man, had come to their attention during an investigation the previous spring. Homeless and suffering with amnesia, the mystery had been fascinating and, to everyone's delight, had turned out for the best in every way. The young man was a talented artist and had suggested turning the stables into a studio where he could teach guests how to paint and draw. One of his first pupils was the lovely Catherine, whom he'd taken as his wife in December. GJ had also branched out and taken commissions to paint landscapes. In between times, he restored paintings blighted by dust and age and, as an extension to his skills, was learning the art of bookbinding. Although GJ was well-off as the result of an inheritance, James was pleased to see he had had a work ethic instilled in him by his adopted parents.

James reached out to the glass jug that held iced water, slices of lemon and sprigs of mint. He topped his glass up and caught the last bit of Didier's menu choices.

'*Oui, oui,*' he finalised. 'I think our guests would like the summer chicken pie over the beef dish. The ingredients are more suited to the season, *non?*'

'This is Grandma Harrington's chicken pie?' asked James.

'Mais oui.'

'Splendid. We had that the other day and, you're right, it's a perfect dish for a summer's evening.'

'That brings us on to the Midsummer Ball,' said Beth. 'Is everything in place?'

Adam, a young man in his early twenties, had recently begun sitting in on the various meetings over menus and events at Harrington's. He'd expressed a keen interest in moving up the ranks and James and Beth had encouraged him to do so. After a quiet word with Paul, the *maître d'* had taken the waiter under his wing and begun guiding him on the ins and outs of hotel management.

Taking his lead from Paul, Adam cleared his throat. 'I contacted the Mepham Agency on Friday. The Johnny Johnson Big Band is all signed up and eager to perform. They're arriving here at six o'clock to set up the stage and they're bringing their own lighting and sound people. My mum and dad said they're a good band. Have you seen them?'

'We certainly have,' said Beth recalling the upbeat music they played. 'They don't stick to swing music either. They've recently hired a couple of jazz musicians.'

'They're quite a forward-thinking band,' added James. 'They know the rock 'n' roll music and some of the jazz standards are beginning to have an influence so they include them in their repertoire. It'll be a wonderful night.' He gazed at the sky. 'Let's hope the weather stays dry; we can have the doors open and people can dance on the terrace.'

'How wonderful,' said Beth. She turned to Paul. 'Are we full?'

'Every room sold out for the week. About two thirds of them booked last year by the same people who came before. It's turning into a small community and the guests all seem to know one another simply by coming to the ball.'

James asked if his sister, Fiona, had booked her room. Although she was always welcome at their own home, Fiona loved to stay in what was the old family pile. Paul confirmed that she had booked a double room with her husband, William. Beth expressed disappointment that their nephew, Christian, wouldn't be joining them.

James reminded her that Christian would be looking after the farm. 'It's not his sort of thing anyway. I can't see Christian dressed appropriately for dinner, can you?'

She let out a laugh. 'No, I can't. He's more at home in wellingtons and carrying a shotgun.'

He turned to Didier. 'Are you doing the normal sort of thing?'

'*Oui, oui,* a buffet of the highest order.' Their chef twisted in his chair to take in the dining room. 'The length of that wall will be given over to the tables with sweet and savoury delights.' He puffed out his chest. 'It will be a masterpiece of culinary expertise.'

James couldn't help but admire his chef's confidence. Didier was not shy in extolling his own talent and, if he was honest, he had every right to boast. The man was a marvel and could turn the humblest sausage roll into a dish of ecstasy. He knew that every pastry, tart and cake would be hand-made and eye-catching.

He turned to Beth. 'Did Anne say she's doing the flowers?'

Beth said that both she and Anne would be making posies to set off the buffet.

Didier took a sharp breath. 'Do not use perfumed flowers on the buffet table,' he implored. 'I do not want the fragrance of fresh sponge mingling with strong floral aromas. They do not mix.'

'We'll take that into account,' said Beth.

James took one last look through the menu and asked for clarification on a couple of things. While Didier answered his questions, he noticed that Adam was distracted by the young waitress preparing the tables for lunch. He was sure this was the lady Adam was courting but he appeared worried and she would not meet the young man's eyes.

Didier and Paul rose from their chairs and murmured their need to get on with their respective jobs. Adam was slower to get up. He went over to speak with the waitress but she scurried away.

Beth had also noticed. 'Isn't that young lady you've been courting?'

'Yes, it is, Lady Harrington.' He broke eye contact.

'Are things not going well?'

He started placing the empty glasses and jug of water on a tray. 'She's refused me a date on a couple of nights recently. She's been going over to that Celestial place. Have you seen it?'

James got up from his seat. 'How long has she been involved in that?'

'She's only been a few times but . . . well, she seems a bit besotted by the bloke that runs it. Father Sun, she calls him. I'm all for having an interest but when I see her it's Father Sun this and Father Sun that. I think she's more interested in him than me.'

Beth went round the table to face him. 'You mustn't think like that, Adam. That Father Sun man is much older and may even be married.'

'And we've met him. Not everyone is as they seem, Adam. You may want to remind your girl that she has someone just as charming here.'

'More than charming,' added Beth. 'You're more of a catch than he'll ever be.'

The young man blushed. He'd had a crush on Beth since the day he started at Harrington's. He had just turned seventeen when he had joined them, unable to do National Service due to a medical condition. As a result, he'd put his efforts into carving out a career at Harrington's.

As Adam turned to go, James tugged at his sleeve. 'Do you want me to have a chat with your girl?'

'Oh no, Lord Harrington, I'll sit down with her and see if I can win her round.' He went on his way.

'I have a theory,' said Beth.

'What's that?'

'Adam's girlfriend, Julie Faulkner, and the two widows, Missus Long and Fellowes, they're all naïve women, easily taken in.'

He stared at her. 'How on earth do you know that?'

She linked an arm through his and they

made their way down the steps and on to the grass. 'I had a chat with Julie when she first arrived and she believes everything she reads in the magazines, all the gossip. There was something a few weeks ago about some salacious activity with the Prime Minister. There wasn't an ounce of evidence but she believed the whole thing. Then, of course, it was proved to be absolute nonsense. And then there was that April Fool.'

'What April Fool?' James asked, beginning to think he'd missed out on things.

'The one the children played on Mrs Long.'

James put his head back and laughed. 'Oh Lord, I'd forgotten all about that.'

'I'll bet Mrs Long hasn't.'

The older children in the village had spread a rumour that they'd been doing a project on family history and discovered that Mrs Long was related to the Queen. The majority of villagers had pooh-poohed the idea and cottoned on to the date straight away but Mrs Long had fallen for it.

Beth went on. 'I know that Mrs Long

spoke to Mrs Fellowes about it and they were both taken in. Mrs Long was even going to instruct an artist to prepare a coat of arms.'

James couldn't believe the ladies had been so gullible. It wasn't until Bert Briggs had arrived later that day that he'd put the women straight.

'If you're rela'ed to the Queen,' he'd said, 'I'll run 'round this village green naked. Don't yer know what day it is?'

The two women were noticeable by their absence for a few days after. James conceded that perhaps Beth was right. The women he knew of at this commune were either vulnerable or naïve; both of which would be ideal for Father Sun to exploit. He hoped that Julie Faulkner didn't get drawn in as well.

They found themselves at the old stables where GJ's students had adjourned to the back of the barn for soft drinks. It was a large area that GJ had completely refurbished and painted white. Cupboards and shelves held blank canvasses, paints, brushes and sketch pads. Easels were placed in a circle around a miniature statue of Eros and the students were in various stages of either painting or drawing the image. At the far end were two potter's wheels where Catherine was discussing a piece with one of their students. She waved to them.

GJ wiped his hands on a towel and strolled over. His hair flopped over his forehead and his easy gait encouraged all who came into contact with him to relax before even meeting him. A well-spoken, privately educated man, he had a smooth voice that eased you into the conversation.

'Lord Harrington, Lady Harrington. How are you?'

They spent a good ten minutes chatting before James spotted a sheet of paper with beautiful calligraphy written on it. Careful not to touch it, he wandered around the desk to get a better view.

'I say, did you do this?'

'Yes, I was asked to copy a piece of text as calligraphy. Something to do with a gift for a family member. I wasn't taking much notice, if I'm honest, but the man was paying good money so who am I to argue.'

James scrutinised the various calligraphy pens on the table. 'How long does it take you to do something like this?'

'Depends on the length of the piece. But, this in particular, took around three hours. Some people can do it faster but I prefer to take my time. It's quite a mesmeric process.'

Beth asked if it was someone in the village who had commissioned him. 'Or perhaps one of the guests?'

'No, no, nothing like that. A chap came by. Said I'd been recommended. He wanted to see my work before he offered me anything further. I think if this is to his liking, he may offer me a commission every now and again. I told him that he should have thought about putting this on thicker paper. You know, like parchment?'

James read through the original document. He recognised it as the opening words to *A Tale of Two Cities*. 'It was the best of times, it was the worst of times . . . ' Just one paragraph.

'It's an odd request, isn't it? And he

said he may have more work for you?'

'Yes.' GJ rummaged in his pockets and brought out several scraps of paper. Finally, he pulled one free. 'This is the man. Stuart Drummond. Do you know him?'

James pulled a face. 'No, name's not familiar. He's not local?'

'No. He said he'd contact me.' He thought for a moment. 'That's a bit odd, isn't it? And you, Lord Harrington, have that look about you. As if you have your teeth into something.'

James dismissed the idea. 'Just a couple of things that are making the cogs turn.'

The young man said he should be getting on and gathered his students together for the afternoon session.

★ ★ ★

At home, they found the front door unlocked. Wary of intruders, James crept inside, closely followed by Beth. They tiptoed across the hall and carefully nudged the door to the lounge. The record player was on, Bing Crosby singing Road to Bali.

Outside they heard voices on the patio. The tightness in James' back eased as he rolled his eyes at Beth. Stepping through the open French windows, he gave the two intruders sitting on the patio a knowing look. 'What the devil are you two doing here?'

12

Beth rushed to greet their son, Harry, who leapt to his feet and embraced her.

Bert grinned. 'I saw 'im gettin' off the bus so I thought I'd walk up with 'im.'

Harry hugged James. 'Sorry I didn't telephone but I got leave at the last minute. I have two weeks off and I thought I'd come and stay. Is that all right? Aunt Fi hasn't taken over, has she?'

Henry Jacob Harrington, Harry to all who knew him, stood about the same height as James, just over six feet tall. He had the same dark hair as Beth and had turned from a gangly youth into a handsome young man. He had his National Service uniform on but had slipped his boots and battledress blouse off. His crew cut was beginning to grow out and he'd built up some muscle since being enlisted.

Over tea and cake, Harry updated them on what he'd been doing. When their call-up papers had arrived, both he and his twin, Oliver, had put themselves forward for the Royal Air Force and to James' delight, they'd been accepted. An ex-RAF man, he had a bias toward that particular branch of service and remembered happy days with his comrades even though they had lived through the dark days of war.

Oliver, at the moment, was stationed in Kent and getting to grips with languages; something he hadn't realised he had a talent for.

'Honestly,' said Harry, 'the man is pretty fluent in French, German and now he's learning some Japanese. He still wants to teach but he's beginning to think he should be teaching languages.'

'If he don't do that,' said Bert, 'he'll find something. People with those skills are always useful.'

'And what about you,' said Beth, 'are you still going to join us here?'

It had always been Harry's ambition to help James run Harrington's and keep the family business going. The young man took a bite of Victoria sponge and savoured it for a while.

'This,' he said holding up the sponge, 'is what I miss about home. Good, honest baking. I can taste the vanilla and that buttercream is gorgeous. The cakes we get in the NAAFI are as hard as rocks and just as heavy. But yes, I do still want to do that but I also have something I want to run by you.'

Bert picked up his cap. 'If this is family business, I'll ge' going.'

Harry insisted he stay. 'Bert, you're about as close as you can get to being family without actually being so. And, anyway, I'd appreciate your advice.'

They waited.

He rested his arms on the table. 'I'm apparently in the running for an intelligence role up in London. They like the way I work and I've proven myself as someone who thinks things through. They think I'd be ideal.'

'Is this a full-time role?' asked James. 'I mean, within the Royal Air Force?'

'No, no. They want me to see out my National Service and then go straight to them.'

'That would be a wonderful experience for you, don't you think, James?' said Beth.

'I do,' said James. 'I mean, I know you want to take over here but that's more about when I'm a bit older and need some help. I'd like to think that I'm not at that stage just yet.'

'I think you're far from that, Dad. No, I was thinking that it would be a good thing to do, just for a few years.' He turned to Bert. 'What d'you think?'

Bert appeared impressed. 'Intelligence. That sounds a bit like spy work.'

'Not exactly that. I'm not going to be out interrogating Russians or have a licence to kill. I'm not turning into James Bond or anything. No, it's more about sifting through intelligence that comes in from around the world.'

'Sounds exciting,' said Beth, 'and less dangerous than James Bond.'

'What do you think, Dad? Do you think I should consider it?'

'I think so, yes. It could be a good career until you're ready to take over here.'

Over the next hour, the four of them chatted about all manner of things but the last twenty minutes were taken up with the Celestial Faith Commune.

Bert asked what the world was coming to. 'Who in their right mind goes off to do something like that. It ain't a religion.'

'I don't think they're purporting to be,' said James.

'But why,' said Harry with a frown, 'advertise yourself as a faith? Celestial Faith. It gives the impression that they offer an alternative religion. I can't imagine the Reverend Merryweather is happy about it.'

'I don't think it'll be long before they come to blows,' said Beth.

'I can't imagine our vicar getting heated up over anything. He may be gearing up for a battle that doesn't actually exist. If he's only had two people abscond to the enemy, it's hardly an exodus.'

The discussion continued until the shrill of the telephone interrupted them. James went through to the hall and picked up the receiver.

'Cavendish — '

'They're h-having an open evening,' Stephen blurted out.

'Who?'

'The Celestial Faith Commune. They p-posted another infernal poster on my church notice-board. I apologise for my language but the cheek of it.'

'When is it?'

'What?'

'The open evening.'

'Ah, yes, sorry. I'm s-so incensed by these people, I can't think straight.'

James heard a rustle of paper.

'Right, here it is. Visitors are invited to join the Celestial Faith's evening worship this Wednesday. Are we g-going? It's at eight o'clock.'

'I think we should. Let's chat about our strategy tomorrow night at the rehearsal.'

Ending the call, James returned to the patio and imparted the news.

Bert picked up his tobacco pouch. 'Well, I ain't wasting my time with that. I'm off. I'll see you at re'earsals. I'll see meself out.' He gave a mock salute and departed.

117

Harry played with his teaspoon. 'I think I'll give it a miss. Are you going?'

James said yes and gave his reasons why. 'That board of information Mr Potter compiled about the commune has sparked my curiosity.'

'Mine too,' said Beth.

They were met with a roar of laughter. 'You two have really turned into a couple of private eyes, haven't you? You'll be setting yourselves up as an agency soon, especially now you have that commendation stuck up on the wall.'

Seeing the funny side of things, James had to admit that he liked a puzzle and this was certainly something that had caught his attention. A respected constable, close to retirement, had seen something he wasn't happy with at the commune. A few weeks later, he was dead. Had he asked too many questions?

Fingers crossed, this open evening would give them a chance to poke about and see what was really going on.

13

The next morning, DCI George Lane settled down at his desk, putting a cup of strong tea and a bacon sandwich down before sifting through the paperwork strewn across the surface. To the onlooker, it was a scene of chaos but George knew exactly where to find things. He took a bite from his sandwich and savoured the crispy, salty flavour. A rap on the door-frame interrupted him.

'Fulton, come in.'

PC Fulton, just a few months out of the academy, entered. His buttons gleamed, his shoes shone and his uniform was brand new and pristine. George had seen it all before. The young men and women fresh to the force all embarked on their careers with a need to impress. Commendable in most respects but he knew, a few years from now, that uniform would not be so smart and the eager expression would probably have changed to one of slight weariness.

He took a slurp of tea. 'What is it, Fulton? No work to get on with?'

'Oh, yes sir. I just thought I'd let you know something. I can't find Sergeant Hines so I thought I'd tell you. I'm not sure what I should do.'

'About what?'

'I got called out to a Mrs . . . ' he checked his notebook, 'Millerson. She was quite agitated, said she'd had a drawing stolen by some bloke . . . Cézanne?'

George's head snapped up. 'Cézanne! Are you sure?'

'Yes sir. I've heard the name but I'm not that well up on art.'

'Neither am I but that's one of the famous ones, I can tell you. You said it was a drawing?'

'Yes. Mrs Millerson's father was friendly with the artist and this was something he was given in that friendship.'

'Lucky bugger,' muttered George, knowing that selling such an item would guarantee a comfortable retirement for most people. 'What's the problem? Just file a report.'

'It's not that simple, sir. I did what I needed to do, you know, visit and put me report in. But I've just received another telephone call from her and she says that the drawing's reappeared.'

'Reappeared? How?'

Fulton shrugged. 'She's the only one living in the house. She swears blind she never takes it down. The only time she takes much notice of it is when she dusts; she dusts it but she says she dusts it on the wall without taking it off the hook.'

'And she's sure it'd gone missing?'

'I suggested she'd been mistaken or that her mind was playing tricks but she didn't hesitate to argue with me, sir.'

'And this woman's all right, is she? I mean she's not losing her marbles or anything?'

'No sir. She seemed a very alert and astute woman.'

George had to admit it was a strange one. 'How long was the drawing missing for?'

'She says it could be around a week. She dusts and vacuums the hall once a week. It wasn't there last week; that's why she rang us, because it reappeared.'

George agreed it was unusual but didn't place too much importance on it. 'File a report and put down what you've told me. Get a signed statement from Mrs Millerson. Let's make sure we've covered everything. Like you say, she could have been mistaken. See if there are any fingerprints.'

'Yes sir. Thank you.'

Taking another bite from his sandwich, George began the day's work

14

The church hall positively buzzed. Not one inch of the varnished wooden floor escaped the tread of the throng as villagers went back and forth, taking turns on the stage. In the middle of the floor was a long table where Dorothy Forbes sat. Alongside her was Stephen Merryweather and Bob Tanner, who ran the folk club. Out of the three, Bob Tanner was the most musically talented and, together, they would be finalising the performers to appear at the Old Time Music Hall.

The open windows provided a much-needed breeze.

Most of the children were outside on the green but a handful were sitting at the back playing Ludo. Tommy Hawkins, Charlie's son, had responsibility for Radley while Luke and Mark helped on stage, painting scenery. The dog's tail thumped a rhythm on the floor.

To the side, the WI had set up a couple of trestle-tables with hot and cold drinks and Elsie Taylor had supplied a selection of iced fairy cakes. Elsie, who ran the excellent café on the road between Cavendish and Charnley, had become a stalwart when it came to catering for events in both villages. Refusing to show bias to either hamlet, she simply turned up at every occasion and helped with the catering wherever needed. In her early thirties, she'd chosen to avoid the traditional path of marrying and having children. Instead, she ran her own business and had made a huge success of it.

James admired her greatly and was so in awe of her baking skills that he had entrusted her with some of Grandma Harrington's recipes to offer in the café. They'd become good friends and her establishment was always on his list of places to spend an hour in. He accepted a cup of tea and, putting a few coppers in the 'events' fund, chose a cake with pink icing and a cherry before turning his attention to her.

'Are you doing a song, Else?'

She recoiled. She spoke with a soft Sussex burr. 'Not on your life. You won't catch me singing up there. You'd clear the hall in two seconds.'

They laughed, then focussed on the stage where Bert Briggs was getting ready to perform. James edged a bit closer. He knew that whatever his friend was going to do, it would fit perfectly with the music hall theme.

The villagers hushed as Bert undid his jacket and slipped his thumbs under his braces.

'I'm subject to colds and they make me quite deaf

And then I can't 'ear what you say

A fellow once offered to buy me a drink

(I 'eard that with a cold, by the way)

So we're drinking and talking of women we've known

I described a sweet girl dressed in red

My description was good, and my pal went 'alf mad

It was the girl he was planning to wed!

He said 'I'll punch your head!'

I said 'Whose?' He said 'Yours!'

I said 'Mine?' He said 'Yes!' I said 'Oh?'

He said 'Want a fight?' I said 'Who?' He said 'You!'

I said 'Me?' He said 'Yes!' I said 'No!'

So we then came to words, he said 'You're a cad!'

I said 'Cad?' He said 'Yes!' I said 'Who?'

He said 'Who?' I said 'Yes?' He said 'You!'

I said 'Oh?' So, of course, then I knew.'

James had seen Bert perform this before; not on a stage or in public but in his own front room. They'd been talking about monologues and poems and Bert had launched into 'Back Answers' by Robb Wilton. Clearly a favourite, he'd decided this would be his piece for the Old Time Music Hall. At the end, the villagers erupted in cheers and shouted for more. Bert perked up and grinned. Even Dorothy Forbes was in tears of laughter and actually rose to her feet to applaud. She turned to the villagers.

'I think we've found our star turn.'

Shouts of encouragement demonstrated support for the decision.

Bert froze. 'Oi. No. I don't wanna be a star turn. I'm not even a resident.'

'Nonsense,' said Stephen, 'you s-spend half your life here and everyone considers you part of this family.'

'Pure music hall,' added Bob Tanner, his deep voice resonating. 'Who better to be our last act than a true cockney. Come on, Bert, don't let us down.'

Beth handed him a cup of tea. 'You'll be perfect.'

Bert accepted the cup and saucer and, egged on by all and sundry, announced that he would do it and that he could lay his hands on a pearly jacket to look the part. 'The Pearly King and Queen are friends of mine.'

'Of course they are,' said James to himself, wondering if there was anyone Bert didn't know. He'd seen several Pearlies in London; traditional East End fruit and veg sellers who wore magnificent suits covered with pearl buttons. Many were sewn on in designs depicting flowers, stars, suns and mystic symbols.

'Oh, that would be wonderful,' Dorothy almost gushed. From someone who wasn't terribly enamoured by Bert Briggs, she now appeared to be in awe of him. She settled back in her seat. 'That's a huge weight off my mind. Can you deliver two more monologues or songs?'

Bert, now basking in the praise from the Cavendish Players, suggested it would be best to have a couple of songs. 'I can start off with 'Back Answers' but you need to 'ave a proper knees-up, you know, a good sing-song to round the evening off.' He came down from the stage. 'Leave it with me and I'll think about it.'

Dorothy swung round and waved. 'Lord Harrington? You're doing something with George Lane, is that correct?'

James sought out George. 'Come along, old chap, it's our turn.'

George rolled his sleeves up and joined James on the stage. Mr Brownlee, the church organist, took the music from James and set it on the old piano to the side of them. James announced that he and George had opted for a song written by Weston and Lee.

Brownlee pounded down on the keys and the pair of them broke into the chorus:

'All I want is a proper cup of coffee
Made in a proper copper coffee pot.
I may be off my dot,
But I want a proper coffee in a proper copper pot.
Iron coffee pots and tin coffee pots, they're no use to me.
If I can't have a proper cup of coffee
In a proper copper coffee pot,
I'll have a cup of tea.'

As they sang, James had to admit that it sounded rather good. They'd perfected the song years ago and, after a few drinks, the pair of them had occasionally sung out a rendition much to the delight of whoever was in James' lounge. Their audience, tonight, was no exception. A raucous round of applause broke out and Dorothy's face again lit up.

'What a wonderful evening this will be,' she said, before suggesting a short break.

'I'm off to ge' a pint,' said Bert.

Stephen stretched his long limbs before getting up. He went straight over to

James. 'We d-do have some very talented people here, don't we?'

Beth, overhearing, approached them. 'I think Dulcie's influence is paying off.'

'I think so too,' said James. 'I understand that she's been quite inspirational.'

'Who's that?' asked Anne as she joined them, fairy cake in hand.

'Our talented actress, Dulcie Faye.'

'Ooh, yes, I went to one of her little drama workshops earlier. She showed us how to enter the stage and sit down on a sofa. I've never really thought about it before but it's surprising how wooden everyone looked. We all sat on that old sofa as if it were going to collapse. But when she came on, she made it flow. It was so natural.'

'She a-also gave some lessons about calming the n-nerves. I think that'll help a lot of the Cavendish Players.'

James winked at Beth. 'Perhaps she'll convince you to tread the boards, darling.'

She playfully slapped him. 'I'm more than content with costumes. I'm going along to learn a little more about make-up and wigs. Dulcie's doing an hour-long demonstration and we're all being given the opportunity to experiment. I'll leave you to show off on stage.'

The door to the hall flew open and, to everyone's astonishment, Father Sun entered. He was dressed in a golden ankle-length gown with motifs of the sun, moon and earth embroidered on it. Made of shimmering satin, any movement seemed effortless as he sailed across the floor.

He extended a hand to Stephen who reluctantly took it. 'Reverend Merryweather, it's good to see you again.' He scanned the room. 'You're putting on a production?'

James observed Stephen forcing politeness from every pore.

'Yes. Old T-Time Music Hall. The Cavendish Players put on a show two or th-three times a year. We're very community-spirited.'

'It's a wonderful way to bring people together,' Father Sun said. 'I'm a huge fan of the cinema myself but never had the inclination to act. I don't think I would have been seen as a talented thespian.'

'We're fortunate,' said Beth, 'that we have a talented professional here in Cavendish. Dulcie Faye.'

His lips parted. He seemed genuinely star-struck. 'Dulcie Faye! Really? I didn't know she lived in Cavendish.'

James watched as the man almost fell over himself with adoration of the young actress.

'I'd love to meet her, get an autograph. Is she here?'

Charlie announced that she'd popped home.

The man's posture sagged.

'I-If you were to involve yourself in our community rather than shutting yourself off in that old m-monstrosity down the road, you would have known.'

James and Beth gave each other a sideways look. Stephen was certainly doing his best to express his opinion.

Father Sun stared at Stephen. 'The commune takes time and effort to run. It's not a hobby; it's a way of life, a vocation that you commit yourself to all day every day. Like you, I need to be there for the members of our commune.'

Stephen put his shoulders back. 'How d-dare you liken your activities to those of my own? A commune is not a vocation, Mr . . . Father . . . oh, whatever your name is. A commune is simply a group of people living together.'

'A group of people who follow a spiritual path and commune with nature.'

'There is no spiritual path that I c-can see,' said Stephen. 'All I see are a bunch of misled individuals parading around in ridiculous gowns and refusing p-people access to their family.'

Father Sun's jaw tightened.

James noted his reaction. Stephen had hit upon a nerve but the man quickly recovered. He pulled a handful of leaflets from his pocket.

'The olive branch is extended. You obviously see me as the enemy, Vicar, so I'm here to provide a welcome to all. Closed gates will always encourage gossip and conspiracy but that is simply ignorance.' He addressed everyone in the hall; by now they were transfixed by the altercation. 'To convince you that we mean no harm to anyone and that we treat our commune members with love, we're having an open evening. Please join us and have a look around. We've nothing to hide.'

With a flippant salute toward Stephen, he placed the leaflets on the table and disappeared through the door.

Stephen pursed his lips. 'He's got a n-nerve. He's deliberately goading me.'

A word from Anne settled him down. 'The best thing we can do,' she said, 'is go to that evening and do what he said. Look around and satisfy ourselves.'

'He's right about one thing,' said James. 'Ignorance does have a way of leading us to make assumptions.'

'And so far,' Beth added, 'he's been nothing but gracious with all of us. Shouldn't we give him the benefit of the doubt?'

Stephen tipped his head back and sighed. 'Of all people, I should be the pragmatist, the one clearing the path of c-conciliation. But there's something about that m-man that gets my goat.'

Bert came through the back door and picked up on an atmosphere. ' 'ave I missed something?'

'A treat,' said James. 'You missed Father Sun from the Celestial Faith Commune.'

Bert smirked. 'Load of old cob . . . ,' he stopped. 'What I meant to say was it's all a load of rubbish.' He prodded the vicar gently. 'You don't wanna take any notice of 'im. Those sort are two a penny, 'ere one minute and gone the next. Right, I'm getting another cake and a cuppa.' He veered toward Elsie.

James said that Bert was right. 'How many of these sorts of things ever last? I can't think of one, can you?'

His friend brightened. 'No. No I can't. You're right, I shouldn't be so intimidated. I shall attend the o-open evening with an open mind.'

Good for you,' said James who was thinking along an entirely different line for his reason for attending. Yes, he'd go with an open mind but he'd also put on an enquiring head and start asking some probing questions. But before he did that, he wanted to have a good look at the information PC Potter had collated.

He went over to George who was studying the leaflet. 'I say, George, have you had any complaints or concerns about the Celestial Faith Commune?'

George brought out his pipe and they made their way out into the evening sunshine. Preparing the bowl with tobacco was a ritual for his friend and James knew that this was not just George lighting a pipe but considering his response. He lit the tobacco and the nutty smell of Barney's drifted up as he spoke.

'We've had a couple of complaints about noise at night.'

'By night, do you mean the evening or . . .'

'Late night. There are a few cottages to the rear of that property. I think they're the first houses that lead into Loxfield but they reckon they hear chanting and car engines about that time.'

'Have you gone over to investigate?'

George pulled a face. 'Not me, no. One of our uniforms went over to ask a few questions. That Father Sun bloke said it was when they worshipped at dawn and dusk; that the engines were the comings and goings of people who weren't yet full members.' He chewed the stem of his pipe. 'There wasn't anything suspicious; no crimes committed. They're doing what they say they do.'

'Nothing done then?'

'Just a request that they keep the noise down.'

James tipped his head to the hall. 'What did you make of that in there?'

'Two people with different perspectives. It was just a dispute, nothing more. I think Stephen's getting het up over nothing.' He checked his watch. 'Are we needed anymore? I could do with an early night.'

'You toddle off home. I think we already have our song fine-tuned. Will you be coming to this open evening at the commune?'

The look he received told him that George would not be attending. The church clock chimed eight. He really wanted to have a look at some of Potter's notes and, on returning to the hall, struck an agreement with Beth. He would return home and Harry, who was in the Half Moon with some old school chums, would drive her home in his newly-acquired Popular.

With a farewell to the Players, he marched purposely to his car.

* * *

At home, he poured a Scotch on ice, wandered through to the study and pulled up his Captain's chair. Putting his inkwell, pens and various papers to one side, he set out the items Mrs Potter had given him. He picked up the leaflet.

'*Celestial Faith Commune*
Connect with the Universe
Speak with the Galaxy
Ground yourself with Mother Earth
The sun nourishes you; the earth feeds you
Worship them, they are your power, your celestial soul.'

He raised an eyebrow. It wasn't his sort of thing but he couldn't see that this place would be a hive of criminal activity; it was simply a bunch of lost souls who had found a common interest. He leafed through the photographs.

Father Sun exuded appeal, even in black and white. The man had been charming and gracious when they'd met, yet he did feel that there was something beneath that magnetism. He'd seen it, tonight. That comment about the commune refusing access to families. That had certainly hit home.

He sifted through the photographs and slid the image of Mother Moon toward him. Similar in age to Father Sun; she had an elegance about her, and beauty too. Were they married? Had they set up this commune together? Flicking through the remaining photographs, he decided this wasn't telling him anything. He'd yet to meet these people and had no idea if they were members or fellow owners.

His eyes settled on Sister Bellatrix — Wendy Potter. This was a family photograph taken on a street. It was drizzling and Wendy was dressed in a wool overcoat and holding a handbag. She had shoulder-length hair with a slight wave and posed awkwardly for the camera: a plain girl with no notable features. The way Mrs Potter spoke about her, he had concluded that although she was in her mid-twenties, she was quite young for her age. She'd grown up in Loxfield, hadn't moved out, no mention of a boyfriend, hadn't travelled, which could mean she was not wise to the world. Was she naïve? That word had come up a couple of times where this commune was concerned. Mrs Potter had herself described Wendy as vulnerable. Stephen insisted the commune was picking on innocent and susceptible people. Was Wendy one of those?'

And her mother was right. She'd given up her job to stay at the commune which begged a more important question; one that he had struggled to answer no matter how many times he considered it. How on earth did these Celestial Faith people manage to purchase such a large house and how did they maintain it? They might sustain themselves where food was concerned but what about heating, electric, gas and all the other bills associated with owning a property?

He moved to the newspaper clippings that presented various accounts of cults across the world. Many of them detailed movements within the United States but there were also several dotted around the globe, including in England. Bernard Potter had circled one particular article by an eminent psychologist that gave an overview of the personality traits of a cult leader. It was a three-page article and, fortunately, Potter had made notes of things he felt were pertinent:

Has delusions of power.
Revels in admiration.
Asks for money from members and/or relatives.
Sensitive as to how he is seen by others.
Likes to be the focus of attention.
Can be overdramatic.
Has the best of everything.
Controlling.

Superficially charming.
Refuses members contact with
family.
Hides family background.

Another scrap of paper caught his eye. Bernard Potter had tried to get information on Father Sun but officially channels were blocked. But he did have a name: Johnny Barton.

He heard the front door close and a cheery hello from Beth and Harry.

'I'm in the study.'

She breezed through and, in a horrendous cockney accent, broke into song:

''My old man said follow the van and don't dilly dally on the way . . .''

He couldn't help but burst out laughing and noticed Harry roll his eyes. She did her best to look insulted but, eventually, couldn't contain her own laughter.

'Anne tried to persuade me to go on stage and sing with Bert who attempted to teach me an East End accent.' She plonked herself down opposite him. 'Your reaction tells me that I should stick to sewing costumes and putting on make-up.'

'I'm sure a few lessons with Dulcie Faye would help,' he said with a cheeky grin.

'Now you're digging yourself into more trouble. You're saying I can't act or sing now.'

'But you are a mean seamstress and, if you left that skill to tread the boards, we would be lacking in the wardrobe department. And, anyway, you did tread the boards during the last pantomime. Didn't you enjoy that?'

She tutted. 'Too many people talked me into that. Including you. I've never been so nervous.' She came around to his side of the desk and studied the items.

Harry pulled up a chair alongside. 'Have you come up with anything?'

He handed Beth the article. 'This is rather interesting. Our man, Potter, perhaps believed that some of these traits relate to Father Sun.'

'All of them, I'd say.' She sat on the arm of Harry's chair and flicked through the article. 'I'm sure if we got to know

Father Sun more, there'd be a few additions to the list.'

Harry, studying the text, added: 'Including sex.'

'Do you think so?' said Beth.

'From what you've said, the man is charming and good-looking. If he's both of those, and he has those traits, he'll relish power and control. What hot-blooded male wouldn't take advantage of that?'

'That's true,' said Beth.

James displayed the picture of Wendy and a couple of the other female members. 'They're not Marilyn Monroe, darling.' He held his palms up. 'I'm not saying that looks are everything but if you're Father Sun, wouldn't you be in a position to pick and choose?'

His son stopped him. 'But vulnerable women are probably easier to manipulate. Don't you think they'd be easily flattered?'

James conceded this was true.

His son then went on to describe a cult in South America. 'I can't remember the name of it now but it was in the middle of nowhere, in the jungle, and they were into some extreme form of worship.' He gestured at the articles and lists of traits. 'But that all fits in with the cult mentality. One of the women escaped and spent a few days, on foot, getting back to civilisation. She arrived at the nearest town and the residents alerted the police. They made some sort of raid and found that their leader was power-crazy and had several children by various women in the commune.'

'Oh,' said Beth. 'D'you think that's what's happening here?'

'I'm absolutely certain it's not,' said James. 'Father Sun is not in the middle of the jungle so he's under closer scrutiny. I didn't see any children there. And he's invited everyone to an open evening which hardly implies he wants to hide the place away.'

Beth picked up the photograph of Mother Moon. 'You think they're married?'

He shrugged. 'I've no idea. The only way we're going to get further with this is by snooping around on the open evening.'

'Then that's what we'll do.' She placed the papers down and picked up the smallest item on the table — the piece of paper with fragmented writing. 'I wonder why Bernard Potter found this so interesting?'

He took it from her and placed it in an envelope. 'It's something he thought was important so we'll take good care of it.'

Harry tutted at the pair of them.

'Are you making fun of us, Harry?'

Harry slapped him on the back. 'I wouldn't dare. And I wouldn't have my mother and father any other way. Do I prefer ordinary or adventurous? I'd say you were the latter. Although 'adventurous' could be replaced with 'foolhardy'.'

They went through to the kitchen where Beth asked if they would like some warm milk before bed.

'Not for me, thanks,' said Harry. 'I'm taking a glass of brandy up and having a read.' He kissed Beth on the cheek and told James not to think too much or he wouldn't sleep. 'Put a tot of brandy in your milk or you'll be playing Sherlock all night.' He went through to the lounge.

'I think hot milk will be fine,' James said to Beth, 'but I do have all sorts of things buzzing around in my brain. I may pop over to the library and see if Charlie has something about the Druids. That Celestial Faith Commune appears to be very similar and I wonder if Bernard Potter was simply chasing something that wasn't there.'

'Worried about his daughter. It could well be.' She filled the saucepan with milk and brought out two mugs. 'There was one thing in that article that Mr Potter didn't put down on his list.'

'Oh?'

'Cult leaders tend to locate their communes away from civilisation; in the middle of nowhere so they can't be seen. I know he's not in the jungle but that farm is out of the way, isn't it? And he keeps the gate locked.'

15

The huge wrought iron gates to the Celestial Faith Commune were open and a number of people from Cavendish and the neighbouring villages of Charnley and Loxfield had decided to attend the open evening more out of curiosity than because of any underlying suspicions.

The lawn at the front of the converted farmhouse was freshly mowed and half a dozen trestle-tables stood there, with commune members behind them. The first four offered soft drinks and cakes for a small contribution toward the commune. The last two had vegetables and fruit for sale from the allotments and leaflets about their beliefs.

James, standing with Beth, Stephen and Anne, gazed around. Approximately fifty people had arrived so far, the majority of them gathering by the refreshments. He approached one of the commune members. Her blue robe depicted colourful images of the planet Saturn.

'Welcome to the Celestial Faith Commune,' she said. 'Can I offer you some lemonade? It's home-made; a little sour but very refreshing.'

'Not for me thanks,' said James, who wasn't a big lover of sour drinks. 'We were wondering what was on the cards for tonight? Is Father Sun going to make an appearance?'

Mother Moon, identified by the beautiful embroidery on her gown, approached from the stall next door. Her eyes sparkled. 'I'm Mother Moon; my husband's on his way.'

She had a typically English peaches and cream complexion, with soft brown eyes and full lips.

'Your husband is Father Sun?'

Before she had a chance to answer, Father Sun strode toward them and proffered a general greeting to everyone. The chatter hushed as he made it clear that the open evening was there to quell any concerns or fears the villagers might have about the commune.

'You're free to roam the grounds and

the house. Our members are scattered around, doing their chores.' He checked his watch. 'At nine o'clock, we'll be gathering here to go through a shortened version of our dusk worship. A little earlier than normal but it gives you time to ask questions after. Some of you will know that we're a group that honours our Mother Earth. She and the universe provide us with nourishment, heat, shelter and clean air. As part of our daily ritual, we give thanks to her and to our sun and moon. Please join us here at nine and witness this gathering. We'll wrap things up at ten o'clock. In the meantime, enjoy your visit and do ask us anything.' His eyes sought out Stephen. 'Anything at all.'

People began to meander off but a clap of the hands signalled that Father Sun had one last thing to say. 'When I say roam the grounds, please take care not to enter the ruins at the back of the house. You'll see that the council have put up notices to say that it is deemed unsafe. We are seeking permission to knock it down and build an accommodation block in its place.'

Stephen held a hand up. 'Could I ask, how a-are you getting the money to pay for that? You must struggle to make ends meet.'

Again, James noticed a slight twitch of irritation in Father Sun. 'Reverend Merryweather, how much does a vicar earn in one year?'

'I-I don't think that's anything to do with you.'

'Exactly.' He addressed the crowd. 'When I say that we are open to questions, I mean about our beliefs and how we live. Our financial records are confidential and between me and our accountants.' He invited everyone to disperse.

James sidled up to his friend. 'I think he won that one, don't you?'

Stephen reluctantly admitted that he hadn't handled the question well. 'I suppose i-it isn't any business of mine. I would be interested though, wouldn't you?'

'Yes. But I think a subtler approach is required.' With Beth and Anne to his side he made a suggestion. 'Look, Stephen, why don't you and Anne go and find out about the commune. Ask the members what they get up to, find out about the faith side of things and anything that you feel needs answering to satisfy your concerns.' He linked hands with Beth. 'Meanwhile, we'll nose about where we're not supposed to be, see if we can track down Wendy, Sister Bellatrix, and ask a few questions.'

'Meet back here for the dusk worship?' asked Anne.

'I wouldn't miss it for the world,' said Beth pulling James toward her. 'Come on, Sherlock.'

As they separated, James felt in his pocket and brought out a slip of paper. 'Bernard Potter listed a few of the commune members on his board so why don't we try and seek them out.'

'Who's first on the list?'

'Sister Jupiter.'

Beth asked one of the members serving at the trestle tables and then returned to James. 'She's in the kitchen making supper with Sister Venus.'

'Jolly good. She's another on the list.

We can kill two birds with one stone.'

'And nose around the house.'

The old farmhouse was an impressive structure, a large stone building that had been renovated to a good standard. To the side was what James presumed to be the old cowshed that had been tastefully converted. They followed a number of intrigued people through the front door.

In the hallway were photographs and paintings of various natural and planetary images. At the far end someone had painted a mural of the earth surrounded by various stars, comets and nebulae. James had to admit that it was a stunning picture and summed up what the commune was all about.

A pleasant aroma reached them and, following the scent, they found themselves in a traditional farmhouse kitchen. An Aga dominated the room and, on its top, were a number of huge saucepans and pots bubbling away.

Beth breathed in. 'Mmm, that smells lovely. What're you cooking?'

A woman in her early twenties answered. 'Chicken soup.' She beckoned them over and lifted the lid on a pot.

The scent was enticing and they immediately complimented her. She handed them two spoons.

'Here, have a taste.'

They accepted their respective spoons, caught a sample, then allowed it to cool before trying it.

James sipped his and closed his eyes. 'I say, that's absolutely delicious.'

Beth agreed.

James noticed the embroidered design on her robe depicted the blue/white planet of Venus and there was another design, a much smaller image, showing the Roman goddess Venus. Sister Venus was a plain-looking girl with short dark hair cut in a pudding basin style which did nothing to flatter her. She wore no make-up but had caught the sun.

He put his spoon in the sink. 'You keep your own chickens?'

'Just started,' she gushed. 'I've never kept them before but they're great fun. I've given names to all of them, although someone said I shouldn't do that because I'll get too attached, you know, when we come to eat them. They're probably right but it's difficult to latch on to a bird, isn't it? I mean, when we start getting sheep and lambs, I will definitely not be naming them. Lambs are so sweet and I'm sure when we bring them in I'll find it difficult to prepare them for dinner if they've got names.'

'You've presumably never worked on a farm.'

'Oh no. I lived in Bognor Regis. I've always loved the countryside though and I'm not squeamish about animals and preparing them. My gran showed me how to do quite a bit when she got rabbits from the butchers. She used to prepare them from scratch.'

Beth replaced the lid on the pot. 'You live here permanently?'

There was an eagerness about her and James hoped that she would be as talkative when he asked her specific questions.

'Mum and Dad weren't happy with me coming here at first but they've had to learn to like it. I got fed up living at home and always having to answer about where

I'm going and how late I'm going to be. I mean, I'm twenty-three, not seven. I started coming here a couple of months ago and Father Sun told me I've to think it over before committing myself to anything but I knew straight away, this was the place for me.'

James frowned. 'Because you wanted to get away from your parents?'

Sister Venus checked the contents of the oven. 'That's right, yeah.'

It was said in such a matter-of-fact way that it surprised James. He couldn't help but ask why she simply didn't move out and rent a room. 'I mean, how on earth do you live? You're a young woman who must want to experience life and meet a chap or something.'

'Oh no. I'm really happy here. I'm learning all about growing vegetables and looking after animals. I love all the worshipping Mother Earth; it's really interesting.'

Beth asked what would happen if she decided she didn't like it. 'Can you leave?'

The young woman pretended not to hear and carried on with her chores.

James wasn't going to let her get away with that. 'You're not free to leave?'

'We have allocated days off where we do the commune work and distribute leaflets.' She continued busying herself although there didn't seem to be much to do.

'On your own?' asked Beth.

'No, no, normally with Father Sun or Mother Moon.'

'Do your parents visit?'

'No. The elders don't allow visitors. They call them a distraction and, to be honest, they are. They think what we're doing is peculiar and make fun of us. I'm sure you'll do the same when you get home.'

James convinced her otherwise. 'We're interested in what you're doing but we have a measure of concern too. Only because a friend of ours has a daughter here and he worries.'

'Well, he shouldn't.'

Beth couldn't help but let out an exasperated groan. 'A mother or father will always worry about their children, no matter how old they are. Unfortunately, our friend was killed recently and his last thoughts were for his daughter.'

That startling piece of news had shaken Sister Venus. James hoped that she was imagining being in the same position. It irked him that she had no consideration for how her parents must be feeling. But, he thought, not everyone had the same relationship with their children as he and Beth were fortunate to enjoy.

'Can I ask,' said James, 'are you not even permitted to write to your parents?'

'No contact with the outside world.' Her eyes began to dart here and there. The bright and happy demeanour was slipping.

'You have a good community here?' asked James.

Feeling the topic had landed on safer ground, Sister Venus was eager to say that they did. 'We are truly brothers and sisters in every sense of the word.'

'And yet you've not asked who our friend's daughter is. A brother or sister would surely have asked and be there to look after her.'

Although little needed attending to, the

girl wiped surfaces that were already clean, checked the soup for the umpteenth time, then shouted for Sister Jupiter. 'Honestly, that woman is supposed to be in here helping me.'

James caught Beth's eye. It was she who spoke next.

'Don't the leaders allow their members time to visit their families after a bereavement?'

To pile on the pressure, James suggested that Mother Earth would surely feel this would be beneficial. 'This commune is all about love and community, a spiritual togetherness. A number of animals on this planet come together to mourn.' He wandered around the kitchen. 'I read an article the other day about elephants and how they gather to lament a lost family member; I believe that monkeys do the same thing. The whole world is made up of family units and — '

'You'll have to speak to Father Sun,' she bridled. Aware that she had let her guard drop, she brushed away a stray hair. 'I'm so sorry. It's been rather busy today and I'm not used to so many strangers.'

Before they had time to ask anything further, a woman in her fifties scuttled in like a nervous sparrow. Her robes told them this was Sister Jupiter. Although Jupiter was the biggest planet, this woman was the smallest they'd seen in the commune and her behaviour was jittery to say the least. She reached into a large bowl, brought out some dough and slammed it down on the work surface.

'Sister Jupiter?' enquired James.

Sister Venus replied. 'Sister Jupiter is quite shy. You're unlikely to get much out of her. Sister, the bread should have been in the oven by now.'

'Yes, Sister Venus.' She sounded almost childlike.

'You have a beautiful robe,' said Beth.

This seemed to soften the lady as she kneaded the dough. She went on to separate it out into small balls for rolls. 'I made it myself. I like sewing.'

'Me too,' said Beth, and went on to explain how she loved making the costumes for the Cavendish Players.

James watched as she gained the woman's trust. A few visitors entered.

After a couple of minutes of idle chat about dressmaking, Beth asked: 'Do you both know about Sister Bellatrix and what happened to her father?'

The baking tray Sister Jupiter was holding crashed to the floor. She snatched it back up and shot an anxious look at Sister Venus who grabbed a cloth and, once again, cleaned what appeared to be a pristine worktop.

'Of course we know,' Sister Venus said. 'But it's nothing to do with us.'

'What isn't?' asked James.

'Father Sun and Mother Moon look after our welfare. Ask them.'

More visitors began arriving and had general questions to put to the women. James didn't think they'd get any further so he and Beth thanked them for their time.

'What did you make of them?' asked James as they wandered through to the room opposite.

'Suspicious. As if they know more than they're letting on.'

'Mmm.' James scanned the room. It was a sitting room with a three-piece suite, a wireless and a small television. The bookshelves held a variety of popular paperback novels and quite a few hardback books on gardening, animal husbandry and spirituality. He tapped the spines. 'You know, everywhere I look, I see what appears to be a legitimate business. This Sun and Moon couple are clearly trying to set up a self-sufficient commune.' He swung round. 'But, like you, I feel as if there's something odd going on.'

They returned to the hall and made their way to the rear of the house where they found two more doors. One opened in on a room that had been converted into a classroom. The blackboard bore a number of facts about looking after poultry and on some of the desks were leaflets from the National Farmers Union. On another board were discussion points about the Celts and Druids.

Beth flicked through a leaflet while James tried the other door. The sign on it simply read: 'Office'. He twisted the doorknob. 'Blast. Locked. Shall we see if we can find the others on our list?'

'Yes, let's. This leaflet is all about dairy farming. Do you think they're going to expand some more?'

'Perhaps. It all seems quite enterprising. I know Stephen's perturbed about the whole thing but, apart from that nagging doubt, I'm actually quite impressed.'

'I wonder how Stephen and Anne are getting on.'

16

'I-I feel as if I've let you both down in some way,' said Stephen.

He and Anne were sitting on some wooden folding chairs, speaking with Mrs Long and Mrs Fellowes.

Both were astonished to learn that he felt this way and, between them, they assured him this was not the case.

'We're not deserting you,' said Mrs Long. 'We've always loved your services and you provide such inspiration.'

'A breath of fresh air compared to the last vicar,' added Mrs Fellowes.

Anne tilted her head. 'Then why on earth are you thinking of moving in here? You have a faith that you follow.'

'Oh, but Father Sun says that we can continue with that.'

'While you're trying it out,' reminded Anne. 'We were of the understanding that you had to make your mind up about whether to move here permanently or stop coming. That sounds like an ultimatum to me.'

'It'll m-mean that you'll miss our Sunday services and the v-village activities,' added Stephen.

Mrs Long scoffed at the notion. 'I'm sure Father Sun will allow us to carry on as normal. He's a very nice man, very accommodating.'

'Yes,' her companion said. 'He went through everything with us yesterday afternoon.'

An elderly lady, in long blue robes depicting a swirling galaxy, asked if she could join them. Stephen retrieved a wooden chair and held it as she sat down with a groan. 'Getting old is not an enjoyable experience,' she said with a thin voice. Stephen couldn't place the trace of an accent but, if he had to guess, he would say Yorkshire or Lancashire. 'Can't get about like I used to. I'm much better at planning things out than being practical.'

She introduced herself as Sister Andromeda.

'How long have you been a member?' asked Anne.

'Three years. I was one of the first.'

Stephen sat up with a start. 'But th-this commune has only been here a few months.'

'Oh, we moved from the Midlands. Father Sun had a property leased to begin with but it wasn't right. Too near the city and main roads. It wasn't conducive to any sort of spiritual needs and certainly not if you wanted to sit quietly.'

'H-How did he come by this place?'

'You'd have to ask him.'

Stephen returned his attention to his two parishioners. His sole reason for coming to this open day was to bring his lost sheep home. Unless he'd got the wrong end of the stick, these two ladies were under the misconception that they were free to come and go as they pleased.

'You d-do realise that, once you sign up for this . . . affair, you're not permitted to leave.'

Again, the ladies laughed at him.

'Of course we can.'

Anne turned to Sister Andromeda. 'Can members come and go as they please?'

She gave the ladies an old-fashioned

look. 'We're a closed community. I suppose it may be similar to a convent. Nuns don't go out much, do they? And everything's here for you. Why would you want to go back to the outside world when things are so perfect here? Almost like paradise, especially here, in the countryside.'

Stephen felt his stomach twist in knots. It wasn't often that he had to be firm or argumentative but what he was hearing was unacceptable. With a quiet assertiveness he reached for Anne's hand and addressed the three women.

'I must correct you, Sister Andromeda. Many of the c-convents are closed communities but they do not stop their sisters from mixing with the general public and doing good work for them too. My parishioners here are valuable members of the Cavendish community and enjoy the events we h-have within the church and the village.'

'Then they have a choice to make.' She reached out an arm. 'Would you help me up?' Stephen did so and she went on her way.

Mrs Fellowes had a look of alarm on her face. 'Is she saying that once we make our commitment to this commune, we can't go out?'

Anne pulled her chair closer. 'Mrs Fellowes, what exactly did Father Sun say to you yesterday? I mean, what are the terms of you being here permanently?'

They listened as the two ladies recited their chat with Father Sun. He had extolled, with considerable charm, the virtues of living in the commune. They had, he'd said, experienced the sheer wonder and delight of sharing their lives with like-minded people. He promised them rejuvenation and happiness beyond anything they had now. He and Mother Moon had complimented them on their skills and thanked them profusely for what they brought to the commune.

Stephen stopped them. 'What does he mean, what you bring to the commune?'

'Our experiences,' said Mrs Long. 'He told us that people our age had so much wisdom and knowledge and that he can see us being elders.'

'An elder,' said Mrs Fellowes, 'is

someone the members can confide in. Like a favourite aunt. I quite liked the idea of that.'

Anne asked if she could put a delicate question to them. They invited her to do so.

'We heard, when you commit yourself full-time to the commune, that you have to give up your home. Is that right?'

'Oh no dear,' said Mrs Fellowes. 'I rent so I would simply give up my flat and move in here. I have a pension and a percentage of that goes to the commune every week. It's only fair, to help with rates and bills.'

'B-But you own your home, Mrs Long,' said Stephen. 'Surely you w-won't sell your house.'

'I'd rather not. I've lived there for years. Father Sun suggested that if I don't sell it, then I could rent it out.'

'How m-much would he take from you if you sold it?'

She shifted in her chair. 'He didn't specify.'

'Oh ladies,' said Anne, 'would you please allow us to sit with you when you're speaking with Father Sun? If you truly want to live here then we would never stand in your way but I'd be much happier knowing that you're appraised of all the details. Will you allow us to do that?'

Mrs Long said she would have no issue with it but asked her companion what she thought Father Sun would make of it.

'I'm sure he would be most amenable.'

Stephen couldn't help but think the opposite. As they left the ladies to their contemplation he sidled up to Anne. 'Father Sun w-wouldn't allow us within a hundred yards of that discussion.'

'Perhaps James and Beth could try. I mean, they haven't antagonised him in any way so he may be more open to them.'

'That's t-true. I wonder how they're getting on.'

⋆　⋆　⋆

James and Beth found themselves at the allotments, a huge area around the size of a tennis court consisting of orderly vegetable patches along with orchard trees and bushes full of summer berries. In the centre was a makeshift shed. It certainly seemed well-organised. A number of commune members were planting, cutting, weeding and preparing the soil. These people had discarded their embroidered costumes and wore simple brown robes, similar to those worn by monks. James checked his list of people.

'We're looking for Brothers Neptune and Mars.'

'Without their gowns on, we won't know who's who. We'll have to ask.'

Before they had a chance to speak, a man in his late teens came over with a hoe. He had a ruddy complexion and, James guessed, he spent the majority of his time outside.

'Hello,' he said. 'Have you come for the open day?'

He was a Downs Syndrome lad with a round, dumpy face and an air of wonder.

'Yes, we have,' James answered. 'What celestial body of the universe have you chosen?'

He grinned proudly. 'I'm Brother Neptune.'

James gave Beth a sideways glance. *That was a stroke of luck,* they were thinking.

'I chose it because it's a mysterious planet,' continued the young man. 'Neptune is the God of the Seas.'

'In Roman mythology yes. In Greek, he's Poseidon. Did you know that?'

The lad's eyes opened wide. 'No, I didn't know that. Are you really intelligent?'

'More well-read, I think' answered James.

Beth asked how long he'd been at the commune.

'Three years.'

He went on to explain that the commune had begun life just outside of Birmingham and he'd thought of Father Sun as his own father.

'But he's only a little bit older than you,' said Beth.

Brother Neptune gently dug the hoe into the earth. 'My dad was cruel to me. Said I was simple and no use to anyone.'

'How dreadful for you.'

'And Father Sun took you under his wing?' An eager nod backed up James' assumption. 'And your job here is to work on the allotments.'

'Father Sun said I'm a natural.'

'And does Father Sun ask you to contribute in any other way? Do you have to pay bed and board?'

'I don't have much. My mum sends through a couple of pounds now and then and I give that to him.'

'You don't keep anything back for yourself?'

He beamed. 'Don't have to. I don't go anywhere. I stay here where I'm safe.'

'And do you notice anything odd going on at all? Anything that strikes you as out of the ordinary?'

'Sometimes I hear noises in the night.'

'What sort of noises?' asked Beth.

'Mother Moon says I'm dreaming but I'm sure I hear them. Engines.'

'I say, do you know where we can find Sister Bellatrix?'

A change came over the lad — not a hostile or angry one but more one of trepidation. James sensed it straight away and quelled any concerns in an instant.

'We know her mother. We said we'd have a chat with her today, seeing that it's an open evening and all that. We thought she'd be here.'

A shake of the head is all they received in return.

'Is Sister Bellatrix not here?' asked Beth.

They were interrupted by Brother Mars who, James guessed, had taken the name to match his temperament. So far, the people they'd met had been gracious and polite but the man who had appeared from behind them was not of that ilk. He wore a dark blue robe scattered with images of the red planet. Enveloped in the gown was a middle-aged man with a face as red as the planet he'd chosen. James didn't know him from Adam but his complexion indicated he was a heavy drinker. He had an unnaturally flushed face and nose, and broken veins across his cheeks. If he wasn't a drinker now he certainly had been in the past.

'What's this 'bout Sister Bellatrix?' He had a Yorkshire accent.

'We're friends of her mother,' said Beth. 'Mrs Potter is a little worried. Wendy's . . . Sister Bellatrix's father was killed and she claims she was refused access to her daughter.'

'No, no. Wouldn't refuse access for something like that. It's prob'ly t'other way around. Bellatrix wants time. She decided not to come out tonight. She wants time t'grieve.'

'But surely she has time for her own mother!' exclaimed Beth. 'She's distraught and needs her family.'

He gave a dismissive wave. 'That's nowt do with me. Or you.'

'Could we see her just for two minutes?' asked James.

Brother Mars asked Brother Neptune go return to the allotments. The young man, oblivious to the tension, beamed at Brother Mars and waved a friendly goodbye.

'Sister Bellatrix doesn't want to see anyone,' Brother Mars said.

As Beth went to challenge him, James

interrupted. 'I say, what's all this about engines in the middle of the night?'

The man put his head back and laughed. 'Brother Neptune and his dreams. No one else hears 'em.'

'The neighbours hear them. They put a complaint in to the police.'

'Nowt but cars, that's all.'

He reminded them that the sun worship was due to begin in ten minutes. 'Don't tha' be late.' He turned and trudged back toward the front lawn.

James grabbed Beth's hand and led her behind the house.

'Where are we going?'

'I'm having a nose about. Come on.'

They made their way toward the dilapidated building. It was an old brick-built barn that had seen better days. Some bricks had fallen away and the few windows there were had been boarded up.

'Look at this,' said Beth.

They perused a notice from the local council:

KEEP OUT

This structure is considered dangerous.

No trespassing without written authorisation.

A number of bylaws and conditions were contained in the notice. James threaded a path to the side where he found one of the windows had a wooden slat missing. He peered in and wished he'd brought a torch. From what he could see, though, it was a dusty old ruin ready for demolition.

'HEY!'

They turned to see Father Sun striding toward them.

'Can't you read? This building's not safe. What're you doing poking your nose around here for? Our worship's in a few minutes. Make sure you're there. Once that's finished, I want all visitors out.'

He turned on his heels and marched off.

James pulled a face to indicate that he was pleased to have evoked a reaction. 'We're seeing a different side to Father Sun, aren't we? I thought this evening was between eight and ten o'clock. Why's he turfing us out so soon?'

'Do you think we're all asking too

many questions?'

As they made their way to the front of the house, James stopped in his tracks and squatted down. 'Look at this?' He picked up a couple of pieces of torn paper, each the size of a postage stamp. 'This looks similar to the paper that Mr Potter found.' They scanned the grounds.

Beth picked up another fragment and gave it to him. 'Looks like someone tore up a document. Here's another.'

He slipped the pieces in his pocket. They'd reached the edge of the lawn when James pulled Beth back. 'There's a garage over there. Let's take a look.'

The garage was another rickety wooden building, big enough to house four cars. Only one took up a space in there: a new Hillman Minx, hot off the production line. Its grey paintwork gleamed.

Beth told him to hurry along. 'Father Sun will be more annoyed if we arrive late for this worship thing.'

The sound of a resonant bell warned them that the ceremony was about to begin. As James turned to join Beth, he noticed a bowl of clear fluid on the ground. He gingerly lifted the bonnet up. Careful not to get dirty, he checked over the engine and then the tyres. He closed the bonnet and, to his delight, the driver's door was open. He slipped into the seat and checked the dials.

Beth glared. 'What on earth are you doing?'

She dragged him out of the garage and back to the main grounds.

'A new car with less than ten miles on the clock. It's either been delivered here or he's purchased it at a local garage.'

'What has that to do with anything?'

'I'm not entirely sure. But I don't understand how they can afford all of this.'

'You're making something out of nothing. Unless we see their accounts, we can't know.'

When they reached the main lawn, the ceremony to worship the setting sun was under way. They tiptoed toward Stephen and Anne, who both had questioning frowns on their faces.

'Where have you been?' mouthed Anne.

'Snooping,' whispered James with a grin.

Feeling Beth's urgent tug on his arm, he turned. 'What is it?'

'Look.'

He followed her eye-line to catch a glimpse of Mrs Potter hurrying from the old cowshed toward the woods at the side of the house.

17

While James and Beth were visiting the commune, GJ was tidying up the oils and canvasses from that day's session. He was enjoying his new livelihood and the fact that he'd been given the opportunity to work in such beautiful surroundings. This last year had seen so many changes and he'd gone from being a homeless itinerant to finding his family and having a home of his own. Added to that, he'd been delighted to meet Catherine who he was now proud to call his wife. She kissed him on the cheek.

'Lord and Lady Harrington have gone over to that Celestial Faith open evening. Did you fancy going?'

He checked his watch and pulled a face. 'I'd rather not. I'm not that interested, are you?'

'Not really. I know one of the waitresses is quite keen. Adam's girlfriend, Julie. I wonder if she's there tonight?'

GJ said he thought she was working 'I'm sure I saw her at the tables earlier.'

She hugged him. 'I'm going to cycle home. Do you fancy a sandwich when we get in? I've got some sausages left over from yesterday.'

'Anything you make is all right. I shouldn't be too long. You eat when you get home if you're hungry.'

She left and GJ did what he always did at this time; one last sweep around the barn to ensure everything was in place for the following day. He had students of various standards and had to make sure he not only appealed to the beginners but also those who showed an aptitude for painting or had some prior experience. It was a difficult balance but one that he was beginning to master.

Ten minutes later, he slid the barn doors closed and secured the padlock. A man approached from the side and he recognised him straight away. It was Mr Drummond, the man who had offered him the calligraphy work.

'Good evening,' the man said. 'I was hoping to catch you. Do you have a few minutes?'

'Literally a few,' said GJ. 'My wife's at home making supper so I don't want to be late. Were you happy with the calligraphy work?'

'Extremely happy.' The man followed GJ to his bicycle as he went on. 'It takes a special talent to create calligraphy so beautifully. You clearly have all of the correct equipment.'

Putting his bicycle clips on, GJ shrugged. 'The correct equipment is simply a selection of nibs. Granted, if you have superior nibs, your calligraphy will improve. It's difficult to write accurately with sweeping movements if you have a cheap pen. I'm fortunate that I work with the best tools.'

'Would you be interested in doing more work for us?'

'Us?'

The man ignored the question and carried on. 'We have quite a bit of work to do and wondered if you could pay us a visit.'

GJ said he would be delighted. 'If you're paying me the same money that I got for this last commission, I'd be very interested.'

'Some of the documents would be longer, more time-consuming for you.'

'That's fine, providing you give me enough notice.' He picked up his knapsack. 'Do I have to come to you? I have a studio here where I work. Can you nip by here tomorrow?'

'I'm afraid not. I need you to meet someone. How about I pick you up at ten o'clock tomorrow night.'

'That's a bit late, isn't it?'

'It's the only time I can do. Before you go, could I ask; I notice you teach painting and drawing. Are you able to replicate pictures?'

'As in copy them?'

'Stroke for stroke.'

'I've never really tried but, yes, with some artists I probably could. Not all I hasten to add. Why?'

Without another word on the subject, the man took a step back. 'Until tomorrow.'

GJ cycled away from Harrington's with more than a trace of concern lodged in his mind.

*   *   *

That night, in a windowless room, an elderly woman studied a number of paintings and documents under a bright desk-light. In the distance was the gentle sound of the ocean. She held a large magnifying glass and scrutinised the artwork and the papers.

'I'm pleased with this,' she said. 'But orders are coming in from the Continent. We need two or three more people to help.'

'Don't worry,' said a younger man. 'I think I have another person. We're paying a considerable amount though. That'll eat into our profits.'

The old woman smirked. 'For what we'll get for this painting alone, we'll make a mint.' She swung round. 'Talking of mint, how's everything going with the silversmith?'

A confident grin. 'The one-pound

notes haven't been spotted. He's working on a metal plate for five-pound notes now.'

'We must be careful. Shifting art is one thing; funnelling money through shops and banks is dangerous.'

'We won't do anything rash.'

An elderly man approached the pair. He spoke to the woman. 'I find these late nights debilitating at my age. Can't we do this earlier in the evening?'

'No,' came the reply. 'We'll take you home.'

The young man placed a blindfold over the old man's eyes.

'Is this really necessary?'

'Yes,' the young man replied as he guided him through the doorway.

* * *

Late the following morning, James and Harry were supervising the dismantling of the old barn, two fields from Harrington's country hotel. The previous summer, James and Beth unearthed a dog-fighting ring that had taken place there. They'd been pondering, for some time, about pulling the thing down and replacing it with a bird-watching area. That unfortunate discovery had made their minds up.

Bert caught up with them. 'Yer finally got the old shambles down then?'

'Yes, not before time,' said James.

'Dad, what exactly are you going to put here?'

'Another enterprise to entice our guests.' He described a sanctuary in another county that had managed to attract a number of birds on their summer and winter migrations. 'The chap had a low-level wooden hut covered in a camouflage netting. The length of the hut had shoulder-height windows that looked across the field and toward the hedgerows.' He pointed to the edge of the field. 'We're letting those hedgerows grow a little more so it'll attract insects for the birds. Our gardener, Appleton, told us to let the grass grow a bit and to get some wild flowers in to attract the bees. It'll become a giant meadow.'

'And what's going in the 'ut?' asked Bert.

'Chairs and a place to rest binoculars.'

'Blimey, that sounds good, don't it 'arry?'

'It does sound good, yes. You could also have a few books in there about the different sorts of birds.' Enthused, Harry clicked his finger and thumb. 'And, you could ask an expert to come down and give a talk.'

'Your mother has already suggested that,' said James. 'GJ has also asked that we extend the hut so that some of his students could try their hand at painting our feathered friends.'

'And it's an economic use of the field,' replied Harry. 'I mean, once you've built the hut and have everything in place, it's not going to take a lot to keep it running. Didier could provide refreshments or flasks of hot drinks.'

After a few more minutes discussing how they felt the venture would go, they returned to the terrace at Harrington's to join Beth and the Merry weathers.

With everyone reunited, Bert asked

them about the Celestial Faith Commune. 'Did you go to that open evening?'

Stephen groaned. 'It w-was supposed to put my mind at r-rest but I'm even more annoyed about it now.' With help from Anne, he went on to describe the chat with Mrs Long and Mrs Fellowes. 'I do f-feel that this Father Sun man is leaving out vital information where contributions are concerned.'

Beth told Harry that the Merryweathers had suggested that she and James should sit in when the ladies next spoke with Father Sun. 'We haven't upset the man as much as them.'

'Oh, I don't know,' James said. 'I think the four of us were snooping around a little too much for his liking.' He described their chat with the Brothers Neptune and Mars; the reluctance to speak about Sister Bellatrix or even allow them access.

Harry's brow knitted. 'Do you honestly think they're stopping this Wendy girl from seeing her own mother? Her father's only just died.'

'That's exactly what we're saying.'

'And don't forget,' Anne said, 'we saw Mrs Potter scurrying toward the bushes last night.'

Bert's interest was piqued. 'Scurrying toward the bushes!'

'She said she's not been allowed in to see her daughter. We think she got in around the back and tried to contact her.'

James told Harry and Bert that they'd driven back that way to see if they could find a gap in the fence. 'Sure enough, there it was. Not a natural break either. Someone had been down with wire cutters.'

'That could have easily been Mrs Potter,' said Beth. 'A mother can be quite persistent if she's denied her right to see her own flesh and blood, especially as she's so distraught.'

Harry poured a glass of wine. 'Dad, d'you think something's going on there?'

'I've no idea. I would have said no a couple of days ago. I mean, I know that Stephen here is outraged at the notion of this commune but there was nothing to suggest anything underhand. But all this business with Bernard Potter being killed and the investigation he was undertaking, well, he clearly thought something was awry.'

The tap of metal heels on the patio caused them all to turn. Although it was a warm and balmy day, George still had his suit and tie on and looked hot and flustered as a result. 'How the other half live,' he quipped.

James told him to pull up a chair and he ordered a beer from Adam.

George changed it to a lemonade. 'I'm on duty. I can't go drinking beer halfway through my shift. I'll fall asleep at the wheel.'

Adam placed a glass of iced lemonade down and George promptly swigged the whole lot in one. 'I didn't realise I was so thirsty.' He declined a refill. 'I can't sit here chatting. I knew you were here and wanted to update you. First,' he turned to James, 'I've learned the coffee cup song off by heart. I was singing it over and over in the bath last night and it all came back to me. That'll stop Dorothy Forbes nagging.'

The group congratulated him. George's

profession did not always allow for him to sit and learn his part as quickly as the rest of the players, so he was often on the end of a ticking off from the Cavendish Players' director. Although he was a gruff individual and well used to dealing with criminals and louts, Dorothy always put the fear of God into him.

'And what's your second piece of news?' asked James.

'The mechanics have been over Bernard Potter's car. No obvious sign of trouble but the man had forgotten to top up the brake fluid. It was empty.'

'Oh dear,' said Stephen. 'That means, down that bendy road, he w-wouldn't have stood a chance.'

James twisted in his chair to face George. 'But that makes no sense. Bernard Potter taught road safety; he was a traffic constable. His wife said that he always checked his car.'

George got up from the table. 'It doesn't matter how much you check a car, breakdowns happen. I know that from my own experience.'

James asked him to wait. 'You can't

dismiss this. You do know that Bernard Potter was investigating that commune.'

'So I've heard. And for no reason except that he couldn't see his daughter. The man that runs it . . . what's his name?'

'Father Sun,' the group chorused.

'Yes, him, he put in a complaint about PC Potter and he was told on more than one occasion to stop harassing them. I've got to go, I said I'd meet my boss in half an hour and I'm cutting it fine.'

With George gone, James caught Harry's grin.

'What're you smirking about?'

'I'm not doing anything for a week. I was going to help out here but I think I might sign up for that commune — see what's going on. What d'you think?'

Bert rolled some tobacco in a cigarette paper. 'I'll come with yer.'

James sat up with a start. 'Are you serious?'

'You can't do that,' Beth said, 'you'd stick out like a sore thumb.'

Anne agreed. 'And anyway, they know who you are.'

'No, they don't,' said Harry. 'Neither me nor Bert have been near the place and, if they've been in the village, we've not been there.' He turned to Bert. 'Are you having me on, Bert? Did you really want to come in with me?'

'Why not? Gladys is busy at the mission and I've got a few days I could spare. It'll be a laugh if nothing else. And if there's a hole in the fence, I can always go AWOL.'

A smug look settled on Harry's face. 'I think I'll be Brother Pluto, he's all about the underworld, isn't he and we're looking for something underhand. What'll you be, Bert?'

'You can be Pluto, mate, and I'll be Goofy. Must be Looney Tunes to sign up for this.'

They all laughed.

18

Paul interrupted their laughter to announce that James' sister, Fiona, had arrived. He went to get up but found that she had followed their *maître' d'* on to the terrace.

She hooted. 'I might have known you'd all be out here swanning around without a care in the world.' At the sight of Harry, she dropped her handbag and held her arms wide. 'Harry, darling, how wonderful to see you.'

Harry leapt to his feet and embraced his aunt. 'Good to see you, Aunt Fi. Are Uncle William and Christian with you?'

Fiona was a buxom woman with a ruddy complexion. Marrying a landowner-come-farmer and a keen farmer herself meant that she was outside most of the time. Her hair was short and styled and she wore a colourful floral skirt with a thin sweater.

'William took the bags upstairs ages ago and Christian is looking after the farm. He might have had second thoughts if he'd known you were here. What are you doing here? Your father didn't mention you were on leave. Is Oli with you?'

'No, no. I was given leave last minute. Oli's in a different squadron. Just because we're twins, doesn't mean we're stuck together for life. We're not in primary school now.'

James remembered the twins' first day at school, dressed in uniform and holding hands as they made their way, with some trepidation, toward the playground. The teacher at the time had been besotted with twins and seemed to think that, because they looked alike, they must be paired together at all times. Fortunately, she had realised that although similar in many respects, the pair of them had their own personalities. Both had inherited their parents' sense of fun and adventure but Oliver had proven to be a more serious and mature individual whereas Harry had a more adventurous, mischievous side. Where Oliver excelled at the academic aspect of things, Harry was more into sports and the arts. But, where Oliver had a somewhat low boredom threshold when it came to certain things, Harry was happy to spend an inordinate amount of time on a conundrum. James thought that it was this attribute that had led him to being scouted for the Intelligence Unit.

Harry and Oliver were two years older than Christian and the best of friends but their cousin was a farmer through and through and the thought of having to dress for dinner and attend the Midsummer Ball would have filled him with dread.

'I'm sorry, darling,' said Fiona, 'but you know what Christian's like. If he'd have been allowed to pitch up in wellington boots and a moth-eaten jacket, he would have been here in an instant.' She helped herself to lemonade. 'What are you doing with your leave? Have you a young lady?'

Harry shifted in his chair. 'Not at the moment, no.'

Bert nudged him. 'You 'ave though, 'aven't you? You're looking too embarrassed.'

'It was nothing serious, just a girl from the NAAFI.'

'Name?' asked Fiona.

'For pity's sake,' said James, 'stop interrogating the man.'

His son grinned. 'It's all right, Dad. My aunt doesn't scare me as much as my Squadron Leader.' He leant toward his aunt. 'Her name was Millie, she was very nice and we took tea together a few times. Now I'm billeted at another station.'

'More fish to fry,' said Bert with a wink.

Harry became a little uncomfortable under the gaze of his parents. James gave him a sideways glance. 'We're all adults now, Harry, spill the beans.'

The young man laughed. 'There isn't anyone.' He jabbed his glass toward Beth. 'And don't make assumptions that there is. If there was, I'd be spending my leave nearer her.'

Beth acted coy. 'I don't know what you're talking about. I wouldn't dream of making assumptions about my son's love-life.'

Fiona roared with laughter and James,

as always, wondered where his sister had got her loud persona from. She bellowed greetings from across fields, whooped in hysterics if things were funny and had a particular no-nonsense stiff-upper-lip approach where emotions were concerned. Harry was taken by surprise by the slap on the back he received from his aunt.

'So, you're running Harrington's and getting some practice in.'

'Actually, I'm not.'

Over the next ten minutes, Harry disclosed what he and Bert had planned to do at the commune. He had piqued Fiona's interest straight away.

'I have to say, that does sound exciting. This is you doing some sleuthing, isn't it, James. Trying to find a mystery where none exists. Honestly, Beth, you should get him digging fields to tire him out. He's obviously got too much free time.'

Bert sat back, enjoying the exchange.

This rankled with James. 'I am sitting here, Fi. You've no need to talk about me as if I'm one of your sheep.' Another whoop of laughter caused him to join in.

'You really are the limit, Fi. And where's William? Shouldn't he be down here by now?'

'You know William, he's probably gone wandering off. You know he always does things out of sequence.'

He scanned the fields and spotted his brother-in-law chatting to GJ. It was true what Fi said. William had the knack of disappearing and it was simply out of interest and being unable to sit still for five minutes. James knew the chap would have parked the car and dumped the luggage and, instead of popping on to the terrace to say hello, wandered off to see what was new. No doubt, he would have seen the activity with the barn in the far field too.

William was forty-five years old and came from farming aristocracy. He stood the same height as James and looked, every inch, the farmer, in his tattersall shirt and flannel trousers. His family had farmed a huge area in Wiltshire over the course of the last three hundred years and he had carried on the family business. He'd sectioned off a chunk of land for

Christian to run as his own smallholding but, eventually, the whole lot would go to their son.

James reached him. 'William, I don't see you for a month or two and the first person you come to is GJ.'

'Sorry, yes, yes, I know but I saw GJ here and was wondering how he was getting on with the workshops. Turns out to have been a good idea.' Before James had a chance to answer, he turned to face the old barn. 'I see you're knocking that monstrosity down, good riddance to it.' Again, James didn't have a chance to speak. 'Is that right, you're doing an Old Time Music Hall. Fantastic. Are we going to be here for that?'

Before he could change subject again, James took his chance to answer. 'Yes, you'll be here. It's on just before the ball so you'll have to come along and support us. Listen, I'll give you a tour of the far field but why don't you pop up and say hello to Beth? Harry and Bert are there too.'

With a nonchalant wave to GJ, William marched toward the patio, mumbling that

Fiona should have told him Harry would be there.

GJ was open-mouthed. 'He's difficult to keep up with, isn't he?'

'Damned frustrating at times. Lovely chap but his mind works faster than anyone else's. Before you have a chance to answer anything, he's on to the next topic.' He tilted his head toward the studio. 'How are the classes going?'

When GJ had suggested painting workshops to him, he wasn't altogether sure they would work but, fair play to the man, many of his guests had shown interest and some booked at Harrington's specifically to learn how to paint. Along with Catherine, he was expanding their potential to make money from their talents. Catherine had become a keen potter and, with the profits from their business, they had purchased a couple of potters' wheels for those who fancied making a jug or vase to take home.

GJ wore the expression of a contented man. 'The whole enterprise has taken off well. I knew I was taking a chance with this idea but I had a suspicion that it'd work out well. It's thanks to you taking a risk on me and I'll be forever grateful.'

'It was a risk worth taking, GJ. Stabling horses would have been a loss leader. Our guests certainly love the idea of being able to paint. I don't hear so many wives bemoaning their husbands going fishing now because they have something to do themselves.'

'Lord Harrington, do you recall me speaking about a man called Stuart Drummond?'

'He's the chap that offered you the calligraphy work, isn't he?'

'That's the one. Well, he was here last night, after I'd locked up. Offered me some more work?'

James noted the reluctance in his voice. 'Is that not good news?'

'I'm not sure what to make of it.'

'What's he asked you to do?'

'More calligraphy. Longer pieces.'

'And what's your concern?'

'He asked me if I ever copied paintings, you know, stroke for stroke.'

It took a while for James to understand what the problem was but, then, the lightbulb flickered. 'Do you mean an exact copy?'

'I think that's what he was driving at.'

'But isn't that illegal?'

'It is if you're going to sell it as an original but if it's just for your grandma to hang on the wall, it's fine. Most artists that do that tend to put something in the picture to denote it's not the original, or even sign it as themselves.'

'And you don't think that's what this Drummond chap wants?'

'He seemed to avoid my questions.'

James asked if he would be seeing him again.

'Yes, he's picking me up this evening and we're going to go over everything.'

James' gaze settled on the grounds where he saw Harry and William strolling toward the far field to where the barn had been dismantled. 'As I see it, GJ, you've not said yes to anything and you haven't signed a contract. Why don't you pop along with Drummond and see what he has to say? If it's all above board and you're happy, it could be a good source of income for you.'

'Ye . . . s, yes, you're right. I haven't committed to anything. Sometimes it's good to talk these things through. I'll let you know how I get on.'

With a 'You do that' and a cheerio, James returned to the terrace. Poor GJ had not had the best of starts in life. Adopted by a couple who were at odds over their reasons for taking the boy in, he'd been a runaway in his early teenage years and finally homeless until taken in by the East End mission run by Bert's betrothed, Gladys. The young man had come to look on James as a father-figure and often confided in him. So much so that James was proud to have been asked to be best man at his wedding the previous year.

He checked his watch, and got Beth's attention. 'I'm popping over to the library and then on to see Mrs Potter. I'm interested to hear what she has to say about her clandestine behaviour last night.'

His sister threw her head back. 'Oh James, I do love it when you're pursuing lines of enquiry.'

He gave her a mock look of reproach. His sister couldn't help making fun of his sleuthing antics. 'I have a commendation up on the wall after all that business over Easter.' He gave her a superior look. 'Even you got tangled up in that one and don't tell me you didn't enjoy it.'

Fi conceded that she had and instructed him to get stuck in. He grinned back. It was good to have Fiona here. He loved her dearly; when their older brother Geoffrey had died, they'd vowed to remain as close as possible.

Beth picked up her handbag. 'I'm going to make use of the facilities. I'll see you out front by the car.'

He threaded his way through the dining room where preparations were being made for lunch. In the far corner was Julie Faulkner, Adam's girlfriend. He made a detour and asked how she was getting on.

She was only five foot tall and quavered a little in James' presence. He was over six foot and although he did his best to make staff feel one of the family, people like Julie always put themselves into a servant mentality. He knew he wouldn't change that. All he could do was be himself and hope that she relaxed a bit.

'You certainly seem to be settling in well. Paul always speaks of you in a positive way.' She remained quiet. 'Adam tells me you're interested in the Celestial Faith Commune. That's a fairly new thing, isn't it? Are you enjoying your evenings there?'

'Oh, yes, your Lordship. Everyone's very friendly.'

'How often do you visit?'

'Twice a week.'

'I hope we don't lose you. You know they ask that you commit full-time after a while.'

Her voice had a slight tremor. 'I'd have to speak with Mum and Dad. I don't think they'd approve.'

'I suspect that Adam would prefer to see more of you too.'

Her eyes dropped as colour crept over her cheeks. James knew he'd gone too far. The girl was too timid for such a comment. Thankfully, though, she would have the sense to speak with her parents.

The consensus so far was that the commune leaders recruited naïve and vulnerable individuals. He hoped that Julie didn't fall into that category.

'I'll let you get on, Julie. Pleased to hear you're enjoying it here.'

★ ★ ★

At the library, James had selected a couple of books to read and he joined Beth and Charlie at the front desk where they were leafing through some reference books. Charlie had just made a pot of tea and popped to his cottage next door to retrieve the biscuit barrel. He offered the biscuits round.

'Freshly baked ginger biscuits. Here, have one.'

Beth helped herself. 'Charlie, I have to ask you. Are you and Dulcie courting?'

'Honestly, Beth,' said James, 'let the man have some privacy.'

She had the grace to appear embarrassed but Charlie didn't mind. 'I don't think it's a secret that we've become friendly. I do really like her but I'm taking it slowly. I've got so many things to think about. For one, I'm thirty and she's twenty.'

'But,' Beth said, 'as you get older, the age difference doesn't matter.'

'No, I know that but it's still a consideration. And I've got to think of Tommy and Susan. If it's not right for them it doesn't matter how I feel, they come first.'

'And what's your gut feeling about that?' asked James.

'Oh, they think she's wonderful and she loves them. She's an only child and she's always encouraging them to play together and she's been teaching Susan how to bake. They both did these biscuits. But I've still got to go slow because I don't want any heartache. Do you know what I mean?'

Beth said they did. 'We know you went through a terrible time when you lost Gillian. I can't imagine what you must have gone through.'

A sense of sorrow came over his face. 'I still miss her. I've found it difficult to let her go. No one can replace her, see, and I don't want Dulcie to feel she's second best.'

James rested a book on his thighs. 'I don't think you should think of Dulcie as a replacement, Charlie. Gillian will always be the love of your life, the mother of your children. Dulcie wouldn't want to take that away. This would be a different sort of love for you, don't you think? Have you spoken to Dulcie about that?'

Charlie almost flinched. 'Ooh, no, not yet. I'm not ready to do that. I've only known her a few weeks. I'll keep things ticking along until we know each other better.'

'I think that's a good idea.'

'Me too,' said Beth. 'As much as I love the idea of you finding someone to share your life with, I promise I won't broach the subject again.'

Charlie thanked them. 'Now,' he said sitting up, 'Beth's been asking me about Druids.' He pulled out a reference book. 'Shame Professor Wilkins isn't here, he'd be a good person to speak with about this.'

Professor Wilkins ran the local museum.

'Isn't he at a conference?'

'Yeah, up in Oxford, I think.'

'The Jacksons are away too,' said Beth, adding that they were visiting Philip's parents.

Philip Jackson was Cavendish's doctor; his dark, smouldering looks melted the hearts of all female residents, young and old. The village was, this week, reliant on a locum, an elderly man who looked closer to death's door than any of the patients.

They perused the books, many of those repeating small fragments of information but James found one volume that provided an extended version of the movement.

'It says here that scholars know very little about the original Druids because they didn't write anything down. It looks like, back in Roman times, they offered up human sacrifices but, thankfully, that was centuries ago.' He scanned the text. ''These days, they delight in the simple pleasures of life, mainly nature, dawn and dusk, the sound of water. Most like to spend time meditating outside.'' He closed the book. 'Well, that sounds like the Celestial Faith Commune, don't you think?'

Beth referred to the book she had. 'I have one here about all faiths and beliefs. This section is about the American Indian and it likens their culture to that of the Celts and others like the Mayans, the Aborigines and Egyptians. They all tracked the stars and planets in the sky. This apparently helped with their every-day lives, like rituals and when to plant and sow.'

'You think,' said Charlie, 'that this Father Sun bloke has combined the two?'

'I think he's combined several ancient belief systems and made up his own.'

'I think you're right, darling, and I can't see the man is doing any harm. On the surface, that is.'

'Do you really think that Bernard Potter found something untoward going on?' asked Beth.

He saw confusion cross their friend's face and gave him an update on Bernard

Potter. 'I mean, he's been a policeman for years; close to retirement. His wife described him as a sensible sort of chap, not one for exaggeration, a traditional copper. I know he was worried about his daughter but worrying about someone wouldn't make you open up an investigation, would it?'

Charlie said that he didn't think it would. 'He didn't give his wife any explanation for what he was doing?'

'None at all.'

'Is it worth bothering with? I mean, there's been no crime. It seems a strange set-up but, like we've all said, they're not doing any harm.'

James exhaled heavily and Beth asked him what the problem was. 'You have an expression that says you're not happy to leave it.'

'It's something that Potter said when he was in the car. Oh, I know he was drifting in and out of consciousness but, now we know he was investigating this place, it seems pertinent.'

'What was it?'

'"It's not what you think it is."'

He met the expectant gaze of Beth and Charlie.

'That's what he said, after talking about Wendy: he said, 'It's not what you think it is.' I think he was talking about the commune. I mean, we didn't even know that Wendy was part of the Celestial Faith. He hadn't changed the subject so he must have been talking about the commune.'

Beth tidied the books up. 'That list compiled by those psychiatrists is probably what he's talking about. Once you sign up to be a member, you're practically a prisoner. Who knows what goes on when those gates are locked.'

Charlie began stacking the books back on the shelves. 'D'you think they're in danger then?'

James had no idea but Beth's comment had a ring of truth about it. 'That list of the attributes of a cult leader is telling, don't you think? This Father Sun has moved everyone from the Midlands to a remote residence when he could easily cut people off.'

'And the more I think of that list,' said

Beth, 'the more I think Father Sun ticks every attribute on it.'

Charlie sat back at the table. 'If this is a cult, that would be good reason for your copper to look into this more. The way you've described him tells me that he wasn't just worried about his daughter but the other members too.'

'Mmm,' said James announcing that they had to pay a visit to Mrs Potter.

They were interrupted by a group of children, led by head-teacher, Mr Chrichton, marching in pairs across the green.

'Looks like you have a class visit.'

'Oh yeah, that'll be form 2B. Did you get everything you needed?'

They said they had and left the library. Mr Crichton, a jovial bachelor who relished his role as head-teacher, greeted them. He shoo'd the children into the library.

'I saw Graham Porter on the way here. He says that your cousin's in the village, the one that wears the checked suits.'

James groaned. That could only mean one person. Only Herbie Harrington wore garish checked suits. 'What the devil is he doing here?'

Crichton shrugged. 'No idea. By the way, I was sorry to learn about Mr Potter. You were in attendance at the accident, I hear.'

'You knew him?'

'He used to come in and do our road safety demonstrations, help with the cycling proficiency test.'

'He struck you as a down-to-earth individual?'

Chrichton afforded him a surprised look. 'Well, yes. Always good with the children, firm and fair, and the children loved the cycling tests. He'd bring in miniature traffic lights and road signs and mark out routes for them. You'd think they were actually cycling on the road. Very inventive.'

James had seen the layout and had been impressed. It confirmed how passionate Potter was where the road safety aspect of his job was concerned. He must have demonstrated that in his own life too, which made the car accident all the more puzzling.

Chrichton said that he must be getting

on and followed the children into the library.

'Shall we pop over to see Mrs Potter?' asked James.

'Yes, let's. I'm curious to know if that was her we saw at the open day.'

★　★　★

'Oh yes,' said Mrs Potter, inviting them to take a seat in the lounge, 'that was me. I'd found a hole in the fence that leads out to the footpath. It's a bit narrow but I took a pair of Bernard's pliers with me and widened it a bit.'

'That's good thinking,' said Beth. 'You were obviously determined to get in.'

She drew herself up, but then the life seemed to drain out of her. 'Didn't do me much good, though.'

'Why's that?' asked James.

'I didn't know where to look, did I? Bernard had all those notes on that board, photographs and information, but I didn't really know where things were. I couldn't go to the open day because they'd all recognise me and I have to say . . . ' her bottom lip trembled. She pulled out a handkerchief from the sleeve of her cardigan and blew her nose. 'I don't know how I would have reacted if they'd have asked me to leave. I don't think I could have coped.'

Keen for her not to go to pieces, James asked what exactly she had managed to do. 'We saw you dashing toward the fence when that ceremony was starting. You'd managed to get into the building?'

'In the old cowshed. I went through a side door but there was nothing to say who was sleeping where. I thought they'd have their names on the doors but it was numbered and I didn't know what number Wendy was in. I knocked gently on the first two or three but no one answered. I went a bit further in and put my ear to the doors. Trouble is, with that open day going on, everyone was out.'

Beth asked if she had called out for Wendy. 'I don't mean literally call out but perhaps a loud whisper or something?'

'I daren't. What if that Father Sun had come in? He would have had my guts for garters.'

'Would he?' asked James. 'Is he that against you visiting your daughter?'

She responded with a firm nod. 'Do you think I should ask the police to go in there?'

Beth pulled a face and looked to James for an answer. 'Is there good reason to visit officially?'

James said he didn't think there was. 'I can check with George. The only think I can think of is that you can say you're fearful for Wendy's safety; that you haven't seen her and you're worried about her. That might prompt a visit simply to ensure she's safe.'

'Would your friend let me come with him?'

'I honestly don't know. Leave it with me, Mrs Potter, and I'll see what I can find out.'

In the hallway, Mrs Potter opened the door and thanked them for coming. 'Did you make any sense of Bernard's investigation?'

James said that he hadn't but that he really needed to sit down and understand how Bernard thought things through. The fact that Mr Potter had indicated something was not what it purported to be piqued his interest but what else could there be? They'd spoken to a few commune members and all seemed perfectly happy, albeit naïve. What he really could do with was a list of who these people really were. Were they running away from something? Did they have a history? Perhaps a criminal history? On the doorstep, he asked Mrs Potter if Bernard had discovered any actual real identities.

'Bernard was trying to find out who they all were. He'd just found out who Father Sun was.'

'Yes, I saw that, Johnny Barton.'

'Well, that was what he was going up to the commune about the day he . . . ' She blew her nose then grabbed James' arm. 'Do you think he found out something about Father Sun and they killed him?'

'My word, that's a rather strong accusation, Mrs Potter.'

Beth informed her that the police were certain it was an accident. 'Why would you think such a thing?'

She'd regained her composure and with an assertiveness they hadn't heard before, she said: 'Because I know my husband. I know the checks he does on his car whenever he goes out. He doesn't speed either. He knows that road like a pigeon knows its way home.'

'Try not to worry,' said James. 'We'll see what we can do and I'll get on to George straight away.'

But the telephone call to George was not a constructive one.

'James, I can't go blundering in there without good reason. One of my uniformed officers was there to break the news to Wendy. She was upset, of course she was, but she wasn't showing signs of being held against her will.'

'Can't you pop in and make up a reason for having to speak with her? I mean, was she on her own when your constable chap broke the news?'

His friend admitted that she wasn't. 'I think that Mother Moon woman was with her.'

'There you are, she may have felt intimidated in some way. Can't you call in on the pretence that you have confidential matters to discuss, regarding the will or something?'

George groaned. 'All right. You're not going to leave me in peace until I settle your mind so I'll call in when I'm down tomorrow.'

James insisted that it wasn't *his* mind that needed settling. 'It's Mrs Potter's. She's distracted with worry. She even broke into the commune on the open evening.'

George couldn't help but laugh. 'Why didn't she just walk in the front gate like everyone else?'

He described Mrs Potter's position. 'Listen, George, Bernard Potter was on to something, I'm absolutely sure of it. Can you not find out something about Father Sun's background? His real name's Johnny Barton. He's from the West Midlands area. He may be a master criminal or something.'

'I know you've solved a few mysteries James, but you're not in London or Chicago. Not every master criminal makes a beeline for Cavendish. I can't go requesting background checks on people who haven't committed a crime.'

Knowing his friend would not budge, he reluctantly let him go. Beth stood in the doorway of the kitchen.

'No luck?'

'No. The trouble with George is he does insist on playing everything by the book.'

'And that has nothing to do with him being a Detective Chief Inspector?' she said with a hint of sarcasm.

He took her comment in good part. 'Well if Harry and Bert are thinking of going under cover, perhaps they can find something out.' He started. 'I forgot. Herbie's in the area. Do you think he's gone back to London?'

'Perhaps. It's odd for him to be down this way. He never leaves the city unless it's absolutely necessary.'

'Must be an auction or something going on.' The telephone rang beside him and he lifted the receiver. 'Cavendish 261.'

'Dear boy,' came the pompous voice of his cousin, Herbie Harrington. 'I'm chasing you around this village like a greyhound seeks a dead rabbit.'

'Unfortunately, we had no idea you'd be visiting. It would be preferable if you had given us notice.'

'I'm doing that now, James. Don't be tedious. I'm sitting on the village green watching an awful game of cricket.'

James could have clobbered him. No doubt the children in the village had started an impromptu game and it clearly didn't live up to Herbie's standards. 'We'll be with you in a few minutes.' He replaced the receiver.

'I'm guessing that's your cousin,' said Beth. 'Are we going straight out?'

James grabbed his keys. 'You know what he's like, Beth. Thinks everyone's at his beck and call.' He checked his watch. 'And it's lunchtime — shall we have a ploughman's?'

'Ooh yes, and a stiff drink. I always feel I need one when we socialise with Herbie.'

19

By the time they'd arrived at the village green, the game of cricket had turned into a game of rounders and a few villagers had been cajoled into making up the numbers. Stephen and Anne were field while Charlie, Graham and Kate Delaney took charge of their respective bases. Even Mr Bennett, James' old fishing tutor, was in the field. Radley simply raced from pillar to post, barking in excitement and wagging his tail.

Charlie's son Tommy dashed toward James. 'Are you going to play with us?'

He ruffled the boy's hair. 'I may do once I've had a chat with my cousin.'

'Is that the man in the checked suit?'

'That's the one.'

'He doesn't look much like you, does he?'

'No, I don't suppose he does.'

Charlie waved Tommy over. 'You're next up to bat.'

Tommy raced back to the group. Beth slipped a hand through the crook of James' arm. 'He's become very fond of you.'

'As has his sister of you.'

They could see Herbie Harrington sitting in the shade of a large shrub at the end of the cobbles outside the Half Moon. He had his regular daytime tipple of a glass of cream sherry in front of him, a drink that James found heavy and syrupy for such a beautiful day. Indeed, it seemed an odd sort of drink for a man to choose except as an aperitif before dinner or at a wedding. But Herbie was a regular imbiber and, if sherry wasn't on tap, he had a hip-flask filled with the stuff.

Unlike James, he was a short, balding, bulky man with an egg-shaped florid face and always wore brightly-coloured checked suits that made him look like Max Miller, the music hall entertainer. If he weren't such a boor, James would have invited him to do a song at their old-time music hall evening but just the thought filled him with horror.

'I should have told Fiona he was here.

Do you think I should call Harrington's and let her know?'

Beth thought it unwise. 'She has the same feeling about Herbie as you do. I can't imagine that she'd want to interrupt her day to spend time with him unless she actually has to.'

'I've a good mind to get her over here. It's about time she put a shift in. He's her cousin as well.'

'Don't be so grumpy. Anyway, he hates village life so I can't imagine he'll stay long.'

Knowing Beth was right, he gave Herbie a welcoming handshake and asked if he needed another drink. 'We're having a ploughman's; did you want one?'

Herbie scoffed. 'How rustic. I'll stick to sherry and await my duck *à l'orange* when I return home.'

James put an order in with Donovan for two ploughman's lunches and joined Beth and Herbie on a bench seat. 'So, Herbie, what brings you down here? Have you been nosing around The Lanes?'

'The Lanes' was a collection of narrow alleyways in the centre of Brighton, renowned for the jewellery shops that sold both new and second-hand gems. It also had the reputation of being a place where stolen goods were sold on, but how true this was, James didn't know. But the area itself was a splendid place for browsing.

Herbie said that he had, indeed, been down to The Lanes but he'd also visited a private art gallery to view several pieces there.

'Is this with a mind to purchasing?' said Beth.

'It's unlikely I'd have a hope of buying. The owner is adamant he wants to keep his collection although I did make him an offer for a Stubbs.'

Herbie had his own art gallery in London which opened by appointment only. Most of his paintings were by prominent artists so putting a bid in for a Stubbs would have been routine for him.

'I take it,' James said, 'that your chap isn't taking the bait.'

'You take it correctly.' Herbie watched as Donovan approached with two plates.

He placed them in front of James and

Beth. 'There you are,' he said, 'two ploughman's with some of me ma's pickled onions.'

They thanked him. James scrutinised the plate. Two thick slices of bread, butter, two slabs of cheddar and Cheshire cheese, pickles, pickled onions, tomatoes, cucumber and home-made chutney.

Herbie's lip curled, as if James had crossed from good evil. 'Dear boy, when on earth did you start eating peasant food?'

Beth playfully waved her knife at him. 'Herbie, you really are such a snob. You can't beat home-baked bread, butter and cheese from the local farm and chutney made by the land-lady.'

'Peasant food,' Herbie reiterated, looking down his nose at her.

'It's nothing of the sort,' said James. 'And Beth's right, you're becoming a boorish snob since you've cocooned yourself in London. It'll do you good to get out of the city for a while and experience the simple things in life.'

'Like a slice of bread and cheese. Yes,' he said with a hint of sarcasm, 'I can see that I'm missing out on something wonderful.'

James let the comment wash over him. If he allowed his cousin to annoy him, he'd be in a bad mood for the rest of the day. Instead, he asked why Herbie had bothered stopping off. 'I mean, if you've gone to Brighton, why not go straight back?'

'I was asked by a detective at Scotland Yard to come down to Haywards Heath and identify what might be a fraudulent painting.'

James put his knife and fork down. 'I say, that sounds rather intriguing. What's all that about?'

Herbie sipped his sherry then twitched as a shout warned him of an approaching rounders ball. James, being an excellent cricketer, simply reached a hand out, caught it and threw it back. An apology came from someone on the green.

'Come on, Herb, spill the beans.'

Astonished at James' catching abilities, Herbie took a moment to answer. 'There are three individuals at Scotland Yard who investigate art fraud. They've asked me a couple of times to verify certain pieces. As you know, that's my area of expertise. I mean, I can't go around stocking paintings in my gallery without knowing they're the genuine article, can I?'

Beth agreed. 'And what did you look at down here?'

'A piece by Mondrian.'

'Original or fraud?' asked James.

'Fraud.'

'How can you tell?' said Beth.

'Experience. I couldn't possibly explain it to someone who hasn't studied the painter.'

James bit back a retort. Neither he nor Beth were experts on the art world but he was sure they would understand, even if Herb explained that the brush work was substandard.

'I say, Herbie, have you had a few of these requests, you know, to check up on works of art?'

'Just recently, yes. It's been rather interesting, if I'm being honest. It's taken me to a number of private collections and it's like being taken into an Aladdin's cave each time.'

'How many?'

'Mm?

'How many have you been asked to verify?'

'Oh, at least a dozen.'

'All in private collections?'

'That's right.' He swigged his sherry. 'Are you able to give me a lift to the railway station? The police drove me to Haywards Heath but when I wanted dropping off here they said they weren't a taxi service.'

James stared at his half-eaten ploughman's. 'Not until I've finished this, no. What time's your train?'

Herbie checked his fob watch. 'Half an hour.'

Haywards Heath station was a good fifteen minutes from Cavendish. James knew there were two London trains every hour so if he missed this one it wouldn't matter. He wanted to know more about these paintings.

'Are you saying that the owners of these collections are wondering if their paintings are real? Has some sort of crime taken place?'

'I've no idea. I think so, yes.'

'And all of those paintings you went to verify were fake?'

'Is that not what I've been saying?'

Beth buttered her second slice of bread. 'How did this all come to light?'

'The private collectors are like an elite club. Two owners had decided to sell a couple of their pieces and the auction houses had proclaimed them as fake. The owners insisted their experts were wrong and offered a record of provenance to prove the art was genuine. Both Sotheby's and Bonham's studied the paintings concerned and both assessed the artwork as being fake.'

'And they,' presumed James, 'toddled off to the police to report it.'

Herbie peeked at his watch and then at James, who was not going to be rushed.

'You're saying that these collectors think someone has taken the original paintings?' he said.

'Yes.'

'And replaced them with fakes!' said Beth.

'James, all of this talking is not getting

me to Haywards Heath.'

'You're trying to catch the one twenty-five. That's the slow train. Catch the train fifteen minutes later and you'll be in London around the same time. Now, tell us, what happened with the other collectors.'

'Oh, very well. Like I say, the owners feel they're elite. They socialise together and although they are by no means close friends, they are aware of the paintings and sculptures they collectively own. When word got out that two paintings had been replaced, a ripple spread through the ranks of collectors.'

'Who then,' said Beth, 'went on to have their own collections authenticated.'

'Precisely.'

'And,' said James, 'found that they had fake among their collections.'

Herbie groaned. 'Are you deliberately stretching this subject matter out?'

'Absolutely not, we're just interested, that's all. I find it fascinating that a collector can have valuable works under his roof and not notice that something is amiss. I mean, how long do you think those fakes had been sitting there?'

His cousin shrugged and tapped his watch.

James put his knife down. 'Oh, come on, I can see you're champing at the bit to get out of here.'

Brightening, Herbie mumbled that he could put up with no more than an hour of dreary village life. 'The city and my duck *à l'orange* calls. Onward, James, and do not spare the horses.'

James kissed Beth on the cheek. 'I'll be back in a while.'

'But you've not finished your lunch.'

He watched Herbie plod across the green, oblivious to interrupting the rounders game.

'I'd rather give up half a ploughman's than have Herbie checking his watch every two minutes.' He turned and couldn't help but chuckle as a rounders ball caught his cousin in the midriff. Charlie shouted out an apology as Herbie attempted to return the ball. Games had never been his fortè and his limp attempt to return the ball caused Anne to sprint forward to retrieve it.

'What is the purpose of exercise?' asked Herbie as James reached him. 'A lot of effort that causes nothing but discomfort.'

★ ★ ★

DCI George Lane pressed the doorbell. Alongside him was PC Fulton. They didn't have to wait long for Mrs Millerson to open the door and invite them in. The smell of fresh bread filled the hall. After introductions and a general run through of her version of events regarding the Cézanne drawing, she showed them the picture.

They were standing in a long corridor that led from the hall to the room at the back of the house.

George examined the drawing. 'And you're certain that this item was missing?'

'Oh yes,' replied Mrs Millerson. 'I may be the wrong side of seventy but I'm not senile.'

George said he hadn't thought anything of the sort. In fact, he had to admit that the woman was as Fulton had described, astute and alert, certainly not a ditherer or muddled in any way.

'But you're not sure when it went missing?'

'As I told your constable, I walk back and forth every day. You don't notice what's under your nose, do you? I mean, there's an umbrella in the corner there by the front door but I don't notice it. It's only when it's raining, when I need it, that I turn my attention to it. It was the same with this drawing. I dust and vacuum this area once a week. When I dust, I flick the duster over the frames. And last week, there was no frame to dust.'

The picture was positioned between five other drawings of the same dimensions, about the size of a paperback, and all of a similar design.

'Are these all by Cézanne, Mrs Millerson?'

'Ooh no,' she chuckled. 'If they were, I'd sell one and treat myself to a cruise. No, it's just the one.'

'It's just that they seem a similar style.'

She took them through to the back room and pulled out a book from a shelf.

Flicking through it, she handed the open page to George. 'These are also Cézanne. My father traced them off the page and those are what you see on the wall. He wanted a collection, you see, and he didn't want the real one to stand out. If you're an art critic you'd soon see that they're not to the standard of Cézanne.'

George was not an art critic but, when he looked more closely at the drawings, he could see the difference. Cézanne's had something special about his, as if the artist had confidence in what he was doing.

'And your father was a friend of Cézanne, you say?'

'For a short while. They struck up a friendship when my father was posted to France. He was a young man then.' She met George's questioning gaze. 'The embassy in Paris needed someone for a few months while one of their diplomats was in hospital. Father so adored Paris and spent hours watching the artists along the Seine and visiting galleries. He met Paul Cézanne at a café and the two hit it off straight away. His parting gift to my father, when he returned to England, was that drawing.'

George scrutinised the piece. 'And it reappeared.'

'Yes. I don't understand it, Inspector.'

'And you're certain it's the original?'

'Yes. There's a very faint pencil mark on the back, in the corner. I checked it and it's still there.'

'Have you had any visitors or strangers in the house?'

'None.'

'Tradesmen or salesmen?'

'None. I have regular visits from my son, the postman and the baker. They always come in for a cup of tea. Neighbours come and go but I trust them all.'

'No sign of forced entry? Do you leave windows open?'

'I didn't see anything. I do leave the small windows open this weather but no one can get through them. You'd have to be a ferret to squeeze through.'

George brought out his card and handed it to Mrs Millerson. 'If you think of anything, let me know.'

A look of alarm crossed her face. 'You don't think they'll come back, do you?'

George said he thought it unlikely but, at the same time, he didn't like the idea of people's possessions going missing. 'This one was returned, Mrs Millerson, but someone else may have something stolen permanently.'

'Why do you think they returned it?'

'Perhaps it wasn't what they were looking for.'

When the front door closed behind them, PC Fulton followed George to the car. 'Can I be a bit forward, sir?'

'What's on your mind?'

'If the property's been returned, there's been no theft, so why are we taking an interest in it?'

They reached the car where George leant on the roof. 'Because there's been some thefts within the art world, Fulton, and this follows the same pattern. The only difference is the original has been returned instead of the forgery. Get in the car and I'll fill you in on what I know.'

20

GJ scanned the barn to ensure everything was in place for the next workshop. They had some time off the following day and had planned a picnic down by the river. Catherine had already returned home and he recalled their conversation.

'I don't know how long I'm going to be, Cath,' he'd said. 'This man, Drummond, seems a bit mysterious about everything but he's promised to have me back before midnight.'

She'd smoothed his blond hair back. 'As long as he doesn't kidnap you and hold you to ransom. Hasn't he told you anything about where you're going?'

'Nothing. The thing is, there could be some good work in it for me. I'll get him to drop me off at home. I'll pick my bike up tomorrow.'

She'd offered to wheel both bikes home.

He pondered on how lovely it was to

have someone like Catherine to go home to.

'Are you ready?' He jumped at the voice behind him and turned to see Stuart Drummond. Where on earth had he come from? He checked his watch. The man was ten minutes early.

'Are you ready?' Drummond repeated.

GJ felt a chill. If he was being honest, he wasn't sure. He took a deep breath. 'Yes, yes, let's make a start. The sooner we go, the sooner I can get back.'

He followed Drummond to the main road in front of Harrington's where the man had parked his Ford Anglia. The rear light was missing and rust was making inroads on the bodywork.

'Door's open.'

With GJ comfortable in the passenger seat, the man handed him a piece of thick, black material.

'Before we go any further, I need you put this on.'

He examined the cloth. A blindfold. The muscles in his jaw tensed. 'Why do I need this? What's going on?'

'The people I work for are secretive

about they do. You're not in any danger, you're nothing to be scared of.'

'Well at least let me enjoy the ride until we get closer. I'll put it on when we get there.'

'No. You put it on now or you don't come at all.'

GJ stared at the man while trying to process the strangeness of this encounter. The seconds ticked by and Drummond seemed nonplussed about the time he was taking. After a couple of minutes, Drummond opened a window and rested his arm on the sill. He took out a cigarette and lit it. GJ screwed his face up. The bitter aroma of French cigarettes stuck in his throat.

'I can promise you, hand on heart, that I will simply take you to the location, show you what work we have to offer, and bring you back home. Like you say, the sooner we go, the sooner we come back.'

'I don't know you. How can I trust you?'

'You can't but I'm not here to harm you. Search me. Search the car. I don't have weapons here. This is a business transaction and the people I work for ask for the utmost secrecy and discretion.'

'Which can only mean one thing. It's illegal.'

'It can mean another. That the person I work for simply doesn't want publicity. In the art world there are plenty of collectors who like to remain anonymous.' He reached across GJ and opened the door. 'Please, feel free to leave. I won't bother you again.'

GJ considered the options. Leave now and wonder, probably for the rest of his life, what on earth was on offer? Or travel with Drummond and discover exactly what was being proposed? He reached out and slammed the door shut.

'All right,' he said, putting the blindfold on, 'let's go.'

21

James and Beth had invited Stephen and Anne round for supper. They'd enjoyed sardines and salad on the patio where their numerous terracotta containers spilled over with vibrant pansies and marigolds. Luke, Mark and Radley were playing chase on the extensive lawn.

While the boys played, they sat at the table playing Rummy. A bottle of wine stood in the centre, along with a selection of cheese and crackers. As he dealt the cards, James asked if they'd had any more thoughts about the commune.

'Are you a little happier about things?' asked Beth.

Stephen said he wouldn't go that far. 'I still don't like the i-idea of my two ladies having to commit themselves to living there. I mean, why don't they just run it as a club so that people can come and go?'

James reminded them of an earlier conversation. 'Father Sun feels having people come and go would disrupt the group.'

'One thing did strike us,' continued Beth, 'I don't know if you found the same, but the members did seem a little suggestible. I don't mean that to sound disrespectful but we didn't meet anyone that seemed confident of themselves and all of them seemed hesitant around us. I got the feeling that if you told any of them to jump through a hoop of fire, they'd do it without asking questions.'

'We f-felt exactly the same.'

James sorted his cards. 'Apart from Brother Mars. He seemed pretty sure of himself. Your comment, Stephen, about where they get their money from, is one that continues to bother me. That property is big, they have a considerable amount of land and they're thinking of knocking down that ruin down at the back and rebuilding. There's also a brand-new car in the garage. Father Sun could be a very rich man and indulging in niceties or perhaps he has an inheritance.'

'Or,' Anne said, 'someone who believes in what he's doing, who's happy to pay.'

'A philanthropist? Possibly.'

Stephen asked if George had been able to find out more about Father Sun. 'What did you s-say his name was?'

'Father Sun is one Johnny Barton, presumably from the Midlands if that's where the commune first began. I must admit that the name doesn't resonate as a spiritual leader. No wonder he changed it.'

'To be more in keeping with the commune,' said Beth, 'or because he's had to.'

'Running away from something you mean?'

'Yes. We had a businessman in Boston living close to us who closed a company down and set up a new one under a new name to evade the authorities.'

The group reflected on this but no-one had any suggestions.

'I-I think you should press George to get on to his counterpart in the Midlands about Johnny Barton. And if Bert and Harry are serious about going under-cover, y-you'd better give them a list of questions.'

James finished his drink. 'I'd actually rather go undercover myself. Harry could enjoy his leave, keep his hand in by running the hotel and I could join Bert.'

He was met with an incredulous glare from Beth. 'But you're known to the commune. You can't waltz in there without being recognised.'

He felt for his cigarettes and, after lighting the tip of one, grinned. 'Not if I have the help of a professional make-up artist.'

'Dulcie?' chorused Beth and Anne.

'Why not? I could get her to make me look a little older, have a beard and all that, glasses perhaps, and we can spend a few hours here and there having a gander.'

Stephen roared with laughter. 'I'm sorry, James, but the thought of you and Bert dressed in r-robes is one that's worthy of an Ealing comedy.'

Anne joined in with the merriment. 'I do hope you're going to let us take a photograph of the pair of you.'

'Does Bert know he'll have to dress like a monk?' asked Beth.

James waved the tobacco smoke away. 'I wouldn't think so for a minute.' He saw the funny side. 'I suppose we will look a little comedic but for a good cause. I'll have a chat with Bert and Harry. Dulcie's doing more rehearsals in London, isn't she?'

'Yes,' said Beth, 'but I'll pop in to see Charlie and see what days she has off. You must promise not to do anything if she can't do it. If something underhand is going on, I don't want you on the wrong side of the fence. At least Bert and Harry aren't known to the members.'

James thought about Beth's warning. He wasn't about to argue with her. He knew she'd forbid him to do anything unless she was happy with it and he would respect that. But, a big part of him hoped that Dulcie could work her magic. The thought of going undercover with Bert rather appealed. At the very least they could seek Wendy out and report back to Mrs Potter.

★ ★ ★

As the blindfold was removed, GJ blinked several times to adjust to the glare of naked light bulbs above him. He scanned the surroundings. He was in a large windowless room although he could make out the distant sound of waves and seagulls squawking. There was a musty smell, as if the room never had any fresh air.

The area was littered with artists' tools, easels, paints and brushes. On the desk beside him were numerous pencils, brushes and calligraphy pens. An old man with his sleeves rolled up studied a document through a large magnifying glass and picked up his pen to continue whatever it was he was doing. Two other people, a man and a woman, were seated at opposite ends of the room with their backs to him. He realised they were copying the paintings they had propped up to the side of them. Spotlights helped light the areas where they worked.

Stuart Drummond prodded him to sit down on a chair and brought one up to join him. 'This is the operation.'

GJ was still hesitant about what he was

looking at. His muscles had been tense from the moment he'd set foot in the car and that wariness had remained. Indeed, he felt it had worsened since the blindfold had come off. He hadn't a clue where he was but the journey must have been around twenty minutes or half an hour at most with the car radio turned up high. But, judging by the sound, he was on the coast somewhere.

'Look, I'm sorry, Mr Drummond, but this all seems very cloak and dagger. If this is all above board, I have to say it's not convincing me.'

Drummond brought out a hip-flask along with two metal shot-glasses and poured each of them a brandy. 'Here, I'm just waiting for the boss. She'll explain what's going on.'

GJ wasn't a big drinker but the brandy was a welcome relief. He forced himself to relax but found it difficult.

'GJ, what's that short for?'

'Gentleman Jim. It's a nickname given to me when I was homeless. I wasn't seen as a normal vagrant. My accent is too posh for the streets.'

'You're a James, then, and someone shortened it to Jim and then Gentleman Jim. Clever.'

GJ wasn't about to correct him. His real name was Sebastian but the title felt alien to him now. James and Beth had shortened his nickname to GJ and, not only had it stuck, but everyone said it suited him. A door opening brought him out of his thoughts.

An older lady with iron-grey hair entered. She wore an unflattering tweed skirt and a blouse with large floral designs on it. Her flat, stout shoes made no sound as she plodded across.

She held out a hand. 'GJ, I presume.'

He took her hand. 'And you are?'

'Not something you need to know.' He recognised a Northern inflection.

'Then it's unlikely that we can work together. I need to know who I'm working for and what I'm being asked to do.'

She raised her eyebrows. He hoped he wasn't getting into trouble but this whole set-up was leaving him more anxious by the minute.

'You can call me Mrs Latham.'

'That's not your real name though, is it?'

'Call it a nickname.' She flourished the piece of calligraphy that GJ had been asked to complete. 'This is impressive. I ran it by a few experts. They all agreed. Very professional. We need similar pieces done.'

GJ frowned. 'Extracts from books? What on earth for?'

'Not from books. Copies of writings, shall we say, to make something look more genuine.'

GJ turned to Drummond. 'You asked me about copying works of art, like they're doing over there.' He returned his attention to the old woman. 'You want artwork copied. You're talking about fraud.'

She laughed. 'Perhaps when you hear about the offer we'll make, you won't be quite so judgemental.' She suggested a sum of money to him.

The figure was enormous. How easy it would be to say yes. How wonderful to be able to go to a showroom and buy a car hot off the production line or have the cottage completely redecorated. The look on the old woman's face was a picture. She thought he was tempted but, the truth of it was, he wasn't. He might have had a difficult childhood, a stepmother who didn't really love him, a stint on the streets living with tramps and not knowing where his next meal would be coming from.

But he had something else as well. A sense of right and wrong.

Lord Harrington had told him to see what this was all about. If he wasn't happy, he hadn't signed a contract. And he wasn't happy.

He picked up the blindfold. 'I'm sorry Mrs Latham, but I think you've chosen the wrong person. My instinct is telling me to say no. Thank you for your offer. It's kind of you to think about me.'

'We won't ask again.'

'And I won't seek you out,' GJ replied as Drummond tied the blindfold.

He was placed back in the car, the engine roared to life and the radio, again, was turned up high. This time, Drummond took a different route. He only knew that because it took a lot longer to arrive home. Finally, the car came to a halt. He felt Drummond lean across and open the passenger door. He took the blindfold off, grabbed GJ's shirt and yanked him closer. His breath was warm and stank of Gitanes.

'Keep this to yourself, GJ. I wouldn't want anyone to get hurt.'

GJ scrambled out of the car and glared at him. Drummond had dropped him by his cottage. He watched the car disappear into the distance and tried to read the number-plate. But the number-plate had been covered up.

Pushing open the gate, he opted to keep Catherine in the dark. He'd simply say it had been a job that would take up too much time.

But something fishy was going on there. Lord Harrington spoke a lot about instinct and he found he was acting on it more. And instinct now was telling him to chat this through with his Lordship.

22

Elsie Tanner's café was, as usual, humming with activity: pensioners having tea, ladies lunching and two or three men in overalls taking a break from work. She'd embraced the solstice theme and had asked the local children to make some cut-out suns to hang from the ceiling. The result was a colourful montage of the season. Not only full yellow suns but sunrises and sunsets in various hues of yellows, reds and oranges hung above them.

On the tables themselves Elsie had placed her menus in cardboard sunflower holders.

James was the first to compliment her. 'You really do work hard to keep the theme of the villages going, don't you?'

'It makes people come back and reminds the villagers what's going on. Don't want them to miss anything. If they ask me, I tell 'em. Last month was the steam festival, this month is Jonty's parade and I've yet to advertise the music hall. I thought I'd put a few theatre posters on the walls, you know, of music hall artists.'

'Splendid idea.'

'Would you like to have some tickets to sell?' asked Beth. 'I know a few of the Charnley villagers come to our events.'

'Good idea,' Elsie said. 'I tell you what, give me ten tickets for each evening and I'll see if I can sell them for you.'

'I'll bring them down later today,' responded Beth. 'Did you manage to reserve our favourite table?'

'All ready and waiting. Is it just the two of you?'

James said that Charlie Hawkins and Dulcie Faye were with them. 'Charlie's just dragged Dulcie into the woods.' He laughed at Elsie's surprised look. 'All very innocent. There are a couple of skylarks in the opening just beyond the trees and Dulcie's never seen them before.'

'Here they are now,' said Beth.

Charlie held the door open for Dulcie to breeze through. A few of the customers nudged each other, clearly recognising the young British starlet. James couldn't help but notice the pride in Charlie as he steered her toward them.

'Sorry,' he said, 'but I knew that Dulcie would want to see the birds.'

'And did you see them?'

'Oh yes,' Dulcie replied, 'there are two native birds that I've never seen and now I can tick that one off the list.'

'What's the other one?' asked Beth.

'A kingfisher.'

'Well,' said James, 'perhaps the next time I take young Tommy fishing, you should come along. We often have kingfishers down by the river.'

Beth suggested they could arrange a picnic and told Charlie to bring Susan too. 'We'll make it a family lunch.'

They settled in the seats by the bow window looking across the road to the woodland beyond and, after ordering tea and toasted tea-cakes, talked about the old-time music hall and how entertaining it was going to be.

'You know that Bert's got a pearly-king suit already, don't you?' said Charlie.

'Apparently, the people he knows in the East End have a few spares so he's all kitted out ready to go.'

Beth asked if he knew what else their friend would be singing. 'He is our star act, after all.'

'He's keeping quiet on that one but I can't imagine it being anything mundane.'

'Neither can I,' James said, leaning back to allow Elsie room to place their tea and tea-cakes on the table.

Dulcie picked up the teapot. 'Shall I be mum, Lady Harrington?'

'I'll put the milk in,' said Beth.

'I say, Dulcie, it doesn't seem right, you calling us Lord and Lady. There are certain people that I'm quite happy should use our title but you're not one of them. Charlie is on first name terms with us and I'm much prefer it if you were too.'

'I agree,' said Beth. 'I'm hoping that you'll become a good friend if you're thinking of staying in the area.'

Dulcie gazed at Charlie. 'Oh, I've no reason to go anywhere. I'm hoping to be here for a while.' She put the lid back on the teapot. 'Anyway, if I'm going to be your make-up artist, I'll need to stay local.'

James asked if she would be able to make him look convincing. 'I mean, I've been down to that commune a couple of times now and that Father Sun chap would spot me from a mile away.'

The young actress told him that he would be surprised at how a few alterations could change a person's appearance. 'We'll transform you as best we can but you'll need to work on your voice. That's very often the thing that gives people away. Are you any good at accents?'

Charlie mentioned the music hall act. 'When you got up to sing with George, you put on a convincing cockney accent.'

'Mmm, not sure that Bert would agree with you. It would have to pass his test for me to do that.'

'What about a soft Scottish accent?' said Beth.

The idea didn't fill James with confidence. 'I can pronounce some words but tend to revert to what Bert calls my toff accent.'

'What about a West Country one,' suggested Dulcie, 'they can be quite easy to imitate. Unless you're actually from the West Country, they are quite easy to fool people with.'

James sipped his tea and commented that playing a part was clearly not as easy as he thought it would be. 'I'm going to have to be convincing, not just in appearance and speech but also my background.'

Beth suggested he sit down with Bert. 'He knows so many people, James, he should be able to coach you better than any of us. And he's from a totally different background.'

Charlie had a different idea. 'Use a background you're familiar with. Maybe someone you knew in the RAF during the war. It's easier to have a truthful background than a made-up one.'

'Mmm, that's an idea.' He turned his attention to Dulcie. 'Are you free to practise on me? I think perhaps a tramp or someone who's fallen on hard times.'

'Yes. I've already thought about a look that would suit you, especially if you're going to be a vagrant. We can take some photographs of each stage. That way, if I'm working and you need to do this yourself, then you can. Well, Lady Harr . . . Beth can.'

'Mr Chrichton could develop the photographs,' said Beth. 'He has a darkroom at the school. He's developed photographs for us before at short notice.'

'That's settled then.'

Elsie arrived at their table. 'I've just had a phone call from your police friend, George Lane. He's got the afternoon off and he's up at the cricket club; wondered if you fancied a batting session and a chat.'

Beth told him to go ahead. 'We can get the bus back. He clearly wants to see you about something.'

'You don't have to worry about that,' said Elsie. 'He's still on the line. The cricket captain has said he'll come and collect you if you're available.'

'Splendid.' He turned to Charlie and Dulcie. 'You don't mind me dashing off, do you? I think he may have some information about this commune place.'

'We can't stand in the way of an investigation,' said Charlie with a glint in his eye.

★ ★ ★

Thirty minutes later, James was sitting with George on the wooden veranda of the cricket club. A warm breeze kept the heat of the sun at bay.

'I take it that you have some news for me, or was this simply a ruse to get me to play cricket?'

'Both,' said George. 'I thought we could do with the practice, seeing as we have a match next week. We're a bowler down and I think you're in the running.'

'Me! I'm hopeless at bowling. Batting and fielding are my thing.' Seeing George's wistful look, he shrugged. 'I'll give it a go but the team need to know that I'm not a willing volunteer. But never mind about that, what news do you have?'

'Your confounded curiosity took hold of me.' George went on to explain that he had contacted his counterpart in the West Midlands. 'I put the name Johnny Barton to him and, at first, he didn't have anything to tell me.'

'But?'

'He telephoned back about an hour later after he'd gone through some paperwork. He's made quite a transition in his life.'

'Oh?'

'No convictions, not recent anyway. The information they had on file was regarding a couple of cautions, shoplifting when he was a nipper. We don't do anything about that, James. A chat with the parents normally does the trick and I suppose it did this time.'

'So, what do you have?'

'One of the constables up there remembers Johnny Barton because they were in the same school. He remembers him as a day-dreamer, besotted with film stars. A few of the kids used to sneak into the cinema stalls once a film had started and Johnny was one of them. Transfixed he was and always reading film magazines. That's what he was caught shoplifting — film magazines.'

'Does this constable remember him being religious in any way?'

'Nah, nothing like that. They were all supposed to attend Sunday School but half of 'em used to play truant, including Johnny and our police constable.'

'Are Barton's parents still alive?'

'As far as this constable knows, yes. They live in the suburbs of Birmingham; both work in the factories.'

'No rich relatives on the scene?'

'I did ask but he said he didn't know Barton that well. He was simply part of the crowd and, when I say 'crowd', there were about fifteen of them.' He slid a piece of paper across to James. 'I didn't ask for this because, officially, I'm not looking into this commune but the young constable let me have Barton's sister's address. They kept in contact after school. She lives in Godstone.'

'Godstone in Surrey?'

'That's the one. She's a housekeeper at that address.' George reached down to his feet and picked up his cricket pads. 'That's all I know James. Don't ask me to do anything else or my boss is going to be asking questions.'

They got up and sauntered toward the pitch where several items of cricket equipment were strewn across the green. James picked up a red leather cricket ball. If he was going to be picked to bowl he had better get some practice in. But, once he'd done that, he'd see if Beth fancied a trip up to Godstone. It would only take half an hour to get there and they might actually discover the true personality beneath the Father Sun persona.

★ ★ ★

Later George dropped him off at Harrington's and offered to wait while he went to see if Fiona would be free to dine that evening. He found her reading a book on the terrace.

'We have a rehearsal for the music hall but we could eat early, say six o'clock, to have a catch up.'

'Wonderful. I'll let William know. Do get Harry to join us, it's so lovely to catch up with him.'

'I'll be sure to. I must dash, George is waiting for me.'

He kissed her on the cheek and turned to go but was distracted by some frantic shouting. The noise was coming from GJ who was waving for him to come down to the studio and, from his gestures, quite urgently. Hoping he wouldn't delay George for too long, he strode toward him.

'Everything all right?'

GJ met him halfway. 'I need to speak with you about last night.'

'Last night?'

'I went with that Stuart Drummond man to chat about this work he may have for me. You know, the calligraphy and all that.'

'Oh yes, how did you get on.' James noted the concern etched on the young man's face. 'I say, GJ, what happened?'

'I think that something illegal is going on. I was blindfolded when I got in the car.'

'Blindfolded!'

'Yes.'

James turned toward Harrington's and

back to GJ. 'Listen, George is here, he's giving me a lift home. Why don't you come and speak with him about it?'

GJ pulled a face. 'I said I wouldn't. I'm not even supposed to be talking to you. I was sworn to secrecy. I got the impression that it was more of a threat than a request.' GJ checked his watch. 'I need to get back. I'm working on a picture.'

'Leave it with me. I'm back here early this evening. Will you still be here around five, five-thirty?'

'Yes.'

'Meet me at five, on the terrace.'

With those arrangements in place, James slid into George's car with an apology. He remained quiet about GJ but couldn't help thinking about what on earth he could have potentially got mixed up in. George was on the police radio and just finishing his call.

'Right. Listen to this,' he said as he drove off. 'I got Constable Fulton to pop by the commune on the pretence of seeing Wendy Potter. She's alive and well but no longer at the commune.'

'She's gone home?'

'No. Apparently, her reason for leaving was that she wanted some peace and quiet.'

'Isn't that what the commune's for?'

'I'd have thought so, yes, but perhaps grief has got the better of her.'

'Are you putting out a search for her?'

George said that it wasn't as easy as that. 'Mother Moon said she went willingly and assured Fulton she'd be back. I've got no reason to disbelieve her. Fulton's over at the commune now making a few enquiries. Effectively, she's not missing but, bearing in mind what happened to her dad, we'll see if we can track her down. But, James, she's a grown woman.' He swung the car onto James' drive and came to a halt. 'Perhaps things weren't that good with the mum, either,' said George. 'You never really know what goes on behind closed doors.'

'Yes, you could be right. This may simply be an over-protective mother. All the same, I can't help thinking it's odd that she goes missing now. Thanks for the lift. I'll see you at rehearsals later.'

He bounded up the steps and into the

hall. 'Darling, are you down here?'

The kitchen door opened. 'Yes, I've just got back from the village. The fish van was there so I bought some scallops. I thought they'd go nicely with a salad tomorrow.'

'Perfect,' said James who really enjoyed a warm dish of scallops with a plate of salad. It was something they'd come across in an Italian restaurant in London and certainly made for a lovely meal. 'How d'you fancy a trip to Godstone?'

'Godstone? Whatever for?'

'Let me get changed and I'll fill you in on the details.' While updating Beth, he changed into a pair of navy-blue trousers and a white short-sleeved shirt.

Beth faltered. 'Wendy disappearing like that sounds a little peculiar, doesn't it?'

'I thought so at first but George is right. She's old enough to make her own decisions.'

'I guess so.' She collected her handbag. 'Let's go.'

Smiling at her eagerness, he held the door open for her and locked it behind them. Only a year ago he'd had to persuade Beth to allow him to look into things and pursue any investigation. Now she was as keen as him to seek out information.

He put the car in gear and pulled away.

23

Godstone was a pretty village, not dissimilar to Cavendish in that it had the obligatory village green, a pub, a church and individual shops to serve the community. Unlike Cavendish, however, it did have a large pond where waterfowl and Canadian geese made their home.

'Oh, it's beautiful,' said Beth, motioning to various triumphs of architecture. 'It looks very old.'

'Yes, I think it's mentioned in the Domesday Book. Surprised there are so many old buildings still standing, especially after the war.'

He pulled up in a lay-by. 'Beth, could you wind your window down? Let's ask this lady if she knows where we need to go.'

They stopped a passing shopper who was happy to help. 'Just carry on along this road. About a hundred yards outside the village, you'll see a sign for Deeny House.'

The directions were spot on and, as James turned into the entrance, they were met with a view of a large square house, about half the size of Harrington's.

A woman in her late twenties answered the doorbell. Her appearance took them by surprise: baggy dungarees, no make-up, an oversized man's shirt and her copper hair tied back into a loose pony tail. Her owlish eyes smiled a welcome.

'Can I help you?' She spoke with the hint of a Yorkshire accent.

James offered his card.

'I'm afraid Mr and Mrs Deeny are out. They've gone up to London, to the theatre.'

'It's not them we've come to see. We were rather hoping to catch the sister of Johnny Barton.'

She caught her breath. 'I haven't seen him for years. I couldn't even tell you where he is.'

'A little nearer than you may think,' said James.

'He's all right, is he?'

Beth answered. 'The last time we saw him, he was quite well.'

'Any chance we could have ten minutes with you?' James asked.

She swung the door open. 'Yes, yes. Mr and Mrs Deeny won't be home till later but I need to carry on in the garden. Come through to the back. Do you want some tea or something?'

They declined and followed her through to a large area at the back of the house that had been made into a vegetable patch. Blackbirds and starlings chirped. A blue tit flew back to its nest in a bird box nailed to the shed. Two greenhouses stood at the far end of the garden, their doors open. A golden Labrador scampered to welcome them.

'Ah, hello,' said James, fondling its soft ears. 'And who are you?'

'That's Byron. Mr Deeny's a big fan of the poet.'

'He's gorgeous,' said Beth reaching out to stroke him. 'The dog, that is, not Byron.'

The laughter eased the tension.

James introduced themselves formally

and apologised for not doing so at the front door.

'I'm Melanie, Melanie Barton,' she replied.

'How long have you been here?' asked Beth.

'Too many years to remember.' Melanie, it turned out, was quite a chatterbox. They followed her down the path to where she'd left her gardening tools. 'I'm just cutting things back and making sure everything's as it should be. I've tomatoes in the greenhouse that are coming on, the strawberries and raspberries are also ripening. It'll be a bumper crop this year with the warm weather we've had.' She turned. 'Sorry, you want to talk about Johnny. He's not ill, is he?'

'Absolutely not,' said James. 'Can I ask, when was the last time you saw him?'

'Could you pass me that ball of twine please?'

He did so.

She fastened a straying plant to a bamboo stick and shoo'd Byron off to the shade. 'I'm twenty-eight this year so it'll be five, may be six years.'

'Five years!' said Beth. 'Did you not get on?'

Melanie stood and thought for a second. 'You know, I don't think we did. He's a few years older than me so we always had different friends. When I moved up to junior school, he moved to a bigger one. But it wasn't just that.' She picked up her secateurs. 'Mum and Dad despaired of him, because he had his head in the clouds from the moment he was born. Didn't do well at school. Teachers accused him of daydreaming and that's exactly what he did. He was a fan of the cinema, or rather of the matinée idols. He was always trying to be something he weren't.'

'Oh?' said James, taking a handful of cuttings from her and putting them in a trug. 'In what way?'

She picked up a trowel, squatted down and dug out some weeds. 'He was never satisfied with where he'd come from. Upset Mum quite a bit. I mean our parents didn't have much but they did give us a lot of love and, when they could, they'd take us on holiday. It wasn't much but they did their best. But Johnny, well he said once that when he was grown up, he'd stop in a posh hotel, not a crummy caravan.'

'How would he afford that?' asked Beth.

Melanie stood up and stretched her back. 'God only knows. When I was older, I said to him that people like us have to work hard to get anywhere in life, money don't drop out of the sky. Dad had a right go at him once, told him to come to the factories and earn a wage. Told him he needed to help pay the bills.'

'And did he?'

'He did for a while but then the stress of real life got to him. He couldn't cope with life. Nerves got the better of him. Doctor signed him off for a while. Dad was furious. Couldn't understand it and I must admit, I couldn't either.' She secured a stray hair behind her ear. 'He started getting better after a couple of months and then told me he'd had an idea that couldn't fail.'

James pricked up his ears. 'An idea?'

The woman picked up her tools and

marched toward the greenhouse. 'He was going out with a woman about the same age as him. Came from the posh end of town. Her family owned one of the big houses outside of Harrogate.' She put her tools down. 'Yes, I remember it now; they lived in Kendall Manor. He, the father that is, owned one of the factories. Actually, I think it belonged to the grandparents, but they had a lot of money and this woman, the girlfriend, said she'd support him.'

Beth asked what the idea was.

The young woman's eyes went heavenward. 'I don't know the ins and outs of it. He started reading stuff about ancient civilisations and old religions. I thought he'd had a relapse. I wasn't living at home. I'd taken the position here and sort of lost contact with him. He started dressing differently, putting on posh suits. Even had elocution lessons to get rid of the Yorkshire accent. I didn't understand it. Why be ashamed of your roots?'

'Did he stay in contact with your parents?'

'He sent money home every now and

again but they haven't heard from him in two or three years.'

'And you have no idea what he's doing now? Would it surprise you if the idea involved religion?'

She reached for a bowl and picked some ripe tomatoes. 'It wouldn't. Like I say, Johnny had his head in the clouds, always daydreaming. I remember him reading an article once about some bloke in America who charged people through the nose for attending his church. He had an enormous house, new car, rolling in it he was and his poor parishioners were struggling to make ends meet. I mean, that's not very Christian, is it?'

James suggested that not everyone was very Christian. 'I recall a newsreel of a wealthy group of people in Brazil who worshipped regularly but always ignored the beggars when they came out of church. It struck me as a little hypocritical.'

'Exactly,' said Melanie. 'I don't go to church myself but I'll always help people if I can. I'm sure God can see what I do.'

'I'm sure he can,' said James, keen to

get back to the subject. 'This girlfriend of his, what was her name?'

'Oh, she was a Kendall. Beverley . . . yeah, Beverley.'

'What did she look like?'

She poured the contents of the bowl into a paper bag. 'Same age as Johnny. Slim, dark hair, quite dark eyes if my memory serves me right. And elegant. Well, she had the money to be elegant. The Kendalls are coining it in, still are. We can all look the bee's knees if we have money, can't we?' She put her hand to her mouth. 'Oh, sorry, no offence, didn't mean that to be a swipe at rich people in general.'

'No offence taken.'

'You're asking questions about our Johnny but you haven't said why.'

Beth told her the tale of the Celestial Faith Commune, how it had come to fruition in the North and had now set up camp near their village.

On learning of Johnny's new title, Melanie burst out laughing. 'Sounds like he's lost his sanity again. Father Sun, what sort of name is that? Who's he think he is, Sitting Bull?'

James asked if her brother had ever expressed an interest in the structure or meaning of the universe.

'Not that I remember. The only stars he was interested in were film stars. What's he thinking of?' She laughed again. 'I knew it were an idea but I didn't think he'd do anything about it. I thought he'd try and be an actor and make a complete mess of it. Thought he was another David Niven or Errol Flynn.' She chuckled.

'Joking aside,' said Beth, 'it has caused some consternation in the villages nearby and our vicar is a little put out by the whole thing.' She went on to tell Melanie about the commitment that members had to abide by if they joined the commune permanently.

'Sounds underhand.' She picked up another bowl and filled it with strawberries. 'He thinks this religious commune thing is an easy way to fleece people of their money. That's what Johnny's swayed by, money and with very little stress involved, by the sounds of it.'

'Did he ever get involved in any

criminal activity?' asked James.

'That's one thing Mum and Dad did teach us. The difference 'tween right and wrong. He got caught stealing a film magazine when he was younger but that was it. The shopkeeper told the police, who told Dad who gave him a belt.' She tipped the strawberries into another paper bag. 'Do you think he's doing something illegal?'

'I've absolutely no idea. We were hoping you might know more but you clearly don't see him. Do you know if he was friendly with any other people other than this Beverley Kendall?'

'He mixed with that rich crowd quite a bit. She had a cousin she was close to, Simon something or other. He went off to Oxford. He wasn't a Kendall but part of the empire. His aunt owned a factory, round Leeds way it was. I got an idea that one closed down. Our Johnny never kept in touch with anyone from school. I think he thought they were beneath him. He liked being a leader, not part of something. Shame 'cause some were really nice.'

She handed over the two bags. 'There, some fresh tomatoes and strawberries.'

Surprised, Beth thanked her. 'We'll be sure to have these later. They look delicious.'

Melanie led them back through the house and opened the front door. 'Should I go see Johnny? I can't tell Mum and Dad about this, it'll upset 'em too much.'

James convinced her to do nothing for the time being. 'Or if you do, would you leave our names out of it? I rather think we upset him when we were nosing around on the open evening. He won't thank us for tracking down lost family members.'

'Oh, I'm not lost,' said Melanie. 'I've been here for years. He knows where I am. I wrote to him a few times to tell him to telephone our mam.'

'How did you know where to write?'

'I didn't. I just sent it to his old address. Whether it got sent on, I don't know. If he chooses to disown me then I'm not chasing after him. You think that Mother Moon you told me about is Beverley Kendall?'

James shrugged. 'I've no idea.'

'Will you let me know?' She picked up a card from the occasional table. 'That's our phone number here. I'm always here between ten o'clock and five o'clock, except for Monday. After that, the day's me own.'

'You live in?' asked Beth.

'Aye. Owners are retired so I do housework, a spot of cooking and keep the garden nice.'

James commended her. 'We'll let you know if anything further develops. Oh, by the way, do you happen to have any photographs of your brother with this Beverley Kendall?'

'No, I've not, all my old photographs are at home with Mum and Dad.'

'Thank you for these,' said Beth holding up the bags.

On the drive home, James asked Beth for her thoughts.

'She seems down to earth, hard-working and sensible.'

'Do you think she's telling the truth about not seeing her brother?'

'Yes, I do. Don't you?'

'I'm mindful that George regularly reminds me that I take people at face value too much. But, I have to say I agree with you. What do you think our next step should be?'

'Perhaps find out if Mother Moon is this Kendall woman. I've a feeling she is — the description sounded too similar. And she's associated with the Kendall empire. There's money there and that could be how Barton is funding this commune.'

James thought this was a good next step. 'We have dinner with Fi and William tonight. I'm popping up a little earlier to chat with GJ.' He went over the discussion the young man had had with him.

Beth frowned. 'That does sound a little odd, doesn't it? Well, I'll come up with you and have a gin and tonic while I'm waiting.'

James took a left turn and put the Austin Healey through her paces. In the back of his mind, though, the thoughts were whirring as fast as the engine. Wendy had disappeared, the commune was still a mystery to him and this strange meeting of GJ's the previous evening only added to his curiosity.

24

GJ accepted the half-pint of beer and sat at the end of the terrace at Harrington's with James, who'd opted for a gin and tonic. Seeing Beth a few tables down, GJ insisted that she join them.

'I mean I was sworn to secrecy but I know you're not going to spread this about and I could do with your advice.'

With that, GJ spent the next twenty minutes describing his journey to a windowless room and how he had been blindfolded. He explained what he felt was going on and that he'd been offered a substantial sum of money to do more calligraphy work. 'This woman also offered further work, copying artwork. A couple of other people were there and a man was just finishing up on a painting I'd never seen before but it was in the style of Vermeer.'

GJ's gaze went from James to Beth and back again.

'This chap, Drummond, would you be able to sketch him?'

'Probably. He was pretty ordinary, handsome in a rough way. I'll give it a try. Why?'

'I think you may have stumbled across the art fraud ring that my cousin is helping to expose.'

'Oh yes,' said Beth.

GJ almost dropped his glass. He whispered. 'Art fraud ring?'

Beth explained how Herbie Harrington was helping police identify works of art in private collections that had been replaced by fakes.

The young man listened with increasing interest. 'That fits in with what I saw. Let me get this straight. You're saying that people who have private collections of renowned art have a piece stolen and replaced with a fraud?'

'That's right,' said James. 'Good ones too as the owners don't notice what's happened.'

'Does your friend, George, know about this?'

'I don't think so. He hasn't mentioned

it.' James checked with Beth who shrugged.

'He may know of it,' she said, 'but he's not involved. Herbie's been working with the police at Haywards Heath. George is based at Lewes.'

Sipping his beer, GJ continued. 'I haven't told Catherine any of this. I'm telling you because I wanted your advice. Do you think I should report it?'

'You said earlier that you'd felt threatened,' said James.

'That's right. When this man, Drummond, dropped me off he said he wouldn't want anyone to get hurt. And he dropped me by the cottage so he knows where I live.'

'Was there anything about the room you were in that you can remember?'

GJ gazed up to the sky. 'I remember there weren't any windows. It wasn't a long journey there, about twenty minutes but on the way back I felt he'd taken a different route. It seemed to take much longer. Oh, and I heard the sea.'

'Close by?'

He shrugged. 'Sorry, I'm not being much help, am I?'

Beth told him not to apologise. 'It's not as if you knew you'd be in that situation. What about his car — do you remember what sort of car he drove?'

He brightened. 'Yes, it was a pale green Ford Anglia, a bit rusty and one of the rear lights was missing.'

James finished his drink. 'That makes it a little easier to spot. Did you remember to check his number plate?'

'Covered up. Oh, and he smoked foreign cigarettes, those awful bitter things. French. The smell stuck in my throat.'

'Look, GJ, my advice is something you're not going to want to do. Speak to George. He can have a chat with whoever's investigating this art fraud business and come and take a statement.'

The young man lowered his voice. 'What if this Drummond bloke finds out?'

Beth suggested that James speak with George instead. 'That way, if Drummond has any way of checking GJ's movements,

GJ can honestly say he hasn't spoken to the police.'

'Are you happy with that, GJ?'

He let out a frustrated moan. 'I should have left the door open really, said that I'd think about it. Then I could have found out more about where they were.'

'You've no way of contacting Drummond?'

A shake of the head.

Beth asked how Mr Drummond had found GJ.

'I've no idea. He had a leaflet about the workshops so perhaps he just picked one up in the village.'

Fiona and William waved from the dining room.

Before Beth went to meet them, James held her back. 'Can you make my excuses, Beth? I need to pop into the village.' She frowned. 'I promise to update you later.'

'You be sure to. You're missing out on Didier's chicken pie.'

'Don't remind me. Tell Fiona and William that I'll make it up to them. I'll see you at rehearsals.'

James and GJ went to the edge of the terrace where James told him not to worry. 'I'll chat with George, see what he suggests. Meanwhile, do your best to draw a portrait of Drummond.'

Reassured by the advice, GJ returned to the converted stables. Meanwhile, James was in a quandary. Not only was the commune pulling at him, this new information about possible art fraud had piqued his interest.

25

Later that evening, villagers gathered outside the Half Moon where rehearsals were taking place. It was a last-minute change. The glorious summer evening was too good to miss and the Cavendish Players were sprawled across the grass enjoying a drink while Dorothy attempted to fine-tune some of the performances. Beth listened as Dorothy shared her concerns.

'I'm not sure this is a good idea,' she said. 'We seem to be more disciplined in the church hall.'

'You're a force to be reckoned with, Mrs Forbes. I'm sure you'll have them under control. Put your stern face on.'

Dorothy looked over her glasses. 'I will do my best. Is Lord Harrington not coming?'

Beth scanned the area. 'He came earlier. His car's over there but I haven't seen hide nor hair of him.'

'Who're you missing?' asked Donovan as he collected some empty glasses.

'James. Have you seen him?'

'Ah, yer man James disappeared into the vicarage as soon as he arrived. Didn't so much as order a drink, so he didn't.'

Beth thanked him. 'I'll go over and see what's keeping him. No doubt he and Stephen are deep in some philosophical debate.'

When she arrived at the vicarage she was surprised to see Bert open the front door. His smile wavered.

'Beth,' he said in an extraordinarily loud voice. 'Watcha doing 'ere?'

'Looking for James. Donovan said he'd come straight over here.'

'Nah, he went a while ago. He's probably in the back o' the bar with George.'

'I don't think so.'

Anne peered round the kitchen door then rushed toward her. 'Beth, we have a friend of Bert's here. They served in the forces together.'

'That's right,' said Bert visibly relaxing. 'His name's Freddie and we were in the same barracks. Come on in and meet him.'

Beth followed the pair of them down the hall and into the kitchen. She was introduced to a man who didn't look dissimilar to Bert. Quite ragged clothing, musty too, a greying beard, bushy eyebrows and overlong grey hair. He wore a pork-pie hat, round black-rimmed glasses and needed the support of a walking stick. He favoured his right leg. His boots were old and scuffed. When he spoke, his tone was gruff and the accent was a London one, quite rough but not as common Bert's. He avoided eye contact.

'All right, missus?'

'Yes, thank you. Freddie, it's lovely to meet you.' She turned to Bert. 'I've not heard you speak of Freddie before.'

'Nah, strange that, I can't believe he's not turned up in a few of my anecdotes before now.'

Behind Bert, Beth glimpsed Stephen stifling laughter and making a very bad job of it. Her eyes narrowed. 'Stephen, what are you up to?'

She then saw Bert's face crease.

Bridling slightly at being the butt of their humour, she insisted they let her in on their secret. 'You can't simply laugh and not tell me why.'

Bert turned her to face Freddie. 'Honestly Beth, you've met Freddie loads o' times. Don't you recognise him?'

Wary of getting too close to the man, Beth attempted to place him but no-one sprang to mind.

She gave a helpless shrug. 'I'm afraid not, although there is something about him. Perhaps he met James and I wasn't about.'

The comment caused hilarity and Beth closed her eyes in frustration. 'I don't see what's so funny.'

Freddie took his wig off.

Beth gawped. 'James!'

James peeled off the beard and straightened up. 'Well, if I can fool my own wife, I think I can fool Father Sun.'

She playfully slapped him on the arm. 'You really are the limit. Is Dulcie here too?'

Dulcie's head appeared round the door. 'Is it safe for me to enter?'

Beth grinned. 'What an amazing job. And that accent was convincing too.'

James reverted to character. 'I thought it was a good, too, missus.'

She turned to Dulcie. 'How long did it take for you to do this?'

'Not as long as you think. Once I had a name, a region and a character background, it came very easy. And Lord Harrington, sorry, James, came to life as soon as I'd put the make-up and costume on.'

James shrugged the old jacket off. 'It's surprising how your acting skills improve when you have all of this on. I honestly felt the part, Beth.' He picked up his own clothes and went off to change. 'I'll see you in a few moments. Stephen, can I use some of your after-shave?'

'Of course,' Stephen said, holding up a roll of film. 'I've taken photographs from every angle and every stage. Mr Chrichton's at the rehearsal tonight so I'll ask him to develop it for us.'

Turning to Beth and Anne, Dulcie told them that she would supervise a make-up and wardrobe session with them. 'We'll be guided by the photographs so, if I'm busy, you can turn James into Freddie.'

Anne almost leapt for joy. 'How exciting.'

'Hardly,' said Stephen. 'Anne, y-you really shouldn't be so gleeful about what will be a nefarious m-mission.'

Now it was her turn to slap Stephen. 'Don't be so grumpy. Anyway, you're certain they're not what they seem so this will prove it once and for all. You should be just as happy as me.'

A few minutes later, James returned to the kitchen dressed in dark blue trousers and a pale lemon shirt. He retrieved his straw hat. 'Right, shall we toddle over and catch the acts?'

The group made their way across the village green. Anne shook out a tartan travel blanket and she, Beth and Dulcie sat down while Stephen ordered the drinks.

They watched as Charlie Hawkins and his two children sang 'Any Old Iron'. Tommy and Susan sang with convincing Cockney accents. Charlie had also choreographed the whole thing and promised, at the end, they would be dressed for the part too.

James turned to Dulcie. 'I can't imagine that you didn't have a hand in this.'

'The children weren't so keen initially but Charlie won them round.'

'It's delightful.'

The children raced to Dulcie.

'Did you see us?' said Susan, her pigtails swinging.

'We sang really loud like you told us to,' added Tommy, grinning from ear to ear.

'I thought you were marvellous,' said Dulcie, giving each of them a kiss on the forehead.

James caught Beth's eye. They were clearly thinking the same thing. The children had taken to Dulcie and she to them.

Charlie leant over and kissed the top of Dulcie's head. 'You're all right for a drink I see. I'll just go over and get a half then come and join you.'

Dorothy invited Mr Bateson to perform next. The man leapt to his feet. Bateson, in James' opinion was one of the most professional solicitors he'd come across, but also the most madcap. His mass of unruly white hair and wiry frame made him look like a caricature. The thing James loved most about him was that, unlike many professional men, he left his business head in the office. When not at work, he was wonderfully eccentric and thoroughly immersed in village activities.

Much to the delight of the children on the green, Bateson had come dressed in costume. He wore a Victorian frock coat and top hat; thrusting his walking cane forward, he strode across to the makeshift stage which, James realised, was a dismantled cardboard box. Standing tall, he went through a faultless rendition of 'Burlington Bertie'. Bateson would be the opening act and, after singing this particular song, would take up his position as compère.

Bert puffed out his cheeks. 'He ought to go on the stage at the Victoria. That's a little theatre down near Gladys that still puts on the old music hall stuff. He'd go down well.' He turned to James. 'You got some talent in this village, Jimmy-boy.'

The act following Bateson led Bert to change his mind — a couple from the outskirts of the village who crucified 'It's a Great Big Shame'; however, they brightened again when Rose and Lilac Crumb appeared. They emerged from their rusty old vintage Citroen and, five minutes later gave a beautiful rendition of 'The Boy I Love is Up in the Gallery'.

'I say, that was rather good,' said James, who still couldn't get over how much the sisters had changed since they'd first arrived in the village. The pair of them had been nothing but gossips and harbingers of bad news but, with Stephen's help, they had integrated into the community more and were better people for it.

Harry appeared. 'Hello. I didn't realise it was rehearsals this evening.' James stood and clinked pints with him. 'Dad, Stephen said something about you wanting to go undercover instead of me.'

He steered Harry further away from the crowds. 'To be honest, Harry, I know what I'm looking for and what questions to ask. If you go in, I'll simply have more questions and be asking why you didn't do certain things.'

'You want me to keep an eye on Harrington's?'

'You can do as you please, really.'

'You'll have Bert with you though?'

'Most certainly. He stops me from doing anything stupid.'

Harry sarcastically reminded him that it should be the other way around. 'Honestly, Dad, you're the educated estate owner and he's the shifty Cockney. It should be you keeping him out of trouble.'

'I've done my fair share of keeping him on the straight and narrow. Anyway, yes, keep your hand in at Harrington's but Paul and Adam are there. You may want to check that everything's shipshape for the Midsummer Ball. I'd hate for there to be any last-minute hiccups. Have a word with the guests. It'll be good for you to show your face now and then. They appreciate the personal touch.'

'Yes, I can do that. What about Jonty's parade, are you organising that?'

'Not really. I think Graham and Sarah

Porter are in charge of that this year.' He swigged his beer. 'Listen, I'm not spending all my days at this commune place, just a few hours here and there.'

Bert joined them. 'All right, Harry?'

Harry asked that Bert keep his father safe during their exploits. 'I thought parents were supposed to continue being responsible but it seems that I'm having to play the grown-up here.'

James afforded his son a wry smile.

Bert slapped Harry on the back. 'He'll be fine. If 'e makes a pig's ear of it, I'll drag him out and get the professional in,' he elbowed Harry, 'the future spy in the family.'

With a roll of the eyes, Harry went to join Beth.

'So, Jimmy-boy, when are we going in?'

Across the green, James saw George getting out of his car. 'I need to have a word with George but, how about in a couple of days, providing the girls can do this make-up for me? I say, when we do go in, d'you want to stay with us instead of travelling here every day?'

'Nah mate, I'll get the bus down on the

day. I'm gonna pitch a tent in the woods near to that hole in the fence. I can keep an eye on fings there.'

About to go, James turned. 'By the way, that Wendy Potter girl has disappeared.'

'Where to?'

'I've no idea,' he said, passing on the news that George was making enquiries but that Wendy could simply have decided to leave.

'George could be right,' his friend said. 'She's a grown woman. Perhaps she wasn't as close to her mum and dad as they want you to believe.'

'Mmm.' He left Bert and decided to give Radley a walk. Collecting the dog, he wandered over to greet his friend who was beaming from ear to ear. 'What's made you so happy?'

'I am word perfect. I've been singing that coffee song all around the house. If I can't sleep, I run through it in my head and when I'm driving to and from Lewes I sing it. That Forbes woman can't have a go at me for not knowing my lines this time.'

James couldn't help but laugh. His

friend had been on the wrong end of Dorothy's sharp tongue before now and it had clearly rankled with him. He went to march toward the pub but James pulled him back.

'Any news on Wendy Potter?'

'Not so far. I've got a few of the team working on it.'

'Can I have a word about something else?'

The tone wasn't lost on George. 'What's the matter?'

James guided him toward the church-yard, where he let Radley off the leash. 'Do you know anything about some art fraud that's going on?'

The look he received was one of pure astonishment. 'How on earth do you know about that?'

He picked up a stick and threw it. Radley, eager to play, raced after it. While the hound hunted and retrieved, James went through his conversation with Herbie.

George admitted that he'd heard about the investigation. 'Scotland Yard are liaising with the station at Haywards

Heath. Lewes isn't involved at all.' He delved into his pocket for his pipe and sat on a large boxed gravestone. 'But you've not dragged me away from the crowd just to tell me that.'

'There's no fooling you, is there?' James said as he sat down next to him. 'I had a rather interesting chat with GJ who's reluctant to tell you himself due to a veiled threat.'

As James recounted GJ's experience, his friend's attitude changed from one of mild interest to jotting the information down in his notebook.

At the end, George revealed the curious episode with Mrs Millerson. 'She doesn't have a private collection though, just the one drawing.'

Radley pawed James for another game of fetch. He broke off a large stump and hurled it in the air. 'You know, if this Mrs Millerson only has the one drawing, and it was returned, it could mean something.'

It was no surprise to James that his friend had already figured that out. 'It may mean that she knew a person involved. She reckons she doesn't. Only neighbours and close friends visit. Will GJ speak to me privately, no strings attached? I understand he's worried but he's got vital information. It would be good if he could find a way to go back to that building and give us more detail.'

'He's going to do a sketch of the man and he was taken in a Ford Anglia with a broken rear light.'

'Difficult to track down. Anglias are two a penny round here.'

Radley, bored with retrieving sticks, hopped onto the monument and settled by James. He fondled its ears. 'Perhaps this chap thinks what he's doing is legal.'

'No, no. You don't blindfold a man and then threaten him. He knows what he's doing. I'll pass all this on to my colleagues at Haywards Heath and I'll pop in to see GJ at the workshop, see if I can't convince him to make a statement.'

They jumped off the memorial and made their way back to the green.

'Oh, by the way, we visited Johnny Barton's sister.'

George pursed his lips. 'You can't help

yourself, can you? And did you find out anything criminal about him?'

'Not a sausage. He sounds like a dreamer who's latched on to a rich girl. Changed his image considerably and had elocution lessons to get rid of his accent.'

'No crime in that.'

'No, but I still think he's taking money under false pretences.'

'Unless you get proof, you've nothing to go on. You going to leave it then?'

James wasn't about to divulge his plan to go undercover. The man would blow a fuse. Instead, he simply said that he wouldn't pursue it. 'We've too much on here.' Dorothy waved her clipboard at him. 'Come on, I think our illustrious director is wanting us to perform.'

They went through their song with such precision that it caught James by surprise. They were word perfect and even slipped in a harmony here and there. Cheered by the villagers at the end, they gave each other a congratulatory slap on the back and popped into the Half Moon to refresh their glasses. The pub was empty apart from a few locals playing darts.

Donovan reached up for a pint jug. 'Ah, decided to join us now, James.'

'I'm sure you're doing good trade without my contribution.'

Kate came through to the serving area. 'Just in time. Mr Lane, Lewes Police are on the phone trying to track you down. Go through. You'll see the telephone on the table by the back door.'

James chatted with Donovan and Kate. He didn't always get much time to talk with the Delaneys and it was good to catch up on their news. Just a few minutes later, George reappeared and nudged James toward a table.

'Sit down there and listen to this.'

He did as he was told.

'Mrs Potter has officially reported her daughter missing.'

'How does she know she's missing? She didn't get to see her at the commune on the open evening.'

'She received a note from her this morning. Not from the Post Office, delivered by hand.'

James shifted in his seat. Something in

George's manner told him there was more to this than met the eye.

'The note says that she's fine, that her mum's not to worry and she'll be back when she's ready.'

'Isn't that a good thing? I mean, I don't know what the relationship is between mother and daughter but clearly she doesn't want her mother to worry.'

'Mrs Potter's convinced that it's not her daughter's writing.'

'Why?'

'She says it looks like her writing but there's a spelling mistake. Apparently, Wendy Potter was top of her class throughout school when it came to spelling and there was an error. The girl had written that she felt as if she needed a break, a holiday. But she'd written it with a double 'I'.'

'You believe her?'

'It could be an error. Written in haste and shoved through the letter-box.'

'But you're not sure?'

'She's only been gone a day. She's twenty-five. She doesn't need mollycoddling.'

James waited for his friend to decide.

After a weary sigh, George took a good few gulps of his pint. 'It's an official report so I can't ignore it.'

'What happens with missing adults?'

'We get a name, description, last seen whereabouts, what she was wearing, talk to friends, neighbours, that sort of thing. See if we can't get a lead.'

Keen not to sound too interested in this latest turn of events, James didn't dwell on the subject but it was just another thing about this commune that struck him as odd. The sooner he got in there, the better. He spotted Bert through the window. It might be a good idea to ingratiate themselves at the commune sooner rather than later.

26

Fiona had to sit down, she was laughing so hard.

James straightened up. 'I don't see that it's quite that funny, Fi.'

They were at home where Dulcie had come to show Beth how to transform James from Lord of the Manor to a city itinerant. His indignation only added to his sister's hysterics. 'Oh, I'm sorry, James, but you really do look like a country bumpkin.'

Bert nudged him. 'As long as 'e don't look like Lord James Harrington, that's all right.'

Fiona wiped away tears and apologised. 'Honestly, James, you really do take all this sleuthing a little too far.'

Beth had to agree. 'What if you get found out?'

'I won't,' answered James with confidence and, inside, he sincerely believed he wouldn't. 'I fooled you from two feet away. I won't give Father Sun a chance to have any doubts.'

William lit a cigarette. 'What are you looking for? Is there something untoward going on? Won't that man get annoyed with you?'

Before William bombarded him with more questions, James stopped him. 'I'm doing this because of Bernard Potter, a respected policeman who felt something wasn't quite right. If Bert and I head in there and find everything is above board, that will suffice and I'll come out and forget the whole thing.'

Fiona challenged him. 'You can't go rooting around that leader's personal affairs.'

'We're going in to talk to people, that's all.'

'As long as that's all you're going to do,' said Beth, adding the final touches to the costume. She checked the photographs and studied James. 'I think you'll do. Fiona, are you dropping them off?'

She jangled the car keys. 'William and I are taking a drive to Chichester. We're dropping Laurel and Hardy here on the road leading to the commune.' She lowered her voice. 'Apparently, we're not to make ourselves known. The brothers-in-arms want it to appear that they've walked some distance.'

James gave his sister his sternest glare. 'Fi, I wish you wouldn't speak as if I weren't here.'

'But you aren't, darling, you're now Freddie Woods, ex-army . . . what else? Do you have a background story?'

James shuffled on his feet, looked at the ground and reverted to his London identity. 'I'm ex-infantry. Staff clerk, qualified bookkeeper, fallen on 'ard times. Love nature, no particular religion 'cept to be a good person.' He reverted to self. 'Convincing?'

She gently pushed him. 'Come on then, the sooner I drop you off, the better.'

'How long will you be?' asked Beth, wondering whether he would be home for dinner.

James checked the clock. It was half-past ten in the morning. 'A couple of hours I would imagine. We're not allowed to stay for long but if we can get our foot in the door, make ourselves useful, that'll be a start.'

'How will you do that?'

'I get the impression that the members there are more involved in gardening, painting and decorating, that sort of thing. Father Sun mumbled something about not being able to do accounts when we saw him. I'm hoping that my bookkeeping skills may be of some use.'

'To view the accounts?'

'If I can, yes.'

Bert rubbed the stubble on his chin. 'Meanwhile, I'll 'ave a scout round and see if I can't find a good place to camp for the night.'

Beth couldn't help but stare. 'You're stopping overnight?'

'Just by the fence where the opening was. I'm gonna stroll about, see if I can find anything funny going on.'

Her gaze settled on James. 'You're not doing that, are you?'

'I shall be home, darling. Sharing a tent with Bert is not high on my list of things to do.'

She laughed. 'That's good to hear.'

Fifteen minutes later, James and Bert were standing at the commune gates.

'You ready, Jimmy boy?'

James' heart began to race as doubts crept in. 'Are you sure he won't recognise me?'

Bert rang the bell and patted his back. 'I'd tell you if it weren't good enough. Remember what you said at the vicarage. When you're in costume, you become the character. You're Freddie Woods now.'

On that advice, he became more hunched and clasped his nobbled walking stick. To ensure he limped on the correct foot, Bert had sellotaped a minute stone inside his right shoe. Sister Venus, the young woman he'd met in the kitchen, came to the gate.

'Hello, can I help you?'

'Yes, missus,' said Bert, 'me and my mate 'ere are wanting to join your commune.' He waved a dog-eared copy of the leaflet in the air. 'It sounds right up our street, don't it, Freddie?'

'Yeah, it does,' James said. 'Love nature, me. I said to Bert, this is what we've been looking for. What do we 'ave to do to join?'

She hastened to unlock the gate. 'I'm Sister Venus, one of the commune members. Simply follow me.' She locked the gate after them. 'I'll see if Father Sun is free; he's our leader, the one who started the commune up. He likes to have a chat first. Either him or Mother Moon.'

James hobbled along, appreciative that the young lady was aware of his limp. She had slowed to his pace. 'You been 'ere long?'

'A few months now.'

She told him exactly what she'd divulged on the open evening. Keen to find out a little more, he asked her if she had chosen the name Sister Venus.

'Oh yes, we get to pick our own names. You can be anything really, connected with the stars or the planets.'

James suppressed a grin as Bert, in all seriousness, told her he had always loved the planet Neptune.

'I right love that planets suite by 'olst, don't you? Neptune, the mystic.'

'I'm not sure which one that is but I'm sure it's lovely.'

''ere,' said James, 'what's your real name?'

'I left Trudy Pickford behind when I joined the commune.'

'Just the name or yer 'istory too?'

'A bit of both, I suppose. I had nothing in Bognor. I weren't getting on with my parents. I'd been cautioned for thieving, you know, shoplifting and I left school early. Me parents were getting on my nerves and didn't like me coming here. But I liked it and it was better than living at home.'

They reached the house where she opened the door. 'I'll see if Father Sun's here.'

Once out of earshot, James, forgetting his accent, turned to Bert. 'That's one name we can check back on.'

Bert grabbed his lapel. 'Oi. Stay in character. Blokes dressed like this don't go round talking like a toff.'

James slipped back into character and apologised. His stomach lurched as he saw Father Sun emerge from his office.

Would he recognise him under this disguise? If so, not only would it be the height of embarrassment, it would also fuel a good deal of anger.

But Father Sun simply held out a hand. 'It's lovely to have you visit. Sister Venus tells me you're interested in joining us.'

'That's right, guvnor,' said Bert.

'If that's all right,' James added, hoping his accent passed the test.

Father Sun didn't blink an eye. 'It's more than all right. Why don't you come through? Let's get to know one another and I can tell you all about the Celestial Faith Commune.'

Bert helped James up the step and into the hallway. He stopped at the mural of the earth that he and Beth had seen on the open evening. It really was a stunning piece of art.

'Strewth,' Bert said, 'that's a right nice painting. You do that?'

Father Sun turned and admired the art. 'Not me, no, I haven't an artistic bone in my body. No, one of our members did it, Sister Bellatrix.' He opened his study door.

Fortunately, Father Sun had turned his back on James. Although determined to stay in character, he wasn't expecting Wendy Potter's alias to come up so soon.

'Sister Bellatrix, that's an odd name,' said Bert. 'Ain't that part of Orion or summit?'

Father Sun told them to make themselves comfortable. 'Yes, it is. You know your constellations, Mr . . . I'm so sorry, I haven't even introduced myself. I'm Father Sun, and you are?'

Bert held out a hand. 'I'm Bert Briggs and this 'ere is my old mate, Freddie Woods.'

'Well, welcome, Bert Briggs and Freddie Woods. Hold on there for a few moments, I'll just pop into the kitchen and ask Sister Venus to bring some tea. Do you take sugar?'

'None for 'im, two for me,' said Bert.

Father Sun disappeared. James leant into Bert, mindful of staying in character. 'He seems quite a nice bloke, don't you fink?'

'Yeah, he does. Let's see how 'e sells the place. Let 'im do most of the talking.'

Father Sun returned. 'Tea will be with us shortly.' He sat down behind his desk. 'Right, let me tell you all about the Celestial Faith Commune. Actually, before I do that, can you tell me how you found out about us?'

James waved the leaflet. 'Can't remember where we saw it, prob'ly Loxfield. We've been travellin', see.'

Father Sun stopped him. 'I don't need to know your background, Mr Woods. Providing you embrace our way of life, the pair of you will be most welcome.'

'Oh, righ' you are. That's nice, ain't it, Bert?'

'Yeah, it is.'

Sister Venus came in with a tray and set the cups and saucers down. 'There you are. This is the one with no sugar. I hope you enjoy it.'

'Thanks missus,' said Bert.

Father Sun rested his elbows on his desk. He spoke slowly, calmly. 'Right, down to business. Who and what are we?' He sipped his tea. 'We're not a religion, I have to put that to bed straight away. I'm getting a bit of grief from certain quarters about pinching congregation members but that's not who we are. I've never been particularly religious but I do feel that I'm spiritual. I believe in being good, in helping people, that sort of thing. And, I've also got a thing about the universe, the galaxy, the Milky Way. It's immense and we're nothing compared to its vastness.'

Both James and Bert had decided to remain quiet, stay interested and nod in all of the right places and they were doing exactly that now. In fact, James had to admit that the man was easy on the ears. He actually sounded quite genuine.

'I went to a few churches when I was a youngster but they did nothing for me. I couldn't relate to it. I won't go into my history but an event caused me to look at myself. I suffer a little with nerves. I got a few books out of the library about other religions, Hindu, Buddhism, Judaism, Shinto and anything similar really. Things like the Druids, the Celts, the native Americans, Mayans . . . '

James took a sip of tea. 'Those Druids like nature, don't they?'

Their host brightened even more. 'Yes, yes, they do, as do many of the indigenous peoples around the globe. And that's when I began thinking about my own commune. One that took some aspects of those ancient beliefs and put them into one. The Celestial Faith Commune emerged from that.'

'It's not some sort o' cult, is it?' said Bert with a frown. 'I 'eard about some bloke in America who brainwashed 'is congregation.'

'No! No, nothing like that. I think you'll find that those people who run cults are often delusional. I think I know the one you're thinking of. Didn't he think he was the Second Coming or something?'

'Yeah, that's right.'

'That's where we're different, Mr Briggs. We have no problem with you worshipping your God here although I find that very few of our members follow a religion. That's why they're here.' He steepled his fingers. 'Out of interest, are you religious?'

'Not me, guv'nor' said Bert.

'Used to be,' said James, 'but war makes you cynical, don't it?'

Father Sun said that it certainly did. 'I was too young to serve but we all hear the stories.'

James wanted to make sure he had the gist of things. 'So, you've taken beliefs and practices from the native peoples, is that right?'

'Exactly. The Druids, Native Americans, the Aborigines, Polynesians, Egyptians, they all look to the stars; many of their creation stories tell that they came from the stars.'

'You believe that, do you?' said James.

'I think the idea of it is a good one. Why shouldn't we come from the stars? Religions speak of going to heaven when you die; isn't that about going to the stars?'

'I don't know about that. It sounds right int'resting though, don't it, Bert?'

'You're telling me, mate. But what do you do 'ere all day? I mean, you can't keep praying to the stars, can yer?'

Father Sun smiled. 'No and it's not what we do. We want to honour the earth and the universe and the only way we can do that is to adopt the beliefs of our ancient ancestors.' He checked their cups. 'If you've finished your tea, I'll take you on a brief tour.'

As they followed him out, he asked if they liked gardening.

Bert replied that he wasn't much of a gardener. 'I'm more about fixing stuff, you know, plumbing, that sort o' thing. If someone tells me what to do, I can do it?'

'And you Mr Woods?'

'I don't know a weed from a wild-flower. My thing used to be bookkeeping. Used to be good at keeping accounts. Oh, and I'm fairly good with mechanics. That's what people tell me.'

Father Sun stopped. 'Really? Well, you could be a big help to me. Everyone around here is so invested in the Mother Earth aspect that I've landed myself with gardeners and farmers. Which is lovely but the finance side of things needs looking after. And we do have a car which is working fine at the moment but we want to buy a tractor too. Perhaps you could come with us when we find one. Give it the once-over.'

James couldn't believe his luck. If he could get a look at the accounts, it would answer a lot of questions. 'I'd be 'appy to.'

The tour of the rooms downstairs didn't take long. James found himself back in the kitchen where Sister Venus and Sister Jupiter were preparing lunch. The classroom had half a dozen members there, learning about chickens and how to look after them.

Outside, some members were pruning bushes, cutting the grass and edging the lawns. They were led to the allotments where several people were weeding, sowing, planting and cutting. Two members were securing bamboo poles for the runner beans. Three people were in the large greenhouse watering tomato plants.

All in all, James couldn't help but be impressed by what he'd heard and seen so far. It all appeared above board and well run. Had PC Potter got the wrong end of the stick? Now they had sneaked in, he found the idea appealing.

James hobbled along beside Father Sun. 'Do you do anything else?'

'We're expanding into crafts. You know

pottery, needlecraft, knitting, cross-stitch. One of our members, Sister Andromeda, has given us her potter's wheel. And, of course, if we have enough produce to make jams and pickles, we may be able to sell those as well, to help the funds.'

'Must cost a lot. This 'ouse is enormous, ain't it? Your 'lectric bills must be gigantic.'

Father Sun simply smiled and wouldn't comment.

'Talking about crafts,' said Bert, 'is the lady 'ere that painted that mural in the 'ouse?'

'No.' It was an abrupt answer.

An explanation came soon after, a tad too speedily, James thought. As if the man had realised he'd been short with them. 'She had some family business to attend to so she's left us for a while. Visiting her mother. She'll be back, though, once it's all done.'

Family business to attend to? Not with her own mother. What other family did she have? The doubts James had had when they first arrived resurfaced.

He asked if Sister Andromeda was

here. 'I wouldn't mind 'aving a go at some pott'ry.'

'She's our oldest member and rarely joins us. She's teaching one of our members who will eventually coach everyone.'

The next hour was spent in and around the allotments. Brother Mars took them on a tour of the vegetable plots and introduced them to a few of the members working the fields. They certainly had a huge variety of fruit and vegetables and wouldn't want for much during the winter months. James said as much to their guide.

'It's been a lot of trial and error,' Brother Mars said. 'Some things we planted at the wrong time, or watered too much. We spent a lot of time talking to people at the local nurseries, just getting advice. Should have a good crop this year. I've learned loads over last few harvests so we've fewer mistakes.'

Bert asked if he could smoke. Getting the go ahead, he rolled tobacco and asked why the man had taken the name Brother Mars. 'Bit of an odd name to choose for somethin' like this, innit? It's nicknamed the bringer of war. What made you choose that?'

The man scrutinised him and simply said that the planet had always fascinated him. 'I like science fiction, me. Martians, red planet, I don't know about bringer of war.' He shouted across to one of the men. 'Dig those in a bit deeper and when you finished, let chickens out. Foxes won't come near while we're here.'

James chanced his luck on his next question. 'What was your name, before you joined this place?'

'Kevin. Kevin Winspear.' He leaned on his spade. 'Funny saying name now. Seems like a lifetime ago.'

'What made you come 'ere?'

'Something different. Business had collapsed, don't have qualifications. Had no family and truth be told, no friends neither. I'm all right with this, farming, agriculture. Found me niche, that's what they say, in't it?'

'Wha' business did you 'ave?'

'Delivery van. I had good contract with florist and catering firm but florist went bust. The catering lot expanded, got their own vans. Offered me job but I didn't want it. Don't like taking orders off people. Father Sun put me in charge of allotment 'cause I get things done.'

James spotted Brother Neptune digging a shallow trench. 'He's doin' a good job, ain't he? What's his name?'

'That's Brother Neptune. Bit simple but he loves it. Loves being outside.'

'Watcha mean, a bit simple,' asked Bert.

'He's Down's Syndrome. He's got a lovely way though. Never sees bad in anyone.'

They came away from the allotment and James commented that the commune must have been a huge adjustment for the lad. 'Ain't 'e got no parents to look after him?'

'Gave him up. He'd been in and out of care and foster homes. Father Sun got to know him and when he set commune up, he got the kid to join.'

James went to ask another question but stopped. They'd vowed to limit the number of questions they asked and he didn't want to come across as being too nosy.

'What's tha' over there?' asked Bert, staring at the derelict building behind the main house.

'A heap of rubble that needs knocking down. It's fenced off. Some of it collapsed. Council came round and put notice up. Father Sun wants to clear site.' He called out to a woman; when she turned, James recognised her as Mother Moon.

She glided over to them. 'Hello, you must be Mr Woods and Mr Briggs. Are you enjoying the tour?'

The pair of them complimented the whole set-up.

'Glad I picked that leaflet up,' said Bert.

'Me too,' said James. 'This'll be the making of us.'

Brother Mars said cheerio and left them with Mother Moon who steered them to the side entrance of the house. 'This is where our brothers and sisters sleep.'

James realised that this was the old

cowshed, part of the original farm. It had been completely refurbished and a roof provided a connection to the main house.

'Are we able to look inside one? Just a peek, missus.' He detected a reluctance. 'Don't you bother yourself. We don't wanna be intruding. Is there anyone on holiday or something, you know, not using their room.'

'I'm sure it'll be fine. We do have someone away actually, Sister Bellatrix. I'm sure she won't mind. But I must ask you not to touch anything.'

Selecting a Yale key, she swung the door open. It was a spacious room with a single bed, a chair and a desk. On the wall were photographs of the constellations and a painting of a beautiful woman holding a long, silver sword.

'Blimey, who's that?'

'Sister Bellatrix is a talented painter, Mr Woods. This shows her as her namesake.'

'Is that what she looks like, your Sister Bellatrix?'

'She's made herself a little more

attractive than she actually is but, yes, it's a likeness.'

'Wonder why she wanted tha' name?' said James.

'Each has a reason. It's not our business, providing it relates to the universe,' Mother Moon explained.

James was itching to open a drawer or a wardrobe door but, of course, he couldn't. Within a minute they were back into the corridor. 'What about you, missus. Why'd you call yourself Mother Moon?'

She led them to the end of the corridor and back into the main hallway. 'My husband is Father Sun. He's our leader and inspiration. The sun and moon are vital to Mother Earth. Lose one and the planet would be a very different world. I take my place alongside Father Sun and occasionally lead the dusk and dawn worships. It makes sense for me to take the name.'

'What was your name before?'

'Beverley. Beverley Kendall.'

James couldn't have been more pleased. This was where the investment in the commune came from. 'If you don't mind me saying missus, that's a right nice name. I bet you didn't wanna give that up.'

Her expression was warm. 'She's a distant memory, Mr Woods, and I much prefer Mother Moon. Think of the magic of our moon. The tides, the eclipses, the moonlight walks . . . '

'Yer not wrong there,' said Bert, 'I've 'ad many a moonlight walk in my time.' His suggestive laugh caused Mother Moon to laugh with him.

She opened the study door. 'Our potential members have had a grand tour.'

Father Sun leapt up from his chair. 'Great. What did you think?'

'I right like it,' said Bert.

'Me too.'

'And what is it that you like?'

James knew exactly what he was looking for. 'This belief system: worshipping our mother earth, planting and sowing, living off the land and giving thanks. I couldn't ask for more, could you, Bert?'

'Nah, mate, I fink we'd love it 'ere. Reminds me of my uncle working with the big 'orses. Nothing like the feel of the land to keep you grounded.'

'Well, I've a few things to go through with you first. We don't accept you straight away. We ask people to join us during the day over a few weeks. If you think it's for you, and we like you, then there are finances to think about.'

Bert flinched. 'Wha' sort of finances?'

'Nothing you won't be able to afford.'

'We ain't got much, mister, 'ardly anything,' said James. 'How much would we have to spend?'

'We'd simply ask for a percentage of what you have. Presumably, you have a pension coming in. Do you own your own property?'

Bert roared with laughter. 'Me? Own me own property? You must be bonkers, mate. I own the clothes I walk in and me best suit for weddings and funerals.'

'That's right, 'e ain't got much at all and I ain't got anything. I stay with me daughter sometimes and go' a small pension. Nothing much though.'

Father Sun remained positive. 'I'm sure we'll be able to sort something out. It's midday and time for our worship. Would you like to join us?'

James and Bert said they'd love to and followed Father Sun out to the lawn. James recognised this as where they had witnessed the ceremony on the open evening. The members of the commune had their embroidered robes on and slipped off their sandals as they stood facing Father Sun.

Mother Moon spread her arms, closed her eyes and asked the members to do the same, including James and Bert.

Feeling awkward, James also spread his arms. He squinted through partly-closed eyes. He saw Father Sun, his face directed toward the sky.

'Welcome, brothers and sisters. Welcome to a glorious day and what a beautiful day. Our sun warms us from the clearest of skies, our moon guides our seas and moods and our universe spins its way, watching over us from afar. Let us reach out and ground ourselves with Mother Earth. Mother Earth feeds us, waters us, provides us with the air we breathe. Let us stand in silence to treasure this moment.'

After a few minutes of reflection, Father Sun thanked everyone for their commitment to the commune and asked that they return to their chores. Mother Moon handed him two packages which he promptly handed to James and Bert.

'Two robes. Please wear them when you come to the commune tomorrow.'

'Righ' you are.'

'I gotta go,' Bert blurted out. 'Can I use your lav? Too much tea.'

A little taken aback, Father Sun directed Bert to the house. James wondered what on earth had got into him. He turned to Father Sun. 'Only has to have more than a cup o' tea and he needs the toilet. That's age does that.'

The reason for his concern became evident when he saw Miss Long and Miss Fellowes almost jogging up the drive. Lord, he'd forgotten all about them. They would have recognised Bert in an instant.

'Ladies,' said Father Sun. 'You've made your minds up?'

'We've a few more questions,' said Mrs Long.

'And we wondered if someone could sit with us,' said Mrs Fellowes, who kept a safe distance from James as her eyes travelled over his dishevelled state.

'This is Mr Woods. He and his friend may be joining us too.'

Mrs Fellowes clearly didn't take to James who, mirroring her distaste, stepped back from her.

'By friend,' said Father Sun, 'who do you mean?'

'Our vicar, the Reverend Merry-weather.'

If James hadn't been standing there, he would not have believed it. Father Sun gritted his teeth together and had turned almost crimson.

He almost threw his hands up. 'That blasted vicar is a thorn in my side. No, I'm sorry, ladies, but I will not have that man here. He will do anything he can to dissuade you from joining us.'

'Oh dear. Can we go over there and have a bit of a ponder?' asked Mrs Long.

They didn't wait for an answer and

simply headed across the lawn to sit beneath a sprawling oak tree.

'They not sure, then?' said James.

'Unfortunately, we do get a handful of people who think this is for them and then realise what they're giving up. I believe those two will decide that it's not for them.'

'What d'you mean, giving up?'

'Why don't I go through that with you tomorrow. I think it's a good idea for you to chat about what you've seen today after a night's sleep. I'm sure you'll have more questions for us once you've had a think and a snooze.'

Bert appeared behind him. 'Ready to go, Freddie?'

Outside, they walked for a couple of minutes before stopping. 'Blimey, that was close, Jimmy-boy.'

'Mmm,' said James, reverting to his normal speaking voice, 'I think Stephen needs to distract those two women from coming here for the next few days. What are you doing now?'

'I've put me tent and gas stove in the woods through there. I'll stay 'ere and keep an eye overnight.'

'But it's early afternoon. You can't stay here all day. Come back with me and I'll drop you off later.'

'Yeah, that sounds good.'

A car approached. He watched it go by and did a double-take. A Ford Anglia with the rear light missing. 'Good Lord, that's the car GJ described.'

The Anglia whizzed into the distance and round the bend.

'What car?'

He grabbed Bert's arm. 'Come on, there's a telephone box further along here. I'll ask Beth or Fi to come and pick us up.'

'No, we won't. You don't know who's looking and two blokes like us don't get in posh cars. The bus comes along every half hour. We'll wait for that.' They made their way to the bus-stop. 'What's so special about the car?'

James made his friend promise that if he told him, the information would go no further.

27

The first thing James did when he arrived home was dash upstairs to discard his disguise. Dulcie had given him some cream to help clean up his face and he was thankful to take off the wig which had become quite unbearable in the heat.

After a bath, he dressed in pale linen trousers and a short-sleeved teal shirt. Beth greeted him at the bottom of the stairs.

'Bert said that you'd gone to change. Did you have a successful visit?'

He took her hand and led her through to the study. 'Yes. Before I forget though, I need to add to Bernard Potter's notes.'

He unscrewed his fountain pen and picked out specific photographs. 'Brother Mars is one Kevin Winspear, business fell apart, no family or friends. Sister Venus is one Trudy Pickford, cautioned for shoplifting and, as you know, keen to part with her parents.' He reached for the photograph of Mother Moon. 'And lastly, and more interestingly, Mother Moon here is one Beverley Kendall.'

Beth blew out her cheeks. 'This is where the money's coming from.'

'I would say so.' He picked up an envelope and emptied the scraps of paper onto his blotting pad. Sifting through them, he attempted to make some sense of it. After a bit of thought he discovered where the tear in the paper matched. 'Here, look at this. These bits belong to the piece that Potter found.'

Beth spread the scraps. ' . . . historic piece is found . . . '

He linked a few more together. ' . . . the findings of the . . . ' He eased back in his chair.

'Are you enlightened?'

'Not really.'

A shriek of laughter caused him to look out of the window. Fiona and Bert were playing boules on the lawn. 'Shall we join them?'

Outside, James and Bert updated Fi and Beth on their exploits.

Fiona, again, took great delight in

making fun of James and his undercover activities. 'What are you hoping to achieve? All you've discovered is a group of like-minded people tucked away chanting to the sun. You and Stephen were wondering how they financed themselves and now you know. The Kendall empire. If she's happy to bankroll her husband in his dream, then who are you to argue?'

James suggested they begin a new game.

He picked up one of the round silver balls and studied the distance to the jack. 'The thing is, Fi, I would have thought the same if it wasn't for a couple of things that seemed odd.' He tossed the ball and it came down with a thud about a foot away from the jack.

'Nice one, Jimmy-boy.'

He invited Fi to throw.

She too studied the distance. 'Are you going to keep us in the dark?' She tossed the ball.

'He lied about Wendy Potter. The girl's gone missing and she's certainly not with her mother.'

343

'Perhaps Wendy Potter lied,' said Fiona.

'Good throw,' said Beth. The ball had landed within inches of the jack.

James turned. 'I must admit I hadn't thought of that. George did say that relationships might not be as Mrs Potter had described.'

Beth, who was not taking part in the game, sipped her lemonade. 'What about your general feeling? Did you come away with an overall impression?'

'Difficult to pin down in a couple of words, darling. But if you wanted a broad overview, I'd initially say that this chap Father Sun has set up an excellent enterprise for those people who are spiritual but not necessarily religious. He appears genuinely paternal toward his members. I saw no fear or uncertainty in the eyes of his congregation. Did you, Bert?'

'Nothin'.' Bert tossed a ball in the air and cursed as it landed some way into the distance. 'But the people we did manage to chat to 'ave got history; either petty crime or business going broke; no friends, no family. It's as if this Father Sun is scooping up lost causes.'

James went to retrieve the balls. He rolled them back, raising his voice to be heard. 'We're not going to get much more until we go back. At least we have our foot in the door.' He turned to Fiona. 'Where's William?'

'Horse-riding. You know he can't do anything if there are horses about. I'm going to hike back to Harrington's and gather him in otherwise I shall lose him for the day.'

'Do you want a lift? I'm driving over myself.'

'No thanks.' She picked up her handbag. 'It's a beautiful walk cutting across the fields. I'll see you later for Jonty's parade.'

James straightened. 'Is that today?'

'Had you forgotten?' asked Beth.

He admitted that he had. 'The days seem to blend into one another just lately. Are you coming, Fi?'

She'd already begun striding across the lawn. Her arm waved. 'I'll be there,' she bellowed.

'Are you coming, Bert?'

'No, mate. Not while those two women are about.'

James groaned as he let Beth know about Missus Long and Fellowes. 'Fortunately, Bert was quick-thinking enough to dart out of sight.'

'That's going to be awkward.'

Gulping back the last of his lemonade, Bert asked if he could spend a couple of hours sitting on the patio. 'It'll make tonight's camping out seem less of a trial.'

Beth invited him inside. 'You don't have to stay out here. The newspapers are on the table in the dining room. Make yourself at home, Bert. Do you want some tea?'

A broad grin answered her question.

'Would you like me to polish your shoes?' asked James.

'Don't be sarcastic, sweetie. The man is spending the night under canvas for you.'

James exchanged a chuckle with Bert. 'I'm going over to see if GJ has drawn that portrait.' He swung round. 'I forgot to say, I think I saw the car that GJ had been taken in. We'd just come out of the commune and it sped by.'

'You'd better tell George.'

Before he left, he checked he had his costume for Jonty's parade, grabbed his keys and promised he'd be home in plenty of time.

★   ★   ★

He discovered GJ with a fishing rod down by the river. It was a peaceful spot where the dappled rays of sunshine filtered through the branches. The slow trickle of water provided a sense of calm and the occasional birdsong added to the tranquillity.

James sat on the bank next to him. 'Any luck?'

'Couple of perch but nothing else. My group are in the field over there drawing bits of old tree-trunk. I said I'd leave them to it and come back in an hour.'

'Did you manage to get that drawing done?'

'Yes.' He put his rod down and reached into a battered leather pouch to bring out a notepad. He flicked through a few pages and showed James. 'Stuart Drummond as

I remember him.' He ripped the page out and handed it to James who examined it.

The man staring back at him was in his mid-thirties, handsome in a rakish way with a square jawline and deep-set eyes.

'When are you seeing George?'

'Later this afternoon. He's coming to Jonty's parade so I said I'd see him there. Sounds like this art fraud thing is quite an operation.'

James agreed. 'I'm sure the details you give George will help. At least they now have a description and a car.' He opted not to tell GJ that he'd seen the vehicle. The man was wary of the threat he'd received and understandably so. The less he was involved in this, the better. He decided to leave GJ to his muse. 'See you at the parade. Happy fishing.'

* * *

Later that afternoon, he returned Bert to the outskirts of the commune and gave him a bag of refreshments made up by Beth, and a warm red scarf.

'I know it's the middle of summer but

it can get chilly, especially in the woods.'

'She's a diamond, that Beth,' said Bert.

He rolled his eyes. 'The woman thinks you're hard done by. Little does she know. You get fed and watered down here and I'm sure Gladys doesn't see you starve.'

The suggestive chuckle verified that.

'Are the wedding plans coming along nicely?'

'I'm leaving that to Gladys. Her and her daughter-in-law are nattering all the time about it. I'll just turn up.'

'What's that?' said James looking at a bundle under Bert's arm.

Bert shook out his brown robe. 'I thought I'd put this on. If any of the commune come out and see me I can just tell 'em I can't wait to join.'

James laughed. 'D'you want me to pick you up in the morning?'

'Nah, mate. I'll get the bus and 'ave breakfast at Elsie's. Have a good parade.'

He stood at the edge of the wood and watched as Bert eventually disappeared from view. Before stepping out from the trees, he saw a Ford Anglia approach. He watched as it drove by. Was the tail light broken? The driver was going too fast to notice but, if it was, that could only mean one thing. The chap must be local.

The familiar feeling of adrenalin rushed through him. He'd had it with every investigation he'd ever been involved in and here it was again. To him, this signalled that he'd stumbled across something important. He wasn't sure exactly what that was but time would tell.

First though, he would have some fun at Jonty's parade.

★   ★   ★

Every villager appeared to have turned out. They gathered outside the Half Moon and spilled across the village green. There was a constant hum of conversation. Some had simply come to see the spectacle but those who were taking part sported outfits and costumes in keeping with Jonty's personality. They were easily identified, the popular uniform being capes and ankle-length gowns. Floppy velvet hats were worn by most and the whole place resembled some sort of Bohemian gathering.

James had donned an opera cape and was pleased to have found a new hat for the occasion. Anne and Beth had fashioned a green velvet floppy concoction with a feather in it. He felt as if he were taking part in a Shakespeare play. Harry, standing by some of his old schoolfriends, had opted for the Oscar Wilde look.

Beth had chosen an ankle-length blood-red gown with a hood. He wasn't sure whether to liken her to Red Riding Hood or a vampire. Either way, the outfit flattered her.

He scanned the green and was pleased to see that nearly everyone had made a concerted effort with their costumes. They had all adopted Jonty's preference for a gown but the accessories were getting more exaggerated every year. Brighter colours had begun to appear, feathers and masks were being introduced and even the footwear was becoming outlandish. Pete Mitchell, who owned the local orchard, was wearing boots with buckles and laces that tied to the knee.

Charlie, his children and Dulcie had opted for a more Dickensian look; indeed, they appeared to have walked out of *Oliver Twist*.

Graham, Sarah and the children had decided on an Edwardian theme, all dressed as if attending the opera and holding beaded eye-masks.

Holding trays of drinks, Donovan and Kate emerged in dark blue robes. Their children, Josh and Sally, who had returned from visiting their grandparents in Ireland, were in the same outfits and helped carry the glasses. They wandered around the crowd seeking out their customers. After unloading his tray Donovan sought him out.

'Yer man, James, you'll be wanting a drink.'

James, already sweltering in the heat of the early evening sun, didn't need asking twice. 'I think a pint of bitter shandy would go down a treat.' He turned to Beth. 'What about you, darling?'

'I'll have the same.'

Donovan frowned. 'You're wanting a pint?'

She laughed. 'I couldn't manage a pint, Donovan. Just a half will be more than enough.'

Five minutes later, Kate delivered the drinks. 'I swear this parade gets more outrageous by the year.'

Beth agreed. 'I don't remember Jonty that clearly. I only ever remember him wearing a cloak of some sort.'

James confirmed that her memory was right. 'We appear to be turning it into the most elaborate fashion parade but, you know, I rather think that Jonty, wherever he may be, would approve wholeheartedly.'

Stephen and Anne appeared wearing black robes of a similar style to Beth's.

'This i-is amazing, isn't it? What a w-wonderful thing to celebrate.'

'I don't know how we fit all these festivals and celebrations into the year,' added Anne.

'Mmm,' said James, 'I do wonder if we are a little over-zealous in our community activities.'

'Nonsense,' said Beth, 'at the end of every festival or parade, we all sit back and say how much we enjoyed it.'

Graham and Sarah had supplied home-made pork-pies while the Delaneys had donated bowls of peanuts and crisps. The WI had a small table with cakes and scones. Mrs Jepson, their cleaner, had offered to serve as she wasn't keen in dressing up and, in her words, making a fool of herself.

Bob Tanner and the Taverners tuned their instruments. A few more people had begun joining in with the group so the number of musicians varied from one year to the next. Today, James counted seven, including a couple of fiddle and accordion players.

Mr Bateson, dressed in an elaborate red and gold robe and sporting a feathered tricorn hat, lifted a cow bell and rang it. The villagers hushed.

'Oyez, oyez. Good evening Cavendish.'

The residents chorused a 'Good evening' in return.

'Gather your children please.'

In an effort to ensure the children felt a

part of the event, there was a consensus that they should hold the parade earlier in the evening and actually lead it. That way, it was felt Jonty's name would carry to the next generation and the parade would evolve through the years. Jonty would hopefully become a part of Cavendish's folklore. James wondered if this was how legends were born and ruminated on the Minotaur, Medusa, the Unicorn. Perhaps those myths were once fact. Perhaps, in a thousand years' time, Jonty would have evolved into some sort of seasonal deity.

Youngsters dashed by in robes, masks and hats. There was a sudden flurry as mums and dads pulled out their Brownie cameras and took snaps for the family albums. The local reporter had also arrived and his photographer took the more professional pictures that would appear in the local paper the following week.

Satisfied all the children were where they should be, Bateson continued.

'Summer is coming, to Jonty we cheer.

Raise a toast to the fella with a jar of good beer.

Here's to old Jonty wherever you are,

Here's to your birthday, a toast from the bar.

Glasses were raised as a shout of 'Cheers' resounded and the band launched into the first of many reels and jigs. Their route was a simple one: down to the high street to the end of the row of cottages and back again, around the village green and then congregate back at the Half Moon.

As they joined the parade, Beth said: 'Do you notice that every festival or celebration we have ends up at the pub?'

James said he had. 'I would imagine that's the same in every other town and village. I think a lot of these events are simply an excuse to have a drink.'

Villagers who were not taking part but living on the high street, waved from their top floor windows. Hanging baskets were now in full bloom and, as with the scarecrow festival in the autumn, the music was mesmeric and the costumes colourful.

Returning to the village green, they saw Donovan had pinned an old white sheet to the side of the pub that had been painted with the words 'Happy Birthday, Jonty'.

The band took a break, their first port of call being the bar. Children raced on to the green and discussed which game to start playing. Charlie suggested they play football and retrieved an old leather ball from his garden. With the youngsters occupied, the villagers split up into groups and spent the next hour chatting.

As the evening wore on, a few of the Cavendish Players, a little worse the wear for drink, began rehearsing their songs and monologues for the Old Time Music Hall. Even the Snoop Sisters, with some encouragement, began singing their chosen song. Their voices were weak but the harmonies enthralling.

Sitting cross-legged on the grass, James turned to Beth. 'They sing well together, don't they?'

'Who'd have thought they were so talented.' She twisted around to examine the people.

'You looking for someone?'

'Yes, George. I thought he said he was

coming. If he does, you two could practise your song.'

He absentmindedly picked at the grass. 'I can't imagine George wanting to sing outside a pub. He may end up with his picture in the local paper. Anyway, we don't want to spoil you. All good things come to those that wait.'

'He must be busy, what with all that art fraud business.'

'I don't think so. He told me the Haywards Heath station was looking after that side of things.'

They heard a car door slam.

'Ah, speak of the devil.'

George walked toward them. They got to their feet.

'Sorry I didn't make the parade,' he said. 'I'd just got the opera cape on and the telephone rang.'

'Something serious?' asked James.

George tilted his head, indicating for them to step away. They walked with him to his car. 'Wendy Potter's been found.'

'Thank goodness,' said Beth. 'Where was she?'

'Someone called it in. A telephone box

along the Loxfield road. They found her in the woods with a nasty bump on her head.'

James stared at George. 'Unconscious?'

'No, but very dazed.'

'Heavens,' said Beth. 'She must have tripped. Good job someone found her.'

The look on George's face implied something different.

'You think she was attacked?' said James.

'She had a bump to the back of the head and — '

'Is she all right?'

'She's fine. She's coming round now. They've taken her to the cottage hospital and they're doing some tests, you know, making sure there's no internal bleeding, broken bones, that sort of thing.'

'The woods along the Loxfield road, you say?'

'Yes.' George's eyes narrowed. 'Why?'

'The woods that extend out from the Celestial Faith lot?'

An old-fashioned look. 'Yes, but quite some way. She had a coat on and a suitcase, clearly on her way out.'

'In the woods? Have you spoken with Father Sun?'

'James, we've only just found her. Until we get to talk to her, I'm not about to go blundering in asking if one of their lot attacked her. We got in touch with Mrs Potter and she's making her way over to the hospital now.'

'And you say someone reported it?'

'Yes, odd sort of call. If the woman wrote it down properly, the caller just said they'd put a marker down and an idea of where to find her. The caller said they couldn't stop because they had to be somewhere. That's either genuine or someone knocked her out and feels guilty. But my money's on the former. Left a big stick in the ground with a red scarf and had put a blanket under her head. Listen, I have to go. I thought you'd want to know because you were worried about her. Mrs Potter's pleased. Over the moon. She's got her daughter back.'

He waved cheerio and before James could ask anything else, George had started the car and driven off.

Beth slipped her hand into his. 'Poor

girl. I wonder what happened?'

He watched the children playing ball and sliding in with tackles. 'I'll ask Bert in the morning.'

'Bert?'

'He's the one who telephoned the police. Don't you remember, he had that red scarf. I bet he went for a wander about and stumbled over her.'

'Should we go over and see if he's hurt?'

'Let's say our goodbyes here. If Bert was in trouble he would have waited for the police to arrive. My guess is that he's watching that commune very closely.'

'But what if he was hurt?'

He faced her. 'We'll go to the cottage hospital and make sure Mrs Potter is coping. We'll detour along the Loxfield road so we'll park up where I dropped him off and see if we can track him down.'

* * *

Ten minutes later, James approached the lay-by where he'd dropped Bert off but, seeing a couple of police cars in the area, he drove by. Further round the bend and toward the outskirts of the woodland, James pulled over and turned to Beth.

'I would imagine Bert will have pitched his tent further away from that activity. George thinks there's foul play so those constables will be looking through the undergrowth for clues. Trying to find Bert is a fruitless exercise. He could be anywhere. I trust Bert's ability to stay safe and his message was clear to the police. I'm sure he's fine. Let's get to the hospital.'

28

Matron escorted James and Beth to a room where Mrs Potter was having a cup of tea. A policewoman was with her. James recognised her as a member of George's team and they acknowledged each other.

'Mrs Potter,' said Beth, 'how are you coping?'

She'd clearly been crying and the concern on her face was not lost on James. 'Is Wendy conscious?' She dissolved into tears. James sat alongside the WPC. 'When did they bring her in?'

'About an hour ago. It was quite a bash to the head so they've done some tests to make sure there's nothing serious.'

He turned his attention to Mrs Potter. 'Did you know she was coming out of the commune?'

'No. I've had no contact with her. I tried to speak to that Father Sun man but he wouldn't speak to me or let me see her.'

'Did he say why?'

'No, although it wasn't him I spoke to. I was given the message by one of his members.'

'Can you recall who?'

Another shake of the head. 'He had a brown robe on, not one of the embroidered ones like my Wendy had.'

Beth turned to him. 'Don't the visitors have brown robes? I thought that once you were a member you graduated to the individual designs.'

'Don't forget that those working on the allotments change into plain brown robes.' James rubbed the back of his neck. The sooner he and Bert returned to the commune, the better.

The matron put her head round the door. 'Mrs Potter? Would you like to see her?'

'Oh yes, yes please.' Her look was hopeful. 'Can Lord and Lady Harrington come with me? They've been so kind since my husband died.'

Matron bristled. James knew she ran a

tight ship, no-nonsense and strict with both nurses and visitors. If she said you were not permitted to visit, then you were not permitted to visit. He did his best to give her his most charming look.

She clasped her hands together. 'Very well. But you are not to tire her. Five minutes only. Come along.'

'I'll wait here with the WPC,' said Beth. 'Don't want to overwhelm her.'

James followed Matron and Mrs Potter to a separate room where they discovered Wendy Potter propped up in bed, sipping some water.

Mrs Potter rushed to her side. 'Oh, Wendy, my love.' She stroked her hair back. 'Did someone attack you? Are you hurt?' She sat down on the chair by the bed, her eyes wide. 'You weren't . . . ?'

Wendy, obviously tired by her ordeal, reassured her mother. 'I'm fine, Mum, really. Just glad to be here.' She darted a confused look at James.

Mrs Potter introduced him. 'Lord Harrington is the man who tried to save your father.'

He took her hand. 'I'm sorry I couldn't

do more for him.'

Tears welled. 'Thank you for what you did. He was on his way home from seeing me.' The memory caused the tears to stream down her cheeks. 'I refused to see him. We're not supposed to have visitors and he wanted me to leave with him.' She gripped her mother's arm. 'That's the last thing I'm going to remember about Dad, that I turned him away. If I'd just given him a bit more time.'

Mrs Potter stroked Wendy's hair. 'You weren't to know, Wendy dear, you weren't to know. No one thought he'd have an accident.'

'He spoke about you,' James said. 'While we were waiting for the ambulance. You and your mother were in his thoughts.'

Wendy composed herself, blew her nose and made herself more comfortable. 'He was worried about me, that's all.'

With some hesitation, he asked: 'I don't have daughters, Wendy, but if I had a daughter join this commune, I'd have concerns. Especially if I were not permitted to see her. I'm sure he was simply missing you. When you have children of your own, you'll understand that you never stop worrying.'

She sipped her water. 'Perhaps.'

'And,' said Mrs Potter, 'your father had a bee in his bonnet about that place. Said there was something going on.' She held a hand up as if to stop Wendy from interrupting her. 'No, no, I know you thought it was all sweetness and light there but your father was a good policeman. His instinct told him. I won't have you say a word against him. Even Lord Harrington has taken your father's notes to have a look.'

'What notes?'

Mrs Potter described Bernard's Potter's private investigation.

Matron entered. 'You've had more than five minutes. I think Miss Potter needs to rest.'

To James' relief, Wendy asked for a few more minutes with them. 'I have something important to say to Mum. And to Lord Harrington.'

He turned to Matron. 'I promise we'll be out of your hair very shortly.'

She gave him a stern look. 'Please ensure you do. I can't make exceptions.'

'Of course. We quite understand.'

As the door closed, he brought a chair over and sat opposite Mrs Potter on the other side of the bed. 'Did you discover something that made you rethink your father's stance on things?'

Her gaze went from him to her mum and back again. 'Yes.' She took another sip of her water. 'I quite enjoy drawing and painting.'

'So we understand,' said James, explaining that they had visited the commune during the open day. 'My wife and I admired the mural on the wall. We were impressed.'

Mrs Potter patted her daughter's hand. 'Why weren't you at the open evening?'

'I was sleeping. I'd been up most of the night.'

'Unwell?' asked James.

'No. Working.'

He exchanged a look of confusion with her mother. 'Working at night?'

The story that followed astounded him. Wendy's artistic skills had been noticed by someone, who she didn't recognise, and, late in the evening, she had been driven blindfold down country lanes to a windowless room where she was given the same proposition as GJ: an astronomical sum of money for copying works of art.

Mrs Potter drew back, horrified. 'You were breaking the law?'

'I did one painting, Mum. I didn't think I was doing anything wrong. But then I saw something.'

James instinctively leaned closer. 'What? What did you see?'

Her eyes searched the room. 'Where's my handbag?'

Both James and Mrs Potter began hunting.

'It's here,' said Mrs Potter, opening the small cabinet that held her daughter's clothes. She pulled it out and gave it to Wendy.

'I was waiting for the man to take me back to the commune and I saw something fluttering. A piece of paper had got jammed so I picked it up.' She brought out her purse. 'Here we are.'

She brought out a brand new one-pound note. She handed it to James.

He studied it. A crisp one-pound note, the Queen's image, the elaborate calligraphy, the promise to pay the bearer. He held it up to the light and caught his breath. No security thread.

'Counterfeit.'

Mrs Potter gasped.

'You're going to have to tell the police about this,' said James.

Wendy slid the note back in her purse. 'I will. I didn't realise it was fake at first. I put it in my purse and thought I'd got lucky. When I got back to the commune, I thought I'd put it in my money box. But something made me check it.'

'This place you were taken to. I know you were blindfolded but did you hear the sea?'

She sat up. 'Yes, yes I did. Do you know about this?'

He told her not to get too excited. 'Not as much as you seem to think I do. But a few of the dotted lines are beginning to join up.'

Matron interrupted them. 'Time.'

There would be no arguing with Matron now. As Mrs Potter gathered her things, James chanced one more question.

'Regarding your artistic skills, were you approached at the commune?'

'Yes.'

As he left, he echoed Wendy's mother's instructions that she take it easy and they joined Beth and the WPC who were still in the waiting room.

'Mrs Potter,' said James, 'can we give you a lift home?'

'Thank you but the lovely WPC is here specifically to make sure I'm looked after.'

As they made for the exit, Mrs Potter walked beside him and lowered her voice. 'Are you still looking at my Bernard's notes?'

'I most certainly am. And what Wendy has divulged to us has made me all the more determined to see his work through.'

Tears welled. 'I think you and my Bernard would have got along famously.'

'I think so too. It would have been nice to discuss things with him over a pint.'

The tears spilled and she allowed the

WPC to steer her away. He and Beth watched as they disappeared into the night. Beth turned to him.

'Did you find anything out?'

He beamed at her. 'Bernard Potter was right, darling. The Celestial Faith Commune is not what you think it is. How about you, anything from the WPC?'

'Only that she said someone hit the girl over the head. She was at the bus stop at the time. She certainly wasn't in the woods.'

29

James and Bert, dressed in brown robes, arrived at the Celestial Faith Commune early the following afternoon. Beth, Anne and Dulcie had spent an hour ensuring that James' transformation into Freddie Woods was an effective one and replicated the photographs that had been taken previously. The proof, however, would be in the way Father Sun greeted him. Would he notice anything different? Was the beard longer or shorter? Was he more stooped than before?

To his relief, Father Sun didn't give him a second glance and merely welcomed them as old friends. 'I thought you might have decided it wasn't for you. For some reason, I expected you this morning.'

'I was all ready to get 'ere first thing,' said Bert, 'but Freddie 'ad something he wanted to finish.'

'Right. Well, better late than never.'

James held out a drawing of the house and slipped into the gruff London accent. 'I was working on something for the commune. I like to do a bit o' drawing so I came up 'ere last night and did a sketch. I thought you might like it for your office.'

Father Sun's astonishment was clear. 'You drew this?'

'My 'obby,' said James.

After last night's revelation at the hospital, James had asked GJ to do a sketch of the house. He knew the young man was a good painter but his drawings were also superb. GJ had captured the house and a few trees using charcoal and after two hours of concentrated sweeping and smudging, he'd arrived on the doorstep with the finished article. James couldn't believe someone could conjure up such a wonderful piece in such a short space of time.

'This is fantastic,' said Father Sun. 'Not only have I someone who can help me with the books, he's also an amazing artist.'

'I don't know about that, guv'nor.'

'Don't put yerself down,' said Bert. 'He's had one of his paintings in exhibitions. Not in some jumble sale, neither, proper galleries up in the smoke.'

Father Sun appeared to stand taller. 'In London!'

'It were a long time ago, guv'nor, and not in the famous galleries. My mate 'ere is making me out to be Constable or something.'

'Even so. I'll be proud to have this on my wall.' He examined the corner. 'You've not signed it.'

'Don't sign anything, me. Signing stuff gets you into trouble.'

The three of them laughed.

Mother Moon glided over in her beautiful gown. 'How lovely to see you again. We were wondering if you'd changed your minds.'

Father Sun was adamant they hadn't. 'I think it'll be sooner rather than later that our friends here will join us.' He held the drawing up. 'Look at this. Mr Woods did it last night.'

She gazed at it, as if it were an antique. 'You did this?'

James decided to react in a bashful way while she complimented him on his skills.

Father Sun interrupted her thoughts. 'I wonder if you'd introduce Mr Briggs here to our plumbing.' He turned to Bert. 'You hinted that you were a Jack of all trades and we have a leaky pipe in one of the bathrooms. Are you able to help?'

'As long as you got the tools, mate, I should be able to 'elp.' He playfully punched James on the arm. 'You stay out o'trouble.'

Mother Moon asked Father Sun for a quick word. They were far enough away to be out of earshot. A minute later, they were back.

Father Sun turned to James. 'I've an awful cheek asking you, with you not being a full-time member, but I wondered if you'd take a look at our books.'

'Love to, guv'nor.'

James followed him through to the study while Father Sun chatted.

'We did have an accountant up in the Midlands, but he stopped when we moved down here. I'm trying to do it myself but I'm hopeless at this sort of thing.' They stopped by the entrance to the kitchen. 'Sister Jupiter, any chance of some tea for Mr Woods?'

'Of course. I'll bring it now.'

Not believing his luck, James almost leapt for joy as they entered the study where his host invited him to sit at the desk.

'The ledgers are in the second drawer down on the right.' He examined the drawing. 'Do you paint, as well?'

James heaved the accountancy books up onto the desk. 'Used to. Don't 'ave me paints any more but I still got me brushes. Can't afford it. Paints are expensive. You want a painting then?'

'Not me, no. I do know someone who might commission you, though.'

He sat up with a start. 'Commission? What, like pay me?'

Father Sun laughed. 'Yes, pay you, although if you live here, some of that payment would have to come to the commune.'

'Wouldn't matter about that. I only got me pension so anything above that is pocket money.'

'You're interested then?'

'Oh yeah. Always up for a bit o' spare cash.'

The tea arrived and Father Sun made his excuses to leave. 'See if you can make sense of those. Any help will be appreciated.'

'Right you are. You be long, will you?'

'About half an hour.'

James waited until he heard Father Sun's footsteps reach the gravel outside. The small clock on the desk told him it was ten minutes past one. He put a time limit of twenty minutes to do what he wanted to do.

First on the agenda were the recent accounts. He checked the spines of the ledgers and picked the one relating to the last tax year. He scanned the columns of figures in the pages and concluded that Father Sun wasn't organised and had no idea about bookkeeping. There were ways in which to document accounts more clearly than this and he would make some recommendations. The normal takings and outgoings were listed and included food, refreshment, garden seeds, training books, bedding and household utilities, but everything was haphazard and difficult to make out. The receipts themselves were simply stuffed into an envelope in no particular order.

But it didn't take an expert to see that contributions from members were small. What did surprise him, however, were the one-off payments at the end of each month listed as a contribution. He moved on to the recent ledger for the current tax year. There it was again: five hundred pounds every month. Was this a private benefactor, a philanthropist who supported Father Sun's project? He picked his way through the receipts and invoices. From what he could see, everything was above board but there was nothing relating to these one-off payments. And it was that contribution that was keeping the commune afloat.

He checked the clock. Twenty past one.

Searching the drawers provided nothing of interest so he turned his attention to the filing cabinet behind him. He turned the key, slid open the top drawer and beamed. He chose a specific file.

Beverley Kendall.

Back at the desk, he perused the sheet of paper. It didn't give much information, simply a name, previous address, employment background and contribution payments. Beverley Kendall was, indeed, related to the Kendall empire and worked alongside her father before joining up with Johnny Barton. Alongside the word contribution was an amount: five hundred pounds a month.

He opened the ledger to double-check the figures. Five hundred pounds a month by a contributor. All the other brothers and sisters were listed by name and their meagre contributions listed. Why was hers anonymous?

He slipped the folder back in its place and drew out another: Brother Neptune. He had come straight to the commune, previously unemployed. Skills listed as 'gardening'.

Keeping one eye on the clock, he took a glimpse at half a dozen files. The employment details of all seemed a little sketchy, some had received police cautions, others were truants who had found it difficult to get a job. James was beginning to think this was simply a home for waifs and strays.

At just gone half past one, he locked the filing cabinet and returned to the desk, thankful he'd finished early as he could hear Father Sun ordering tea. A few seconds later the door swung open.

'Ah, how are you getting on. You haven't even drunk your tea.'

'Blimey, I'd forgotten all about that.' He drained his lukewarm cup.

Father Sun drew up a chair. 'What d'you think?'

'Your way o' doing things is a bit haphazard if you don't mind me saying. I don't know why you put some of your columns where you do. Outgoings and income are two different things so they should stay separate.'

'Yes, I'm afraid it's not my thing, accounting.'

'Well, you should 'ave someone do it, then. If you do it wrong, you might have the tax man after you.' He swung the ledger round to face him. 'And what's this five-hundred pounds a month. You've just got that as an ad-hoc payment. I mean, who's giving you that? It's a lot of money to put down without an invoice or receipt or something. Tax man'll be asking questions about that.'

'She . . . the contributor doesn't want to be named. Can it not be from a benefactor?'

James puffed out his cheeks, silently delighted to see the man deflate.

'It's Mother Moon, my wife, she subs the commune. It's my dream and she's in a position to help me fulfil that dream.'

'Oh right. Look, I'm not a qualified accountant but at some stage someone will ask questions about that, I'm sure, 'specially as that's what's keeping your commune going. You take that five hundred away and you're in dire straits. You need to list her as a paying member.'

Father Sun flopped back. 'If I let you stay here for free, can that be in lieu of you doing our accounts.'

'Ah, see, that's your problem, Father Sun. Some of these people are paying a pittance. If anything, you need to increase the rent. Offering me free bed and board is lovely but I got principles. That'd be like robbing a man when he's down.'

James studied the man who seemed to wear a look of resignation. He couldn't help but feel sorry for him. Something was going on here, a man was dead, his daughter might have been attacked and yet there was a vulnerability about the chap that pulled at him.

'You all right, Father Sun?'

Father Sun slammed the ledger shut. 'Yes, I'm fine. Why wouldn't I be? The commune is thriving, Mr Woods. I'll make sure that the contributions are documented more clearly. But, regardless of what you decide to do, I'd like you to do our accounts.'

James got up but didn't confirm. He merely said that it might not be possible if he decided the commune wasn't for him. 'I could be back in the city and I ain't doing long-distance accountancy.'

They wandered through to the front of the building where Bert Briggs was wiping his hands on a towel. 'You just had a couple of loose joints, that's all. I showed that young girl, Sister Venus, how to fix it. Always best to show people how to do things.'

'Wonderful, thank you.'

'Can I use your toilet before I go?'

Without waiting for an answer Bert dashed into the house.

Father Sun watched with some concern. 'He does have a problem, doesn't he?'

'Oh yes, ever since the war, he's 'ad a problem. Always needs to know where the nearest toilet is.'

James' heart skipped as the reason for Bert's sudden disappearance walked toward him: George, accompanied by Constable Fulton. He scuffed his shoes on the gravel and made a point of avoiding eye contact.

George presented his warrant card. 'Detective Chief Inspector Lane and this is Constable Fulton. Sorry to bother you but we wondered if we could have a word about Wendy Potter?'

'Sister Bellatrix? I'm afraid she left us a couple of days ago.'

'I'm aware of that, sir.'

James continued to shuffle under his friend's gaze.

'This is Mr Woods; he and his friend are thinking of joining us.'

'All right, guvnor,' James said, fingers crossed in the pockets of his robe.

George gave James a wary look before returning his attention to Father Sun. 'Is there somewhere we can talk?'

'Of course. My office is at the end of the corridor, on the right. Please, go through. I'll just see Mr Woods off.'

George didn't blink an eye at James and strode into the house.

'I'll be making me way,' said James. 'You'll be busy now.'

Father Sun placed a piece of paper in James' robe pocket. 'I have someone who's interested in your artistic skills.'

He saw Bert peer round the entrance then dash to join them. 'Come on, Freddie.'

James noted the time and date written on the paper. He pulled a face. 'Ten o'clock! That's a bit late, ain't it?'

'Up to you. I'm just the messenger. I have to go and see what the police want.'

Walking toward the iron gates, Bert let out a groan. 'Blimey, it's dodgy this. Every time I've come 'ere there's someone I know pops up. I take it George didn't recognise you.'

James grinned as they made their way to the bus stop. He reverted to his normal speaking voice. 'Dulcie is a marvel. Let me get out of this costume. I haven't had a chance to speak with you yet about last night. Things are coming together.'

'Let's stop at the pub now.'

He turned to his friend. 'Have you any idea how hot I am with this blasted beard and wig? I have the most irritating itch on my head that I'd daren't scratch in case the wig moves. I need to revert to James Harrington and I need to do it *now*.'

Bert's suggestive laugh rang out and James couldn't help but laugh with him. The bus arrived.

'Perhaps Dulcie should have made you up as well. You're getting known in that commune as the man with a bladder problem.'

'That's all right,' said Bert, settling down in his seat. 'If I need to dash off and nose about, I've got the perfect excuse.'

James lit a cigarette. What a productive twenty four hours this had been.

30

Later that afternoon, James and Bert decided to pop to the coast. Beth and Anne had asked to join them, neither wanting to miss out on any news. They'd bought ice creams and found a spot to sit that afforded some breeze. Radley wagged his tail as Anne threw stones that, to his frustration, he could never find.

The sun sparkled off the sea and the air was filled with the sound of children shrieking as they braved the cold waters of the English Channel. Brighton and Hove beach wasn't the most picturesque, being mainly stones and shingle. James recalled trips further along the coast with his grandmother, a keen forager, who had taught him how to harvest cockles. Anne asked how they did it.

'Easy, really. My grandfather made Nanna a wooden board with a handle and I had a wire rack and a rake. Nanna would rock the board over the sand which would help the cockles to surface. I followed on, raking the cockles on to the rack. Fiona, when she wasn't pretending to be a mermaid, brought up the rear with the bucket.'

Beth asked if Geoffrey, his late older brother, had helped.

'Geoffrey hated shellfish. Despised the smell and look of it all. I have to admit that when you look at a cockle or a mussel or anything like that, it does look quite unappetising.'

'Do you miss your older brother?' asked Anne.

It had been some time since Geoffrey had died and James had long since recovered from the shock of his early death. Fond memories took precedence now and he found it was small, incidental things that took him by surprise. A piece of music, a specific smell or comment.

'My father always joked that he and mother brought the wrong child home after he was born because he was so different. The Harrington clan were, and still are in some respects, unconventional. Geoffrey was an earnest individual and took the running of the estate very seriously. I don't mean that my father didn't, it's just that Geoffrey was not someone who relaxed and enjoyed life. I couldn't exchange banter with Geoffrey like I do with Fi. Our relationship has always been closer than the one I had with my brother. But yes, I miss him. I miss having a pint with him. I miss hiking across the Downs and debating politics with him. He was someone I admired, a man I'd discuss things with if I needed advice.' He reached for Beth's hand. 'It was Geoffrey who ordered me to stop dithering and propose to Beth.'

Beth gave him a knowing look. 'You *were* taking your time.'

He grinned. 'Yes, I know. Geoffrey sat me down and lectured me for half an hour on why this lady would be a good wife and mother. I knew that, of course, but marriage was a huge decision for me.'

'No more the gallivanting bachelor,' Bert said.

'Something like that.' He licked his ice cream. 'But it gave me the kick up the backside I needed.'

'That's quite romantic,' said Anne. 'Was he your best man?'

Both James and Beth let out a groan and then laughed.

'Geoffrey performed all of the best man duties by the book. I was hoping for a rather humorous speech with a few anecdotes about our childhood but Geoffrey, true to form, steered clear of embarrassing stories.' He threw a stone for the waiting Radley. 'Now if I'd have chosen George or a chum from university, it would have been a more entertaining twenty minutes.'

'He did what he thought was right,' said Beth.

'And I loved him dearly for it,' said James.

'You should've asked me, Jimmy-boy, I'd 'ave given 'em a few stories.'

'You, my friend, would have been the polar opposite of Geoffrey. I'd have had to gag you.'

Beth gave Bert an old-fashioned look. 'You'll have to tell me some of those stories, Bert.'

'Oh no, not my place to say.'

James cleared his throat and suggested that Beth didn't need a repeat of those exploits. They had no secrets and, before getting close to proposing to her, he'd admitted to being a typical well-to-do bachelor, the man about town; rally driving in Monte Carlo, casinos in Nice, the opera in Italy, a girl on his arm. He was young, discovering life and all that it had to offer. Even his beloved grandmother had encouraged him to go out and live life. He did so but was grateful that Geoffrey had pulled him to one side and drummed a few home truths into him. He'd been courting Beth for several months when he knew they'd fallen helplessly in love with each other. And, although he'd enjoyed the bachelor life, he had become bored with it. Snapping out of his thoughts, he turned to his friend.

'Right, Bert, I'd like to know how you found Wendy Potter. God knows I've been trying to ask you all day but we kept getting interrupted.'

Bert made a fuss of Radley. 'I'd just got me tent set up for the night and thought

I'd go for a stroll. I was down by the fence so I 'ad a good look at the side of the commune. It was all a bit quiet. I think it's lights out at ten o'clock. Anyway, I wandered along the fence and then went deeper into the woods. I 'eard a shout, so I shouted out but no one answered. About a minute later I stumbled across her.'

'What did you do?' asked Anne.

'I planted a stick and tied that red scarf on the end and then went to the phone box and rang the police and an ambulance. Then I sprinted back and took me tent down. Ended up camping about a mile down the road. I didn't want to get involved.'

James asked if he'd gone back to observe.

'I 'ad a word with an ambulanceman. Asked him what was going on. He said they'd found a woman in the woods but that she was all right. I left it. I knew I was meeting you today and thought you'd have more to tell.'

They watched as the Punch and Judy man packed away his puppets, then James described his visit to the hospital and the discovery of the counterfeit money.

'Strewth,' said Bert. 'D'you think that's what's going on at that commune?'

'I honestly don't know. The few files I looked through in the office suggested that many of the members there had skirted the law.'

'But not everyone,' said Anne. 'I mean, Mrs Fellowes and Mrs Long are not criminals.'

'No, and neither am I.'

Beth laughed as Bert insisted he wasn't either. 'I'd class myself as one who's had the occasional run-in but never been charged.'

'Anyway,' said Beth, 'the description we have of this place is that it's by the sea.' Radley dashed about and arrived at her feet, his tongue hanging out as he panted. She leant down and fondled his ears. 'You're going to be dead on your feet with all this running around.'

'Let him run as much as possible,' said Anne. 'He won't need such a long walk tonight.'

Beth tossed a stone. Radley gave chase.

'And Father Sun wants to see you tonight?'

'Mmm, ten o'clock.' He checked his watch. 'It's four now. Would you mind if we made our way back? I'm going to see if we can meet George tomorrow morning for breakfast at Harrington's. I'd like to have a bit of a relax before going out tonight.'

'Are you telling him you're going undercover?'

'Yes. If something dodgy is going on at the commune I'd rather have George knowing. Going by past experience it means I avoid his wrath at me for doing things behind his back and potentially messing up their investigation. I can at least, tonight, try and get some idea of where I'm being taken. I may not be able to see anything but I can certainly listen.'

She pulled a face that told him she was impressed. 'It's nice to hear that you're taking this a bit more seriously instead of rushing around pretending to be Paul Temple.'

He met her gaze. 'Geoffrey was right about you. Not only did he say you'd be a good wife and mother but that you would keep my feet firmly on the ground.'

They gathered their things while Anne ordered Radley to heel and put him on the lead. After dropping Anne and Bert off, they made a call to George who accepted the invitation to breakfast the following morning.

They enjoyed a light supper of poached eggs on toast and listened to the wireless while waiting for Dulcie. At half past seven, she arrived with her make-up box.

★   ★   ★

Father Sun unlocked the gates to the commune. 'How are you Mr Woods?'

James had one of GJ's paintings tucked under his arm. 'Ready for my bed if I'm being honest. I always 'ave hot chocolate and settle down with a book about this time. 'ope I'll stay awake.'

'You won't be out all night. I believe you'll know if it's something you're interested in. If it's not for you, then no harm done.'

'Right y'are.'

Father Sun led him to the side of the main house and to the front of the garage. A tall man had his back to them; the bonnet of his car was up.

'Have you got problems?' asked Father Sun.

'No, just checking the oil.' He slammed the bonnet shut and turned.

James remained as calm as he could. This was the man in GJ's portrait.

31

James shuffled his feet. 'I know a bit about cars. You want me to 'ave a look?'

'It's fine,' the man said. 'Just checking the brake fluid. Wouldn't want to have any accidents.' The last statement was finished with a smirk.

It was all James could do to remain still. Was that a comment about Bernard Potter's accident? Should he have told George about was he was doing tonight? Should he back out now, feigning illness? James mentally gave himself a telling-off. *Don't be so dramatic. No-one suspects me.* Instead he agreed with the man that you could never be too safe.

'You can trust yourself, but you can't trust anyone else.'

He was a handsome chap who seemed at ease. He extended his hand. 'Stuart Drummond.'

' 'ello, my name's Freddie Woods.'

'I hear you're an artist.'

'Oh, I don't know about that. Just dabble about really.'

Father Sun made his excuses. 'I'm not needed here and I've a few bits of paperwork to sort out.' He turned to James. 'By the way, Mr Woods, would you mind spending a couple of hours reorganising my accounts? I took a look at the ledgers and see what you mean about it needing to be better. Once that's sorted, would you coach me on book-keeping?'

James, overjoyed that he would have time in the study, enthused that he'd find it a great honour to help the leader of this wonderful commune.

Stuart said they should be on their way. It was only when James got closer to the car that he realised this was the Ford Anglia.

'You go' a rear light out there.'

Stuart grinned. 'Yes, it's been like that for a while. I'm fixing it tomorrow. Get in.'

James settled back in the passenger seat and breathed in the smell of oil and petrol. He examined the dials and made a note of the time. Ten minutes past ten. He admired the new Hillman Minx parked alongside.

'Cor, that's a nice car, in' it?'

'You like cars, Mr Woods?'

'Oh yes. Can't afford 'em but it don't stop me gawping at 'em.'

The man faced him and handed him a piece of cloth. 'Sorry to ask, but I must insist that you wear a blindfold.'

'Wha' for?'

'The person who wants this work done is a private individual. They want complete anonymity and that includes where they live.'

James happily obliged. The engine started and, once on the main road, Stuart turned the radio up high. Knowing he would struggle to listen for background noises, James decided to try something.

'Blimey, that's 'urting me ears. I got problems with me ears and loud noises give me migraines. Can't you turn it down a bit?'

After a few seconds, the volume decreased.

'Thanks. If you want me painting, I can't do that with a sore 'ead.'

Stuart didn't respond and James wondered if he'd suspected something. They'd only been travelling for a couple of minutes and he'd already lost his bearings.

'I think I'll put me 'ead back and 'ave a snooze.'

Although blindfolded, he closed his eyes and turned his face to the window. A church bell chimed the quarter hour. It wasn't the Cavendish one. That had a more mellow ring. Perhaps the Loxfield belfry, that had a similar tinny sound.

The journey was quiet and he guessed they were going along country roads but which ones, he had no idea. The car turned left and right, crested hills and stopped at junctions. He heard the chirp of a pheasant, the whistle of a train and the rumble of the engine as a locomotive sped beneath them.

'D'you mind if I open the window a bit?'

'Just a fraction.'

He wound it enough to let some air in.'

'Won't be long now,' said Stuart. 'Another two minutes.'

'Right y'are.'

The car veered to the right and James felt the bumps as the vehicle drove over some rough ground. Then he heard the crackle of gravel under the wheels.

'We're here. Keep your blindfold on until we're inside.'

Frustratingly, Stuart decided to be more talkative but he tried his best to engage with him as well as concentrate on his surroundings. He breathed the air. Trees rustled in the breeze. A door opened and he was led down ten steep steps.

Stuart guided him further into the room before he took the blindfold off. The first thing James did was to retie his shoelace and check his watch. Half past ten.

James blinked and saw several naked bulbs hanging from the ceiling. He listened. In the distance, the sea. A foghorn.

An elderly woman approached. 'Mr Woods?'

402

'That's me.' He handed over the painting and scanned the room. In the corner was a man working on a watercolour. The original was to the side of him and he was clearly copying it stroke for stroke. A woman further along sat very still as she worked her magic with calligraphy. She was copying something that had been written on a notepad.

'Blimey,' he said, deciding his character would embrace this. 'This looks right enterprising, don't it?'

The old lady's eyes gleamed at the painting she'd been given. 'This is impressive. I saw your drawing of the commune. It's excellent. Were you trained?'

'Me! No missus. Just a natural. Some people 'ave it, don't they? Me teacher at school helped though.'

'How are you at replicating originals?'

It was now, more than ever, that he stayed in character. He shrugged. 'I dunno. Never tried. I could give it a go if you like.' He turned to Stuart. 'ere, do I get paid for this?'

The man motioned that he should

speak with the lady. She gave him a piece of paper with a figure written on it.

'Blimey. You offering me this to paint a picture?'

'We need to see you replicate something. Can you spend the evening with us tonight?'

Before he knew it, he was shaking his head and sounding panicked. 'Oh no, missus. I need me own brushes. I'm a bit funny about doing stuff on the spur o' the moment. I need me time regulated. You need to give me notice. I suffer with headaches, 'specially if I don't get enough sleep.'

She rested a hand on his arm. 'That's fine, Mr Woods. But you're interested?'

'Ooh yes, missus. Sorry Missus, it's something I've 'ad since the war. I've always got to have a routine. I can't just . . . well, even coming 'ere tonight threw me out of me routine. That's why I always 'ave me mate, Bert, in tow. I'm not used to being on me own. You understand, don'cha?'

'Oh course.' She turned to the man. 'Stuart, give Mr Woods an idea of what he

404

will be required to do.' To James she said, 'I'll see you before you leave.'

Ten minutes later and James had a good idea of what was happening. He didn't take too much notice of what Stuart had said. It was clear he was there to copy artists. He saw four people replicating works of art. The lady closest to him was creating fraudulent provenances to accompany those works of art. The only thing he hadn't seen was equipment to produce bank notes and he guessed he wouldn't see that unless he became integral to the operation.

The old lady returned. 'What d'you think?'

'I think it's ruddy marvellous. You can count me in.'

'We'll be in touch via the commune.'

James continued to be buoyant and strangely drawn to being Freddie Woods. 'You be sure to. I think this'll give me a new lease o' life, 'specially with what you're gonna pay.'

Stuart took the blindfold out and tied it. 'Come on, Mr Woods. I'll get you back.'

Again, James managed to check the time without being seen. Twenty past eleven.

'Where d'you live?'

Thinking on his feet, he said: 'Anywhere and everywhere. I pitched a tent in the woods today, 'bout a mile from the commune.'

He heard a laugh. 'You are keen to join, aren't you?'

'Best thing I've been to in a long time. I feel right at home there.'

'That's good to hear.'

They climbed the steps and Stuart got him comfortable in the car. James slid the window down a fraction while Stuart turned the radio on.

Again, the car made numerous turns and, in some cases, James wondered if it had turned back on itself. Another church bell sounded and with the time taken, he thought this must be a half-hour chime. It rang once and James knew exactly which church it was. They were near Lewes. It was some twenty minutes later when Stuart came to a stop. He took the blindfold off and James checked his watch. The journey home had taken forty minutes.

'That seemed longer coming home.'

'Probably because you have the blindfold on. It can be a bit disorienting.' He held a hand out. 'Good to meet you, Mr Woods. I'll pick you up again when the arrangements are made.'

'Who was the lady?'

'You don't need to know. I told you, privacy is important.'

'Yeah, all right. See you next time.' James waved him off and wondered whether to try and find Bert in the woods. But he had no torch and time was pressing. At the phone box, he dialled home and asked Beth to collect him.

'I was beginning to get worried. Are you all right?'

'I'm fine, darling, but ready to revert to me and snuggle up next to you.'

'Well that's a good excuse for me to come and get you.'

32

The following morning, James and Beth arrived at Harrington's for eight o'clock. They greeted a good many guests who had chosen the same time to start their day. James took his time as he went through the dining room; shared a joke, made suggestions on places to visit, recommended items on the menu and reminded guests of the various activities available to them.

At their table, Harry, Fiona and William had joined them and they ordered fresh orange juice while they waited for George.

Fiona appeared bemused. 'Honestly, James, I can't believe you're gallivanting around the countryside dressed like a tramp. Father would have been appalled.'

'No, he wouldn't. I think he would have found it rather amusing. Nanna would have too.'

'I'll grant you that. She always did

encourage you to be rebellious.' She turned to Beth. 'Has he told you anything?'

'I heard most of it while I was getting all the make-up off. There is definitely something odd going on.'

Harry accepted a cigarette from James. 'It's interesting that Dad has this adventurous streak. From what you've told me of Great Granny, she seemed a mischievous sort herself.'

'She was the worst,' said Fiona, 'although the Harringtons have always been a little eccentric.'

William poured some orange juice. 'Why do you get yourself so involved?'

James started to reply but William had already moved on. 'How do you do it? And why do you do it? You must have a nose for detection?'

Again, James offered to answer but his brother-in-law turned to Fiona. 'Are we staying for this? I wanted to go down to Rottingdean. We could get a couple of horses from their stables and trek across the Downs. What do you think?'

Fiona demanded to know how long James would be.

'I've no idea. Probably an hour, perhaps more.'

'You really are impossible, James.' She got up. 'Beth, can you and I have tea this afternoon and you can fill me in on the details. Come along William. I know you can't sit here for an hour without wanting to move or change the subject.'

James got up and kissed his sister on the cheek. 'I believe you're jealous.'

'Absolute rot,' she responded with a glint. 'Perhaps a little. See you at three o'clock, Beth?'

'Three's fine.'

William apologised. 'I'll get a brief from her highness after she's spoken to you, Beth.'

Both James and Beth grinned as they went on their way.

'He's very twitchy, isn't he,' said Harry.

'William can't sit still for five minutes,' said Beth.

'Yes, he's always been like that,' said James. 'He's a devil to go fishing with. The aim of fishing is to relax and be at

410

one with nature. He manages about five minutes and then he's splashing further down the river, shouting for more tea.'

She laughed and looked past him. 'Here's George.'

Their friend, dressed in his dishevelled suit, joined them at the table.

Adam came forward and raised a parasol to provide shade from the morning sun.

Harry got up. 'I'll do the Lord of the Manor duties. I don't want to sit here and see my father crushed by George.' He gave them all a mischievous grin and departed.

James ignored George's questioning look and asked if everyone was happy with a full English breakfast, to which he received a unanimous yes. 'Adam, can you bring tea and coffee please?'

'Certainly, your Lordship.'

George undid his jacket and breathed in the air. 'Nice way to start your day. I saw Fiona and William. How long are they staying for?'

'They're here for the Old Time Music Hall and the Midsummer Ball,' said Beth.

'Is Fiona doing a turn at the music hall?'

James let out a laugh. 'Good Lord, no. She's happy to push other people into doing things like that but not so keen on doing it herself.'

'It'll be a good evening and I hear that you've got Mr Irwin coming, from the veterans' home.'

James watched as Beth went dreamy on him. 'Oh George, he is such a dear. I wish he lived in Cavendish, the villagers would take him to their hearts.'

James reminded her that the man had the mind of a child. 'He wouldn't cope on his own, darling. That soldiers' home is the best place for him, surrounded by his peers and cared for by dedicated staff.'

She agreed but told him they should make more of an effort to visit.

He said they would. 'Why don't we pop down one afternoon and spend some time with him.'

'That would be lovely.'

George's exaggerated cough caught their attention. 'This is all very nice, but I presume you've invited me here for a reason.'

Adam arrived at their table with a trolley. He lifted the domed cloches, placed the plates in front of them and, from the lower tier, brought out tea and coffee.

'Ah,' said George, 'a proper cup of coffee.'

'Made in a proper copper coffee pot,' sang James.

Adam glanced between the two men and Beth told him to take no notice. Still confused, he retreated.

'Now George,' James said, deciding which part of his breakfast he wanted to attack first. He decided on a piece of fried bread dipped into his egg-yolk. 'You'll admonish me, I'm sure, but Bert and I have gone undercover.'

His friend already had a mouthful of bacon and was in no position to respond except to glare at him.

'George,' said Beth, 'hear him out. He promised, after last night, that he would tell you everything and that's what he's doing now.'

Swallowing his food, George insisted that James could have told him before. 'What are you going undercover for? I've told you there's nothing going on at that commune and yet still you pursue it. That Father Sun bloke'll be putting in a complaint about you.' He sat up. 'You haven't dragged Stephen in on this, have you? I know he's up in arms about the whole set-up.'

As George ranted, James simply poured coffee and waited until he'd finished. 'No, I haven't dragged Stephen into anything. The man would simply explode in anger after a few minutes in Father Sun's company. No, I rather think I've stumbled across your art fraud business.'

His friend stopped eating for a few seconds and just stared at him. 'How on earth did you do that?'

'It wasn't intentional, I can assure you. We'd gone to the commune because of Bernard Potter's notes.' He observed George's frustration. 'George, you said yourself that Bernard was a professional. Why would he be looking into this? One of the last things he said to me at that accident was that it wasn't what they said it was, or words of some sort. But we were talking about Wendy who I then discovered was part of that commune. He'd discovered something.'

'All right. Let's have it.'

'I don't know if you saw the painting on the wall, before you reach Father Sun's office?'

'I did, yes. Very good, I thought.'

James went on to explain who had painted it and, with the discovery Wendy had made, it was clear that she had also stumbled on something. On seeing George's blank expression, he stopped. 'Did you not hear about Wendy's discovery?'

'No.'

Beth described the revelation of the counterfeit one-pound note. 'She said she'd speak to the police about it.'

George slurped his coffee. 'She's still in hospital and, to be honest, if she did call, it would have been put through to Haywards Heath. They're the ones investigating it. Are you sure it's fake?'

'Gosh, yes,' said Beth. 'James said

there's no security strip.'

'It's a damned good forgery, though, George.'

'But is Wendy suggesting this is happening at the commune?'

'Not at the commune, no, but when I went under cover, I took one of GJ's drawings with me. I wanted to test the water. Well, Father Sun was very interested and eventually asked me if I replicated art. I knew this was leading somewhere so I said yes.'

George stabbed a fork into a piece of sausage and swept it round his plate. 'And that took you where?'

James described his unseen journey to and from the windowless room. 'GJ kindly gave me a painting he'd done a few years ago. He'd obscured his signature. It helped me prove my credentials, I think. The thing is, George, I checked the times. It took twenty minutes to get there and forty minutes to return. I did my best to listen for any distinctive sounds but there were none really. The church bells at Lewes, but that was some way into the journey home. When I was at this place, I heard the sea. Inside were a couple of people replicating art and someone forging provenances. I think that's what those scraps of paper are that we picked up.' He sat back with some frustration.

'What is it, darling?'

'I'm not sure. Something just went through my head and it's gone again.'

George asked if they had a map of the area.

Beth slid her chair back. 'We have a few in the entrance for guests to borrow. I'll see if there's one there.'

Before his friend could begin to give him a talking to, James apologised for going behind his back. 'But I didn't have anything to tell you. At least, by going along with this charade, I've seen the operation for myself.'

'One thing that I'm trying to fathom is how you weren't recognised.'

James couldn't help but grin. 'You met me the other day, at the commune.'

George frowned.

Putting on his London accent, he said: 'All right, guv'nor?'

George appeared none the wiser.

'Hold on.' He reached for Beth's handbag. 'I know she keeps a couple in here. I think it provides her and Fiona with no end of amusement.'

'What are talking about?'

He found three photographs and laid them on the table. 'There.' Again, reverting to the accent, he said: 'You 'member meeting me now, guv'nor?'

He was pleased see George had the grace to look incredulous as he picked up one of the photographs.

He stared at James. 'This was you?'

James lit a cigarette and grinned. 'Yes.'

Beth arrived, waving an Ordnance Survey map. 'I managed to find one of the more detailed maps.' She stopped at the table. 'What's the matter?'

George turned the image for Beth to see. 'He fooled me, you know that, don't you?'

She sat down and returned the look of indignation. 'He fooled me too and I'm married to him.'

'Did Bert have a disguise?'

'He didn't need one,' said James. 'He looks like a tramp as it is. You missed him.

He spotted you and suddenly had the urge to visit the lavatory.'

He was pleased to see that George's reaction was one of bemusement and not anger. 'I'll have to have a chat with my colleagues over at Haywards Heath. I may be able to have the investigation transferred over. I mean, the area where the commune is comes under my jurisdiction.'

James slid the salt and pepper pots to one side as Beth unfolded, the map and then refolded it to show only the coastal section. She placed it in the centre of the table. James and George slid their chairs alongside her.

Having acquired a pencil from Adam, James circled a section of the map. 'Here's Cavendish and Loxfield. The commune's along this road here. That's where we started off. On a good run, the trip to the coast is fifteen, maybe twenty minutes so my guess is that, on the way there, we took a direct route.'

Having prepared his pipe, George leant in. 'Twenty minutes would get you to Hove, Portslade, Southwick. Here's Shoreham, that's got quite a few old buildings and warehouses. It's where the bigger boats come in.'

'I got the sense that it wasn't in a built-up area.'

'How?'

'One thing I did notice was the air was fresh and it was quiet. Shoreham is a hive of activity. I heard one fog-horn but it sounded some distance away.'

Beth reminded him that it was late at night.

'You're not convinced, are you?' said George.

James' pencil skirted along the coast-line in the other direction. 'It wouldn't have been Brighton, that's a busy town, even late at night. Then we're up on the hills by Roedean school and on to Peacehaven.' He sat back. 'I wasn't aware of the car climbing at the end of the journey. Which means it must be that stretch of coast near Shoreham. Southwick and Portslade are quite industrial. It could be a building in that area. That would be quite quiet. And I think

Shoreham would be just that little bit too far.'

'You're sure you went through Lewes?'

'As sure as I can be. I recognised the chime of one of the churches there. It's quite distinct.'

'And you're absolutely certain about the timings? You couldn't have made a mistake.'

'I'm as sure as I can be. Why?'

'It's just that Lewes is near Newhaven and Seaford.'

'No,' said Beth. 'It takes some time to get down there. Longer than twenty minutes.'

George folded the map up. 'Are you going down there again?'

'Do you want me to?'

'I'm thinking of putting a tail on you.' James pulled a face. 'You don't think that's a good idea?'

'In the daytime, yes, but at night, no. The roads around here are quiet. Headlights would stand out a mile and I get the impression that this Stuart Drummond man would check his mirrors the whole time, especially as he appears to take the long way around. He'd spot a tail straight away.'

George's shoulders fell. 'Stuart Drummond isn't Stuart Drummond. He doesn't appear anywhere on our records. I checked with Scotland Yard too.'

Beth suggested James check the files in Father Sun's office.

George's jaw dropped. 'What files?'

Over an hour had passed and their fellow diners had long since finished breakfast and headed off to pursue other things. James asked if everyone would like more coffee.

They waited until Adam had placed everything in front of them before James described his visit to the commune and his offer to look through the accounts. 'The place survives on Mother Moon's donations.' He told George their real names and what he had discovered about their histories. 'I didn't get a chance to look at all the files but I can now understand why Bernard Potter began taking an interest.'

'And now,' added Beth, 'his daughter has realised that he was right. I don't think she forgives herself for turning him away that day.'

'George, if you go in asking questions now, that puts me and Bert under suspicion. Can you give us a couple more days to see if we can find out anything more? If you go in now, he could deny everything and give that Drummond chap warning. I'll ask for another look at this place that I was taken to and report back.'

Adding more tobacco to his pipe, George took in the view and mulled things over. Beth opened her mouth to speak but James gave her a subtle shake of the head. His friend was weighing up the pros and cons of the matter and, whatever he decided, James would agree to go along with it.

After a couple of minutes, George decided. 'I'm going ask my boss if I can have a hand in this investigation and the reasons why. You've met Superintendent Higgins; he trusts you so I may convince him. I'll go and have a chat with Wendy Potter to hear what she has to say. You have two more days to do what you have to do, then I go in.'

Ecstatic that he would be permitted to continue his undercover work, James shook George's hand. 'Good chap. I won't let you down.'

'On a side note,' said George, 'was it Bert that contacted us about Wendy Potter?'

'Yes. He's been camping in the woods. He was going to try and have a look round one evening after the lights had gone out. He fell asleep last night so didn't see me take off.'

'Tell him to keep his eyes peeled next time. If this Drummond bloke is picking you up at the commune, I could do with exact times and anything else he might see.' He finished his coffee and stood. 'Oh, and we need to sit down so that I can take a formal statement from you.'

'Right you are.'

'You off to the commune today?'

'Yes, this afternoon. I'll try and get down to that place again tonight or tomorrow.'

'Don't forget,' said Beth, 'we have the dress rehearsal tonight for the music hall. All acts must attend or you face the wrath of Dorothy.'

'I haven't forgotten, darling, but that tends to wind up around nine. I can always leave a little earlier. A good morning's work, don't you think?'

George picked up his fedora. 'You've done well, James. We'll make a detective of you yet. See you at the rehearsal.' He went on his way.

He turned to Beth. 'Shall we go back home and add to Bernard's notes?'

'You do that. I need to get your costume ready for the show. Let's sit out on the patio. I can do my sewing easily out there. I have to be back here for three to meet Fiona.'

He helped her up and found he had a spring in his step. The business with the Livingstones those few weeks ago had rather put him off investigating anything. It had made him wary of encountering such wicked people again. But this? This was fascinating and he was keen to get to the bottom of things.

All roads led to the commune, but where on earth had the road out led him to the previous evening?

33

The doors to the village hall were wedged open to allow what little breeze there was into the main room. The men constructing the scenery had done a marvellous job of transforming the stage into the likeness of a Victorian music hall. GJ, the best artist by far, had finished designing two lengths of board to replicate gold lame curtains and he'd positioned them either side of the stage. The main colour scheme was red and gold.

A placard that ran the length of the stage was being hung from the ceiling. With gold lettering, on a cream background, it read 'Cavendish Music Hall'. Above, fluttering in the through-breeze, were two Union Jacks.

All performers were in costume and Beth, Anne and several other ladies of the WI were checking hems, buttons and seams. Stephen and Graham wheeled the upright piano in from an adjacent room and placed it at the side of the hall.

Rose and Lilac Crumb studied their sheet music. Charlie practised his dancing and Mr Bateson was attempting to make his tall top hat bend a little more in the middle for comedic effect. Many of the children remained outside. The boys had started a game of football and the girls had chalked a hop-scotch grid.

Bert Briggs entered and the place hushed for a few seconds before everyone applauded. James grinned. His friend stood out from the crowd in his pearly king outfit. From his flat cap to the turn-ups in his trousers, the man was covered in pearl buttons forming patterns in the shapes of playing cards, the union flag, St Paul's Cathedral and swirling galaxies.

'My word,' said James, 'you look the part.'

'I borrowed it off a friend of mine, Ronnie Spencer. He's about the same size as me so I've got it on loan.'

Several villagers came across to admire the costume. Stephen asked if he could try it on; when he did, this caused hysterics. The vicar was a good deal taller than Bert and the sleeves and trousers were ridiculously short.

'Mmm, I'm not sure, Stephen,' said James.

Bert positioned the hat on his head at a jaunty angle.

'Ah, that sets it off nicely.'

Stephen narrowed eyes then laughed.

Beth scurried over to him. 'We have your costume ready. Where's George?'

Charlie, overhearing, told them George was backstage. Anne left to take his costume through.

Beth handed James a rather dapper suit on a hanger, a pressed shirt and a bowler hat.

He held the suit up. It was pure Edwardian. A fawn colour with a subtle check. The bowler hat was covered in the same material. He turned to Beth with a look of astonishment. 'Did you make this?'

'I did. I'm afraid the lining isn't terribly professional but it can go in our wardrobe department when we're finished.' 'Has George got a similar costume?'

He learned that his was an identical style except that it was a darker shade. Beth decided that with his larger frame, their friend could do with a more slimming colour.

Dorothy Forbes quietened everyone down. 'I'd like to run something by you. It's an idea that Mr Briggs has mentioned.' She turned to Bert 'Perhaps you'd like to explain.'

Bert, who was retrieving his jacket and cap from Stephen, described some old photographs that he'd seen of music hall theatres. 'A lot of them have got proper tiered seating which you 'aven't got. The shows that were put on in more simple surroundings normally had tables and chairs out. Perhaps six or eight to a table.'

A murmur of agreement came from those in the hall.

Sarah Porter, Graham's wife, suggested that each table have a candle on it. 'And perhaps we could have a plate of snacks, you know, crisps and peanuts. Graham could bring some hot sausage rolls.'

'And rotten tomatoes for the acts you don't like,' said Bert.

Dorothy quashed the idea. 'If you're going to suggest that, you will be the one clearing the hall up afterwards.'

Bert decided it wasn't such a good idea after all. Dulcie appeared from the wings of the stage. 'Can someone show me how to work this machine? I'm hopeless with it.'

Charlie took that as his cue to help and James spotted the anticipation in Beth's face. She was, he knew, hoping that these two would become a couple.

'What machine is she t-talking about?' asked Stephen.

'A reel-to-reel tape recorder,' said Dorothy. 'I think someone needs some background music for their song.' She clapped. 'Come along now, please. Let's start. This is our last rehearsal where I have everyone here. I want to hear that everyone is word and note-perfect.'

James asked if she would mind if he and George performed first. 'I've a couple of things I need to do later.'

Bert echoed the request. 'I need to be doing things too.'

Dorothy harrumphed. 'This should be

in the order we're doing on the night but, if you have pressing business . . . ' She told Bert to take the first performance.

The villagers sat down and enjoyed Bert's complete closing act. He began with 'Back Answers' and followed that with a medley of popular songs that everyone could join in on. A natural performer, he tapped out a few moves and encouraged the audience to join in. A roar of approval rang out when he finished and he took his bow like a professional.

Slipping on his Edwardian jacket and popping the bowler hat on his head, James sought out George and they took to the stage to sing their coffee cup song. Again, they were word perfect and didn't trip up on what was a real tongue-twister. The applause was equally warm and James knew this would be a production that would stay in their memories. There was plenty of scope to play to the audience and mess about on stage and, fortunately, Dorothy Forbes was happy to allow that to happen.

He nipped over to the WI stall and

poured a cup of tea from the urn. He turned to see Sarah Porter mounting the stage. Graham was in charge of the reel-to-reel. The butcher sat down by the recorder. As Sarah sang 'Daddy Wouldn't Buy Me a Bow-Wow', Graham occasionally flipped a lever and the raucous sound of dogs barking was heard. Laughter followed when Radley barked his own response.

James wandered toward the stage, smiling at the exaggerated effects and the occasional mis-timed bark accompanied by an apology from Graham to his wife. He pondered on the performance and a hint of an idea sprang to mind.

He felt his sleeve being tugged. 'Oi, Jimmy-boy, if you wanna get down that commune, you'd better get yourself made up. Dulcie's round at Charlie's now, waiting.'

After catching up with Beth, James followed Bert along the village green to Charlie's cottage.

Dulcie had the make-up, beards and spirit glue to hand, along with an enlarged photograph of James as Freddie

Woods on the dining table. On the sofa lay the outfit James was using for his undercover persona. She pulled out a dining chair.

'Here, sit down. This won't take so long now we know what we're doing.'

Over the next forty minutes, she aged James by at least a decade. Subtle shades of foundation and eye shadow slowly transformed him. He slipped his shirt off so she could glue the beard properly before finishing off with the wig. With a final check of the photograph she sat back and admired her handiwork.

James stood in front of the mirror. Perfect. He grabbed the old clothes and disappeared into the back room before returning as Freddie Woods. Dulcie accepted his discarded costume. 'Beth's coming round later to collect them.'

A sudden panic came over him. He turned. 'Where's the drawing?'

'Calm down, Jimmy-boy, it's 'ere.'

GJ had spent the day sketching a drawing in the style of Edgar Degas. It showed the Celestial Faith Commune from the iron gates looking in. James had, earlier in the day, telephoned Father Sun as Freddie Woods and told him he'd like to visit the place on the coast again and show them some more of his work.

Father Sun insisted that no further evidence was required. 'I think that painting you showed them was proof enough.'

'Just want to be sure, guv'nor,' James had replied, adding that he wasn't confident about his abilities and he didn't want to let them down.

'That's fine. I'll let Mr Drummond know and he can pick you up tonight. Are you coming here?'

'Oh yes. I'm looking forward to it.'

★   ★   ★

Much later, the sun had dipped below the horizon, and he stood at the iron gates that led to the commune. Bert had returned to his tent with a promise to stay awake and keep check on the times and see if anyone else was in the vicinity. He tucked GJ's drawing under his arm as

Sister Venus approached and unlocked the gates.

Stuart Drummond stood to the side of the house near the garage. James hoped the man didn't smell a rat. His demeanour suggested he might do, just something about his body language put James on guard.

'Mr Woods, you want another visit.'

James did his best to look apologetic. 'Sorry, guv'nor, I just wanna make sure that I'm the right person. I brought along a drawing for that woman. If she says I'll make the grade then that's all right for me.'

'I think she already had.'

'I'm right sorry, guv'nor but I'm not good on me own. Bert normally helps me so I have to be sure.'

He followed Drummond to the Ford Anglia and accepted the blindfold from him.

'Mr Woods, you've not asked if what we're doing is legal or not. Does it bother you if we're skating legalities?'

'Don't matter to me. I been in a few scrapes in my time. With all this cloak and dagger business, I thought it weren't right but, look at me. I've not got much and if I can spend me time doing something I like, what's the 'arm?'

The journey down began and James again concentrated. Drummond remained quiet as he did on the last journey and James was happy to simply listen. He wound the window down a fraction and immediately noticed the stillness of the countryside. The odd song of a blackbird shrilled, the hump of a railway bridge, the chime of a church bell. There it was again, the call of the pheasant, such an abrupt chirp. The car came to a stop and Drummond helped him out of the passenger seat.

He made a conscious effort to listen. Down the steps and into the room that he had visited before, the blindfold came off and the elderly lady stood in front of him.

'An unusual request to want to visit a second time,' she said with a slight air of suspicion.

'Sorry, missus, me mate Bert always makes decisions for me and I ain't used to this. I was telling your fella here, I gotta be sure in me own mind. Is that all right?

436

If it's not, take me back and we'll forget all about it.'

The suspicion was replaced with a reassuring nod. 'No more visits. The next one, you start work.'

James took out his drawing and unfolded it. 'I did this for you.'

The woman raised her eyebrows. 'Degas.'

He let out a convincing gasp.

'Don't be so modest about your talent, Mr Woods. You think you don't have what it takes?'

'No, I don't. That's why I'm 'ere. It settles me mind.'

Drummond asked if he had told Mr Briggs.

'No, I didn't. I 'ad a feeling you wouldn't want me to.'

An elderly man with a chalky complexion hobbled across. He handed the woman a piece of parchment. 'This look good to you?'

Without hesitation, James sidled closer to look at the document. 'Blimey, that's good, ain't it?' From what he could see, it was a provenance for a piece of art by a painter he wasn't familiar with. He asked if he could hold the document. It was the same weight and texture of paper that PC Potter had found and similar to the pieces he and Beth had picked up at the commune. This proved one thing. Someone at the commune had inadvertently dropped them.

He handed the provenance back to the lady and faked a yawn. 'Not used to late nights, missus. Does this 'ave to be at night?'

Yes, was the answer he received. 'No one's able to be here during the day,' she said. 'So, will you join us?'

'I think so, missus, as long as it's just once in a while. I'm no good if I'm tired.'

'We won't be here over the next couple of days. We've business up north.'

She tilted her head to Drummond who replaced the blindfold. 'Time we got you back.'

The return journey appeared to duplicate the last in that it took a lot longer to arrive back. James asked him to be dropped on the road by the woods about a mile from the commune.

Drummond untied the blindfold. 'We'll be in touch.'

When the car had disappeared, he heard someone running through the undergrowth behind him. His heart thumped. He swung round, ready to put his fists up, as Bert leapt out from the trees.

Relief turned to annoyance. 'My God, Bert, you frightened me half to death.'

Bert bent over to catch his breath.

'Did you see anything, get timings and all that?'

His friend held a hand up. 'Blimey, I ain't run like that in ages.' After getting his breath back, he dragged James off the road. 'Crikey, you won't believe it.'

'What?'

'You left here, dead on five past ten.' He looked positively elated.

James pursed his lips. 'Well, spit it out. You obviously saw something of interest, or someone of interest.'

'You left here at five past ten. You arrived back at half-past ten.'

34

James almost fell down in shock. 'Half past ten!' He swung to look at the road and then returned his gaze to Bert. 'We came back here? To the commune?'

'Nah, mate, you came back there, to that derelict building at the back. He came in another entrance.'

He couldn't help but laugh. 'It all makes sense. I should have worked it out.'

'Wha' you talking about?'

'Never mind that now, show me the entrance to the building.'

Bert led him through the undergrowth to the clearing where he'd pitched his tent and then led him further beyond. 'Come on, you're gonna wanna see this.'

His friend led him to an area crowded with trees and blackberry bushes. James looked over the shrubs to see that they were now well behind the commune and he was looking at the back of the derelict building. It loomed up and its dark broken windows reminded him of a ghost story that he'd read years ago. With little in the way of moonlight the house appeared menacing. He couldn't see a glimmer of light anywhere.

'Has anyone else come out since Drummond put me in the car to come back?'

'Nah mate. But they might've done when I was running through the woods to catch you. Did you wanna take a gander?'

'No. We're not prepared for this. There are a few people in there. If we get caught, who's to say what'll happen. I believe Bernard Potter died looking into this. I don't intend to end up like that. Can you get me back to the road?'

On the way, James suggested that he and Bert return to the commune the following afternoon. He knew he only had a short amount of time before George waded in. 'I want to get another look at those files and anything else in that study. Father Sun thinks I'm going to spend my time rearranging his bookkeeping but I've already done that. I have everything at home to bring in. If I can convince him

I'll need a couple of hours to sit in his study and finalise everything, that gives me time to rummage about and see if I can locate something about this Drummond man.' He turned to Bert. 'I mean, surely Father Sun knows what's going on?'

Bert shrugged. 'I've no idea, mate. That whole set-up seems a bit odd to me.'

Leaving Bert to return to his tent, James made his way to the telephone box to ask Beth to collect him.

'You're much later than before,' she said, 'is everything all right?'

Assuring her he would tell her when she picked him up, he waited in the trees by the road.

* * *

An hour later, free of his disguise, washed and dressed in pyjamas and dressing gown, he settled next to Beth on the sofa with a large tumbler of brandy as he spilled the beans about his visit and the more exciting observation by Bert.

'How ingenious,' said Beth. 'And you

say you had a suspicion about it?'

'Yes, at the rehearsal earlier. When Sarah asked for the reel-to-reel recorder, you know, for the sound effects. That's when I realised there was something odd about where I'd been taken to. It's just that, inside that building, I could hear the sea. GJ heard it too. But outside, when we arrived, I didn't remember hearing it. I mean, if you can hear the sea inside, you should be able to hear it outside as well. Tonight, I made a point of listening.'

The revelation had left her speechless.

'And I kept hearing pheasant. We have a lot of pheasant around here and they're country birds, aren't they? It's not often that pheasant will settle in a coastal town.'

'You must let George know.'

He squirmed under her gaze.

'You're not keeping this to yourself, surely?'

He outlined what he had planned. 'He gave me two days. It's just for tomorrow afternoon. After that, George can go in with all guns blazing. They're not going anywhere and apparently, they won't be there for the next couple of days.'

'That's good, in a way. We have the music hall to do and Saturday is the Midsummer Ball.'

He turned to her and narrowed his eyes. 'Did you say you'd bought a new dress for this? I haven't seen it have I?'

She took the glass from his hand. 'It's a surprise. A different colour to one I normally have. I'm so in love with it. I hope you will be too.'

He eased off the sofa and locked the French windows. 'I've never known you look anything but stunning. However I shall await your entrance with anticipation.'

★ ★ ★

The following afternoon, he met Bert by the roadside. Beth had become a dab-hand at putting his disguise on and, confident he matched the original photograph, he'd hailed the bus and slipped back into the persona of Freddie Woods.

Father Sun showed the way for Bert who had volunteered to help paint the entrance hall. James was led straight to the study. Knowing Bert would be outside decorating gave him a new sense of confidence. If nothing else, his friend could keep a lookout.

'How long do you think you need?' asked Father Sun.

'Couple of hours, guv'nor.' He gave the man a pleading look. 'Is that all right? I don't wanna intrude.'

'That's perfectly fine. I'm driving into Haywards Heath. I have a few things to get on with there. You have the place to yourself.'

'You taking Mother Moon?'

'She's teaching in the room next door. Meditation and reflection.'

'Right you are.'

He removed his robe and James was astounded to see he had an elegant suit on underneath. 'I have to visit the bank manager. Arriving in my robes instils a panic in that man I've not seen before.' He laughed and said goodbye.

Bert popped his head round the door. 'Everythin' all right?'

Staying in character, James, expressed his concern about Mother Moon being next door. 'She could barge in 'ere any time. I could get caught out.'

'Nah, you won't. I'll put dust-sheets everywhere and put me ladders across the door. You'll be fine. Go and get busy and see what you can find out for George.' He stopped James from closing the door. 'And, when you finished, we'll have a nosy about outside.'

That meant one thing: explore the derelict building.

James closed the door. The image of Bernard Potter came to mind. His assertion that '*It's not what you think it is*' was his motivation. Placing the amended bookkeeping ledgers on the table he opened the filing cabinet.

Now he had a sense of what was going on and where, he could concentrate on the who. He flicked through the files. No longer did he waste precious minutes on the members — his aim was to find out as much as possible about Father Sun, Mother Moon and Stuart Drummond. But the folders he leafed through shed very little on their history. Indeed, there was nothing about Stuart Drummond.

He locked the cabinet and scanned the room. He sat at the desk and rummaged through each of the drawers. The bottom right-hand one was locked.

Dashing to the door, he opened it a fraction and whispered to Bert. 'Can you open a locked drawer?'

Bert, checking behind, slipped into the study and, in a few seconds had released the mechanism, instructed him on how to relock it and returned to the hall.

The drawer contained a number of papers and photographs. He took a handful and began sifting through. The first few were letters, written years ago, from Father Sun's sister, Melanie. She expressed frustration over his decision to leave the factory job and there were several requests that he grow up and return to the family home where their mother and father were. They were, she'd stressed, worried about him. He checked the envelopes and saw they'd been addressed to a former address up north.

Interspersed with the correspondence were black and white photographs of the family when the children were younger.

He put Father Sun at around fourteen and it was difficult to compare that image with the grown man he had met. The boy in the picture was tubby and unkempt. He remembered Melanie Barton explaining how her brother had been influenced by the cinema and began changing the way he spoke and dressed. Father Sun was the end result. James couldn't help but think it unusual that a man so enamoured with the film industry should not try to pursue a career in it. Instead, he set up a commune that made no money and was as far removed from the cinema as he could get.

He put the papers to one side and found little else of interest. Returning everything to its place, he followed Bert's instructions on how to re-lock the drawer and turned his attention to the walls. Most were decorated with various images of the universe, planets and stars but, on the far wall were two large professional portraits. Both were taken by Tinner and Son, Leeds. The first showed Johnny Barton and Beverley Kendall. They looked a few years younger and their expression was that of a couple very much in love; they were stylish too. This is the 'Hollywood' image that Johnny Barton liked to portray.

Turning to the second portrait, he mumbled: 'Well, well.' He lifted the frame from the wall and examined it. The photograph showed a group of people, all ages, standing in front of a large building. There were a dozen people smiling at the camera and one person dominated — a portly old man who, James thought from his expression, would stand no nonsense.

He placed the photograph on the desk and found a small magnifying glass. He had noticed a carving above the huge doors but couldn't make out the name. The magnifying glass revealed it to be Kendall Manor. He studied the faces. The first five he didn't recognise at all but he was brought up short by the next two. Beverley Kendall and Stuart Drummond. At the far end he stopped, and gawped. The elderly lady from the derelict building — the woman in charge. Was she a Kendall?

Taking note of the time, he realised that

over an hour had gone by. He hoped that Father Sun would take the full two hours but to make sure, he opened the door a fraction and caught Bert's attention.

'Can you make sure this door is blocked for ten minutes.'

'Yeah, 'cos I can.'

On closing the door, he heard Bert scuffling outside. He turned the frame over and eased the photograph out, hoping that some clues to the various identities would be given. To his delight, someone had set out the names of who was who and where they were in the photograph. He checked and double-checked. Beverley Kendall was named as a granddaughter but the man standing next to her was not identified as Stuart Drummond. He was listed as Simon Drake, a cousin.

He scribbled the names down. After a moment's hesitation, he drew the telephone toward him and lifted the receiver. A minute later, he was put through to George.

James lowered his voice. 'George, it's James. I'm at the commune and I've found something out that you need to know about'

'Why are you whispering? Are you in trouble?'

'Absolutely not but I don't want to be overheard.' He divulged the real identity of Stuart Drummond and heard his friend let out an enlightened snort.

'Leave it with me, James. I'll see what I can find out.'

'Hold on.' He checked the name of the elderly lady. 'Also, an Agnes Drake. She must be the mother or grandmother.'

Finishing the call, James made sure the telephone was positioned as he'd found it and, returned the photograph to the frame. Placing it back on the wall he stared at Agnes Drake. Who'd have thought an elderly lady like that would be behind all this?

When he alerted Bert that he'd finished, his friend began folding up the dust-sheets. 'I'll start packing up. Let this dry.' He put an ear against the door to the room opposite. 'Mother Moon's still doing a class. Let's go and explore.'

James jotted a note for Father Sun and

left it on top of the newly arranged spreadsheet. He stated that he and Bert were both tired from their exertions and that they would see him the following day. Hoping this would sound convincing, they went on their way.

It was coming up to five o'clock and they wandered out of the front entrance and made their way along the wire fence to where Bert's tent stood. There, they crawled through the opening that Mrs Potter had made and scurried round to the back of the derelict building.

James put his ear against the wooden door that was plastered with council notices warning of danger and falling debris. He went to try the door and noticed a padlock. Signalling to Bert that this was his area, he watched his friend make short work of unlocking it and nudged the door open.

Feeling his coat pocket for the torch, James entered the building with Bert.

35

They carefully descended the steps and entered the windowless room that James was now familiar with. Bert pulled him back, signalling for him to remain quiet and not to touch anything. His friend followed as James negotiated the room and studied specific items, half-finished calligraphy, a drawing awaiting a frame, an easel with a rough sketch of a Matisse. He went toward the walls and shone his torch around the recesses, frustrated that he couldn't find what he was looking for. Finally, when they'd almost completed a circuit, James stumbled upon two reel-to-reel recorders. He switched one on. The unmistakable sound of the distant sea spilled out. Bert stopped it and switched the other one on. Again, the sound of the ocean.

Bert pulled him across to a small archway. They ducked through and found themselves in another room with just one piece of machinery installed there. At the desk, Bert drew his attention to a wooden block with metal plating on it.

James shone the beam and examined the item. Tapping his watch, Bert replaced the block and indicated they should get out. They silently made their way up the stairs and made sure the coast was clear. Replacing the padlock, they scurried through the fence and back to Bert's tent.

Happy to be on familiar ground, Bert said: 'You saw what that was, didn't you?'

'Yes, a template for a one-pound note. That machine is printing counterfeits.'

'You gotta tell George about this.'

'I will, but I'm sure he'll want to wait until the gang is assembled.' He updated Bert on the Kendalls and asked his friend if he thought the whole family was involved.

Bert shrugged. 'Is the Kendall business in trouble?'

'Not that I know of although I've not made many enquiries. It wouldn't take long to find out. Melanie, Father Sun's sister, gave me the impression they were still well-to-do.'

'P'haps there's a couple of bad pennies.'

'Yes, perhaps. Listen, I'm going to pop home. We have the music hall event this evening and I need to get ready. Are you coming to ours or going straight to the village hall?'

'I'll come to yours. Any chance of me having a wash? I 'ate camping and I feel right scruffy.' He stabbed a finger at James. 'Don't say a word. I know I'm no Clark Gable but I ain't a tramp neither.'

James assured Bert he'd get a hot bath. The bus arrived and half an hour later, Bert was upstairs soaking in their guest-room tub while Beth was in their own bedroom peeling the beard off James's face.

'We're running out of this wool stuff, or whatever it is, that you use. Does Dulcie have any more?'

James checked to see how much was left. 'I think what you have there will suffice. I can't imagine that I'll be visiting the commune more than once after today. I've telephoned George and left a message for him to arrive a little earlier.'

He turned to check the clock. 'I'd best get a move on. I'll jump in the bath.'

'While you two are tidying yourselves, I'll make some bacon sandwiches.'

★　★　★

Clean, refreshed and replenished, the three of them set off to the village hall. The evening was overcast but warm. As they'd arrived early, they helped with the last-minute preparations, one of which was securing a large banner across the entrance doors announcing: 'Tonight: Old Time Music Hall'.

Inside, Dorothy Forbes accosted James and told him that George was already getting changed. 'I can't understand why he's so early. You're early too. Did I tell everyone the wrong time?'

'No, Dorothy, we just wanted to run through things one last time.' He cringed as she enthused about his professionalism.

He found George in the corner of the green room, gluing a handlebar moustache to his top lip. After quick hellos to a few of the villagers, he pulled up a chair alongside his friend who was concentrating on the angle of his moustache.

'Simon Drake,' George began, 'is a cousin of Beverley Kendall. An art collector. His mother is one Agnes Drake, all of them from the north and all involved with the Kendall Empire. I've got in touch with my counterpart in the local force up there to see if there's anything I need to know about the two of them. I should get a response when I'm back at work tomorrow.'

James slid his chair closer. 'This is not the place but I have a confession to make.'

George rubbed his brow. 'Now what've you done?'

'I discovered the place where the art fraud business is going on.'

George swivelled to face him. 'You what!'

The few villagers who had arrived looked across. James sat back in his chair and told George to finish getting ready. 'I told you this was not the place. Come back to ours after the show and I'll fill you in. You can't do anything now, anyway, the place is deserted.' Before George could retort, he'd leapt up and grabbed his costume from the rail.

George followed him and whispered in his ear. 'You are bloody frustrating at times. I'm going to be thinking about this all evening now.'

James stared at his friend. 'You're not going to forget the song, are you? I've promised Dorothy we'll be word perfect'

To his relief, he was interrupted by Bert who strode in wearing his pearly king outfit and sent out a general greeting to everyone before selecting some grease-paint.

Charlie popped his head round the door and caught his attention. 'Mr Irwin's arrived.'

James went through to the main hall and greeted 'Fluff' Irwin with open arms. The Great War veteran had attended their Christmas show and his eyes lit up on seeing the brightly painted scenery and the cosy candle-lit auditorium.

'Is there going to be singing?' he

whispered to Beth who had linked arms with him.

'Lots of singing, Mr Irwin. You're sitting at the front here with the Merryweathers. You remember them, don't you?'

His eyes sparkled. 'Oh yes. Are Luke and Mark coming?'

Irwin had regressed to a state of childlike wonder after shell-shock had stripped him of the ability to live a normal life. He identified with children more than adults and James assured him that the boys would be there. 'They'll be along shortly. You remember Charlie Hawkins, he'll be joining you with his two children, Tommy and Susan.'

Charlie, who had tailed James to the hall, introduced Dulcie. Mr Irwin, clearly bowled over by the beautiful woman in front on him, bowed. Dulcie, who had been briefed on Irwin's condition, made every effort to make him welcome.

Leaving them to look after the war veteran, James and Beth made their way to the back of the stage. Beth made a beeline for Anne to help with the costumes and make-up, while James headed into one of two dressing rooms to find his bowler hat.

In the background, he heard the constant hum of chatter as the village hall filled up. Every available seat had been sold and Dorothy had added a few more tables and chairs to accommodate last-minute bookings. He made his way to the front and said a few hellos to friends and residents. Harry, Fiona and William were sharing a table with Graham and Sarah Porter.

Harry gazed up at James. 'You look quite dashing as an Edwardian, Dad.'

'Mmm, I rather like this suit. Perhaps Dorothy will let me keep it. Not so sure about this stiff collar though.'

William laughed. 'I can't imagine Beth will want you escorting her around like some ghost from the past.'

'You're a dandy, aren't you?' said Fiona. 'You look as if you're about to knock on the door to sell a vacuum cleaner.'

Everyone laughed and James allowed them their fun. Once they'd settled down, he reminded them about Mr Irwin. 'Make sure you go over there and make a fuss of him.'

'Already have,' said Harry, who had met the man over Christmas. 'He's a smashing character, isn't he? It's good that you and Mum have remembered him.'

In his peripheral vision, James saw Dorothy hold up her hand: five minutes until curtain up. The music hall evening was a little different to their normal shows, in that the entertainers would sit in the audience and simply go up to the stage when it was their turn. He and Beth joined the table alongside the one where Mr Irwin sat.

The ladies of the WI had done a marvellous job of placing the tables and chairs in a fashion that still afforded a little room for people to go to and fro. They'd set up trestle-tables in the small foyer outside for the interval's refreshments so every available space had been used. The piano was rammed so close to the wall that poor Mr Brownlee, the church organist, seemed to blend in with the paintwork.

Each table had a flickering candle on it although they didn't make much of an impression with the evening summer sun shining through the windows. The suggestion of having crisps and peanuts on each table had been a good one. Donovan and Kate had warmed Graham's sausage rolls in the oven and brought them through from the pub. Anyone wanting alcohol was simply directed to the Half Moon, a thirty second walk across the green.

James settled back on his wooden chair. Joining him and Beth at the table were George, GJ and Catherine and Bert and Gladys. Behind them were Harry, Fiona and William.

Cavendish's own zany solicitor, Mr Bateson, skipped up on stage and caused a ripple of laughter straight away. Bateson had made use of his tall, wiry frame and dressed in a second-hand frock coat and a top hat that leaned to one side. Dulcie had back-combed his longish white hair so that it stuck out at the sides.

Brownlee hammered down on the keys and Bateson sprang to life singing 'Burlington Bertie'. He gaily pranced across the stage and then jumped off it and paraded around the room. As he did so, he placed song sheets on each table. James distributed theirs and gradually the audience began to join in with the refrain.

As the song ended, Bateson returned to the stage, took off his top hat and made an exaggerated bow. Replacing his hat, he took one large stride to the edge of the stage and beamed.

'Good eeeeeevening, ladieeeees and gennnnntlemen, boys and girls, and welcome to the Cavendish Old Time Music Hall.'

Mr Irwin clapped enthusiastically, his childlike wonder spilling over.

'And you have every right to applaud, Mr Irwin, as you are about to experience a torrent of breath-taking talent, an unbridled, ineffable night of ebullience . . . '

James leant in to Beth. 'Good grief, the man's swallowed a dictionary.'

Bert laughed. 'He's doin' it the proper way, Jimmy-boy. Geeing the audience up.'

And he was. With every sentence; every description that Bateson offered, the villagers' *oohed* and *aahed* as if they were watching fireworks. How he had memorised his introduction James didn't know but he couldn't help but be impressed.

'And now, for your delectation and gratification, please welcome to the stage, the captivating, splendiferous, melodious and . . . ' pausing to get a reaction, 'featheracious . . . ' The villagers cheered. 'Please welcome to the stage, Rose and Lilac Crumb.'

The ladies, dressed as Victorians and waving huge peacock feathers, were helped up onto the stage by Bateson who then bowed and disappeared. Putting on their most plummy voices, the sisters sang a rousing version of 'The Boy I Love Is Up In The Gallery'. James spotted that Bert and Gladys didn't need a song-sheet to join in.

To say the evening was an enjoyable one was an understatement. Bateson's introductions became more extreme as the evening went on and the audience became more raucous and happier to heckle. James couldn't remember the last time he'd laughed so much. Every so often, people disappeared then reappeared with trays of drinks from the pub and Anne, along with other ladies of the WI, scurried from table to table replenishing the snacks.

The interval gave everyone time to catch their breaths. Beth and James followed a number of villagers out on to the green. The evening was warm and he, for one, was getting quite hot in his costume.

'What a fantastic evening,' said Beth. 'I think this must be one of the best shows we've ever put on.'

'I think so too. Bateson is pulling the whole thing together nicely. Did you know he was going to litter his sentences with so many incomprehensible words?'

'I didn't, but it certainly brings in the spirit of the music hall. When are you on?'

'First act when we get back.'

George came out of the pub with a pint and made his way across to them. 'Well, I didn't think I would enjoy a music hall event but I have to say, this takes some beating. That Mr Bateson should be a professional entertainer. He's wasted being a solicitor.'

James had to agree. The man was an outstanding solicitor but, unlike many others of the law fraternity, he had a side to his nature that provided those around him with simple joy.

George sipped his beer. 'What sort of time should this be finishing?'

Beth thought it would be close to nine thirty. 'Dorothy didn't want to go on too late because we have children in the audience and some of them are performing. They have school in the morning.'

James didn't think that would make much difference. 'I can't imagine any child sleeping tonight after such a splendid evening but that's handy for us. Are you still coming back to ours later, George?'

His friend gave him an incredulous stare. 'That's one of the most stupid questions you've asked me in a long while, James.'

Dorothy appeared at the door as Kate Delaney banged a metal tray with a wooden spoon. 'Five minutes please.' They returned to the hall.

James caught up with Kate. 'Can I put an order in for a pint of Solstice and a glass of wine?'

'Don't tell everyone I'm doing waitress service.'

He gave her some money. 'Thank you, Kate, you're an angel.'

He and George went straight backstage and awaited their introduction.

Bateson almost vaulted onto the stage. 'Good *Eeeever*-ning . . . Laydeeeeez and *GENT*lemeeeeennnnn, boys and girls!'

The audience members settled in their chairs. From the side of the stage, James saw Irwin laughing with Mark and Luke. The boys had taken a shine to the veteran and had spoken about him before he'd arrived, having remembered him from Christmas. Children, he thought, were far more intuitive than they were given credit for being. Both boys were chatting with him as a friend, not an adult. Bateson's voice brought him back to the present.

'A duo of investigative, inquisitatious, constitutional reprobates.'

James turned to George with a grin. 'Cheek of the man.'

'A positively stylish pair of gentlemen. Ladies, prepare yourself. Gentlemen, bring out the smelling salts for your wives and girlfriends.'

James heard a few giggles from the women.

'Welcome to the stage, Lord James Harrington and Mr George Lane.'

A huge cheer went up as James and George put on their bowlers and strode on stage with their walking canes. Brownlee played the opening chord and the pair of them launched into the coffee song. It couldn't have gone better. The pair of them had known the song for years and they'd rehearsed it until they didn't even need to think about it. The timing, the execution and choreography went like a dream and, to their relief, neither of them tripped over the tongue-twisting chorus, unlike the villagers who were doing their best to join in from the song-sheets. The performance was a roaring success and James and George took their bows like true professionals.

They returned to their seats where James found his drink had arrived. He

468

gratefully gulped the first third of the pint.

The second half seemed to go by in an instant with a number of entertaining singers, poets and sketches on the bill. Bert, in his pearly king suit, left the table and went backstage. The show was nearing its end and James believed everyone was looking forward to his friend's closing act.

'Cocknitotious, pearlyiescent, effervescent and providing the conclusion to this evening's imaginative entertainment, please welcome to the stage, Bethnal Green's Bertram Briggs!'

Bert darted onto the stage and began his act with 'Back Answers'. The audience, by now, were joining in and adding their own version to try and put Bert off. Instead of showing any annoyance, however, Bert gave as good as he got and the performance became more raucous. His second piece saw him invite Gladys up to the stage. Although she had a colourful personality and was no shrinking violet, Gladys seemed a little shy to be the centre of attention as Bert belted out a rendition of 'Daisy Bell' but had substituted 'Gladys' for 'Daisy'. The audience joined in with gusto.

James slipped his hand into Beth's as they joined in with the chorus. At the end of the song, Bert escorted his betrothed to the edge of the stage where James leapt up to help her down.

'Gawd help me,' she said with mock horror, 'what am I doin' marrying the likes of 'im?'

He held her chair out for her. 'I think you know exactly what you're doing and it's absolutely the right thing to do.'

Bert quietened everyone down. 'Now, listen up. I'm gonna finish off the evening now and I want everyone to join in but not before I've said something.' A murmur went around the room. 'Nothing terrible. It's just that I think we ought to give a round of applause to Dorothy for getting this show together. It's been brilliant and we've all had a great time and the people in the background don't get seen. Not just Dorothy but the people doing the costumes and the make-up, and the WI. You've been blinding, you really have. So, a round of applause please.'

The applause went on for some time until Dorothy, true to form, tapped her watch and indicated that Bert should finish.

'Right, here's a song we all know. It's on your song-sheets so let's have a good old sing. This one's for Mr Irwin. We're right glad you made it, Mr Irwin. This is a song that's always sung at the music hall and everyone knows it'

Irwin turned to James. 'He's singing it for me,' he mouthed.

James returned it with an encouraging 'Yes I know' nod.

Mr Brownlee played the introduction and Bert launched into 'Down at the Old Bull and Bush'. James turned to see the villagers in all their finery, swaying to the music and was pleased to see that Charlie was taking some snaps with his camera.

When the song ended, everyone stood to applaud and Bateson went through the names of his fellow performers. 'Give them all a round of applause.' He gestured for those people to come up on the stage, which they duly did.

James stood next to George to take a bow. He scanned the room, delighted to see so many people had enjoyed the evening.

He frowned. Was that Mrs Potter at the back? Once the applause began to die down, he threaded his way through the tables. James saw the worry written on her face from across the hall. He led her out to the small foyer.

'Mrs Potter, is everything all right?'

'Someone tried to attack Wendy tonight!'

'Oh lord, at the hospital?'

She nodded. 'Dressed up like a doctor, he was.'

James steered her to one of the wooden chairs at the back of the hall. The activity of clearing up meant that no one was really taking any notice of the stranger sitting in the corner. He sought out George, dragged him to one side and whispered the news in his ear.

His friend gasped. 'At the hospital!'

'Apparently dressed up like a doctor. Shall we go straight over there?'

'Have you got your car outside?

Stephen picked me up after collecting Mr Irwin.'

'Yes, I've got the Austin. Hold on a moment.' He updated Beth on the news.

'Shall I come with you?'

'No need and I haven't room. You stay here and I'll pick you up from the vicarage.'

Outside, George curled into the tiny rear seat of the Austin, cursing at the tightness of the suit and struggling to put his cane to one side. His moustache had become loose at one side and he pushed it back in place. Mrs Potter took the passenger seat. James threw the walking cane and bowler hat in the back, inadvertently hitting George and causing a mutter of protests. If things hadn't been so serious, James would have laughed. Two grown men dressed as Edwardians shooting off in a sports car. Indeed, this whole affair, if viewed from a distance would have had many in hysterics; the ridiculous outfits worn by the commune members, the daily transformation into Freddie Woods and the look on Beth's face when she encountered his alias.

He fired up the engine, put the car in gear and sped to the cottage hospital. The hospital was situated just outside of Cavendish and it took no more than five minutes. They clambered out and, for reasons they would later reflect on with humour, replaced their bowler hats and strode in with their walking canes.

Matron, lifting a single eyebrow at the sight of the two men, led them down the corridor to a ward. Wendy Potter was in the last bed propped up by four pillows and chatting to a woman police constable. Mrs Potter rushed to her side and gave her a hug before sitting down on a chair.

The uniformed woman came to greet them but not without giving them both a quizzical once-over. George, ensuring his moustache was in place, explained their appearance.

'Sir, she doesn't really remember much about the man.'

'Are you staying here all night?'

'No sir. I'm off duty now but PC Glover should be here to take over in the next few minutes.'

At the bedside, Wendy couldn't help but gawp.

James saw his reflection in the small mirror on the wall and snatched off his bowler hat. 'We've been performing at the music hall evening and came straight here.' He asked her if she thought the man was from the commune. 'You told the lady he was handsome. Father Sun is handsome. Are you sure it wasn't him — in disguise?'

For someone who had gone through such trauma, she was remarkably calm and James wondered if the nurses had given her a sedative.

'No, Lord Harrington, I'd recognise Father Sun and this definitely wasn't him. It was difficult to say although, for some reason, he did seem familiar.'

'Like a chance encounter.'

She locked eyes with him. 'Yes, yes, that's exactly what it was like. I'm sure I've seen him before.'

George put his bowler and cane on the bed and took the seat vacated by the policewoman. 'Would you put him at around six foot two inches, black or very dark brown hair, dark eyes and bushy eyebrows?'

Her eyes became saucers. 'Yes . . . yes, I would. Do you know who that is?'

'Does the name Simon Drake mean anything to you?'

A slow shake of the head.

'What about Stuart Drummond?'

James noticed her brow furrow.

'I'm not sure. Sorry . . . although Drake does sound familiar.'

James exchanged a look with George, one that asked if he could speak. George gave a nod.

'Wendy, Simon Drake and Stuart Drummond are the same person. Simon is the cousin of Mother Moon. Her real name is Beverley Kendall. Do you know that name?'

Wendy reached for her mother's hand. 'Dad mentioned that name to me.'

George shifted forward. 'Who, Beverley Kendall?'

'Yes. He said something about her coming from a rich family. I think he'd just found that out. Her dad owns a few factories up north.'

'And when he chatted with you about her, the name Drake came up?'

'Yes, yes, that's right, I remember now. He told me that the Kendall side were an established family but he'd just discovered that the other side of the family were bad uns. His words, not mine.'

'The bad uns being the Drake side.'

James perched on the end of the bed. 'What else did your father tell you?'

She brought out a hanky and blew her nose. Tears welled in her eyes. 'He told me they were up to no good, using the commune as a front.' She sniffed. 'I wouldn't listen to him. I thought he was telling me fibs to get me to come home.' She burst into tears and flung her arms around her mother. 'I'm so sorry, Mum. If I'd have listened to him, he'd still be here.'

Mrs Potter soothed her, stroking her hair back and telling her not to talk such nonsense. 'Your father would have carried on whether you were there or not. His instinct told him something fishy was going on and, like every copper I know, he wanted to get to the bottom of it'

'Wendy,' James said, 'what exactly happened on the day your father visited? The day he had his accident?'

Wendy took a deep breath and composed herself. 'Dad drove in just after lunch. I think the first thing he did was have a row with Father Sun about not allowing access to me. He couldn't understand why such a spiritual place would be so harsh about refusing access to loved ones.' She stared at her fingernails. 'I must admit, now I'm out of it, I'm not sure that I understood that either. Anyway, regardless of that, I think Dad just shoved him aside. I was working in the allotments and he found me there.'

'You spoke to him?'

Some seconds passed before she continued.

'He saw me from a distance. I'd already started to go back to my room. I didn't want a confrontation. Brother Mars held him back. Dad shouted across, told me to pack my things, that I was to come home with him because things weren't what I thought they were. That they were fraudsters.'

'What do you think he meant by that?'

'I told him he didn't know what he was talking about and that I loved it at the commune. I thought he was just being difficult. Then Father Sun came along. He was really good with Dad, didn't shout or anything and just asked him to leave. He said to Dad that he'd give him a tour of the place to show him that everything was in order but Dad wouldn't have it. Then Father Sun asked him what he thought was going on.'

Another silence followed.

'Dad thought I'd gone but I was listening round the corner. He was shouting that he knew something fishy was going on and he'd already started looking into it. Father Sun didn't have a clue what he was talking about but Dad was waving a bit of paper at him, told him that that should tell him.'

'And Father Sun didn't react?'

'I don't know.'

George asked how long her father had stayed there.

'About twenty minutes I think.'

'Where did he park his car?' asked James.

'By the side of the house, in front of that garage.'

James nudged George. 'Could I have a brief word?'

They went out to the corridor where George asked what the problem was.

'When we went to the open evening at the commune, we had a wander about. Me and Beth. We explored areas that were just away from the main event.'

'And?'

'I saw an old washing up bowl with a clear liquid in it.'

'I'm listening.'

'The car that was parked in there was brand new. It wouldn't have needed any work. I'm certain that it was brake fluid in that bowl. I'm clutching at straws a little but I believe that Simon Drake overheard that conversation and thought he'd scare Mr Potter. Drained the fluid while he was arguing with Father Sun.'

'A bit of a risk.'

'It's a bit of a risk coming in here trying to kill Wendy Potter too.'

They returned to Wendy's bedside where George began questioning her again. 'Miss Potter, you may have seen Simon Drake the day this occurred. Can you recall seeing anyone outside the garage?'

Wendy took some time to think. 'I saw Mother Moon because I remember her robes and the symbol on them. There was someone else there too, a man; she was chatting to him.'

'Did he have a robe on?'

'No, he had trousers and a shirt, he was chatting with her. Yes!' Realisation hit her. 'Oh. He was tall, dark. That was him, wasn't it? The man that came in here.' She paled. 'Is he the man who killed my father?'

'Let's not get ahead of ourselves miss. We're trying to establish the facts so don't go jumping to conclusions. When Drake came in here earlier, did he say anything to you?'

'He said that I knew too much.'

'What does that mean?' asked James.

'I don't know. He was dressed in a white coat with a stethoscope round his neck. He had one of those masks that surgeons wear. He drew the curtains round the bed, picked up one of the pillows and . . . ' she broke down.

Mrs Potter leapt up and held her close. 'I think that's enough questioning.'

'Just one more thing,' said George, 'You had a fraudulent banknote on you. Where did you find it and could Drake have seen you take it?'

Pulling away from her mother, Wendy said that she'd been down in the basement of a building and had seen the note jammed under a table leg. 'It caught my eye because of the colour. It wasn't an ordinary piece of white paper. I was struck by the green and then realised it was a one-pound note. I thought it was good luck at first and pocketed it for a rainy day. But when all this happened with Dad and what he'd said, I took another look at it. It didn't have a security strip so I knew it was fake. I realised Dad was right.'

The clicking of the Matron's heels caused them to look up. PC Glover strode in with her.

'I really must insist that you leave my patient to rest. I have others here who need their peace and quiet.'

James apologised and picked up the two bowler hats. 'Wendy, you have a policeman here with you tonight. You've no need to worry about any more intruders.'

Mrs Potter kissed her daughter on the forehead and gathered her things.

Before leaving, George had one more question. 'Wendy, did you tell anyone, anyone at all, about finding the note?'

'Yes. I was so happy to find something like that I told the first person I saw.'

'And who was that?'

'Mother Moon.'

With Matron tutting in his ear, James asked what her reaction was.

' She was pleased for me and then she told me not to tell anyone. She said that any money found should go to the commune but that she wouldn't let on. I remember her saying that it was a nice amount to find and that I should treat myself to something . . . ' the tears welled. 'Something to remember Dad by.'

'And you hadn't seen this Drake chap before? Who blindfolded you when you were driven to the basement?'

'Some old man. He had ink on his hands.'

James thought that must have been the man he'd seen writing provenances. Mrs Potter again enveloped her daughter in her arms. James pulled George away. 'We'll wait in the car, Mrs Potter, you take your time.'

Outside, George stood with James. 'Time to go in and make some arrests, I think.' 'Not tonight, George, no one will be there.'

'Tomorrow night then, we'll have the gang all there.' He bounced on his toes. 'I'm looking forward to this one.'

James spotted Mrs Potter coming toward them. He held the driver's seat forward to allow George to fold up in to the back. His friend cursed him. 'Why the bloody hell did you have to drive this car?'

'It's only until Cavendish. Are you still coming back to ours?'

'Let's do it tomorrow. Can you come to

the station and we can get it all written up formally?'

'Of course.'

He held the door open for Mrs Potter and, as she started to get in, he squeezed her arm. 'Everything will be all right, Mrs P. I know it doesn't bring your husband back but George is close to shutting the door tight on who did this.'

She gave him a weary smile of thanks.

36

James and Beth sat with Bert, Stephen and Anne at Elsie's café. James had telephoned ahead and asked Elsie to reserve their favourite table.

He and Bert had spent the morning with George at Lewes police station, giving a full written statement of all the details of their escapades at the commune, from the moment they'd first set foot inside, disguised as potential members. It had taken a good couple of hours to go over everything but, after reading the statement through, they were happy with what would be a vital piece of evidence. George had already obtained a statement over the phone from James' cousin, Herbie, and GJ was going in later that day to add his story.

Beth had suggested a change of scenery after having to concentrate on so much detail and the café was an ideal one for James.

Elsie gave them a warm welcome and allowed them a few minutes to make their minds up about refreshments. It had just gone midday and James was peckish.

'I don't know about anyone else, but I rather think I'm going to have lunch. We had an early start and the bowl of cornflakes I had this morning seems a lifetime away.'

'Yer not wrong there, Jimmy-boy. I could eat the menu at the moment.'

'The specials look appetising,' said Beth.

Anne surveyed the chalkboard. 'Fish cakes, rabbit pie and your Grandmother's Welsh Rarebit.'

'Mmm,' said Stephen, 'I think I'll stick t-to the main menu and have my usual, sausages.'

'That's not adventurous,' said Anne.

'Bangers for me too,' said Bert, adding that that was as adventurous as he wanted to be.

'I'll be adventurous w-when I'm somewhere I can be adventurous,' said Stephen.

James turned to Beth. 'What are you having, darling?'

'Rabbit pie.'

Elsie arrived at the table and took orders for two sausage dinners and three rabbit pies.

Stephen leaned in. 'C-come along, James, spill the beans. The last we heard, you and George had raced over to the hospital. This morning you've been at the police station and we are none the wiser.'

Anne asked if the commune was closing. 'With such a bad reputation now, surely they can't continue.'

'I-I certainly hope not.'

'I'm not sure it's as easy as that, Stephen. This Father Sun chap is difficult to pin down. There's nothing incriminating him personally.'

'But his wife!' Stephen said with indignation. 'He m-must know what his wife is up to.'

'Nah, vicar, not everyone's like you lot. And anyway, we don't know 'em — we only know what we see and that ain't a lot, is it?'

Elsie arrived with the meals and James

sprinkled salt and pepper on his pie. 'The thing is, George thinks he has enough to question Mother Moon.' He rolled his eyes. 'I must stop calling them by these blasted names. Beverley Kendall. Although Wendy told her about this one-pound note she found, Beverley could have innocently mentioned it to Simon Drake.'

Beth stared at him. 'Do you think that's likely?'

'Not really, no. I'm just trying to think like George. He needs facts or a confession.'

Anne asked if George had enough to arrest Simon and Agnes Drake.

'If caught in the act, yes.'

'We're going back there tonight, after the music hall,' said Bert, loading his fork up with sausage and onions. 'I'm keeping out the way but ready to pile in should things kick off. I've got me cosh in the tent so I'm kitted out to lend a hand. Jimmy 'ere is slapping on the greasepaint for one last appearance as Freddie Woods.'

'Oh dear,' said Anne, 'is that wise? Could it become dangerous?'

'I don't think so,' said James. 'We need to make sure Simon Drake is there as well as his aunt. The operation doesn't run without the aunt being there and we need all of those involved to be present.'

'What t-time is this all happening?'

'Midnight tonight. Charlie's bringing Dulcie to ours later to plaster on the disguise and Beth's dropping me off by the woods. I'll walk from there.'

'What time is George getting there?' asked Beth.

'He's meeting Bert at half past eleven. He'll have half the force with him. I believe two will stay with their cars to block the front and rear entrances and the rest will be raiding the basement or standing at various exits.' He scooped up some mashed potato and carrots. 'I don't know what Elsie does in that tiny kitchen of hers but everything she brings out here tastes divine. How're your sausages?'

They all had their mouths full but it was clear they thought the same.

Beth giggled. 'I have to say, when you went racing off last night I couldn't help but think of a silent comedy. You and

George in those costumes and bowler hats. It was like the Keystone Cops. What on earth did Matron say?'

He wiped his chin with his napkin. 'Absolutely nothing but there was a hint of resignation about her, as if it wasn't entirely unexpected. Makes you wonder what *would* make her step back in surprise.'

'I-I do hope that commune closes,' said Stephen. 'They are a bad influence. I don't believe people should be m-made to cut off their friends and family.'

'Me neither, vicar,' said Bert. 'But like you said earlier, this may put the kybosh on it.'

Beth asked if the two parishioners had returned to the fold.

Stephen pressed a palm to his heart. 'They didn't r-realise they had to give everything up. I think Father Sun has a way with w-words.'

'And not a little charisma too,' added James. 'Adam's girlfriend was swayed by his looks and charm.'

'Has she stopped going?' said Beth.

'Not yet, but I don't think she's as

taken in by Father Sun as your two parishioners. Hopefully tonight's activities will make her mind up.'

'On a brighter note,' said Anne, 'are you all ready for the Midsummer Ball tomorrow?'

Beth exclaimed, 'I can't wait! Fiona and Harry have been helping to decorate the dining room. They've added a few touches that I hadn't even thought of doing. Are you two going straight there or did you want to come with us?'

'Straight there,' Anne replied adding that her parents would be arriving to sit with the boys. 'I'm so looking forward to a good dinner and dance and an opportunity to dress up.'

'Me too.'

James was as enthusiastic as the ladies. 'I've spent most of my time dressed up like a tramp these last few days. It'll be good to put on a dinner jacket and spruce up a bit.' He checked his watch. 'Darling, do you mind if we skip dessert? I wanted to pop over to Harrington's and make sure everything's in place for tomorrow and we haven't had a chat with Didier for a while. He'll be on tenterhooks about the buffet and will need indulging.'

Beth said she was fine with that. Bert opted to stay with the Merryweathers for ice cream. James settled the bill and opened the door for Beth.

37

The sky was dark, but starlit. James, dressed as Freddie Woods, put on a jaunty appearance as he was welcomed by Simon Drake.

'You look happy.'

'I am, guv'nor. Now I've made me mind up, I'm right looking forward to it. I 'ad a kip this afternoon so I'd stay awake.'

Drake held the passenger door open and handed James the blindfold. 'Let's get going then.'

To stay in character and not arouse suspicion, James wound the window down a fraction. But this time he didn't bother to listen.; he knew exactly where he was going. His main focus was on how George was getting on.

★   ★   ★

George Lane had remained with Bert just inside the wire fence but behind the shrubs. They had eyes on the back entrance and had watched Drake and James drive away. A constable had widened the gap in the fence to make it easier to get through.

Bert checked his watch. 'Right, if 'e follows the same route, they'll be back 'ere in twenty minutes.'

Alongside George was PC Fulton who had now become a regular part of his team. His uncle had played a convincing undercover position in their last investigation and the nephew appeared to be made of the same stuff. The young man leant in.

'Shall I get everyone ready, sir?'

George nodded. 'As soon as that car arrives back here, make sure the entrances are blocked. Front and back.' He turned as two other officers came forward. 'We have about twenty minutes. We'll wait for them to go inside and then give it five minutes before we raid. Wait for my signal. Understood?'

Nods all round. George turned to Bert. 'You stay out here, Bert. If you see anyone getting away, let Sergeant Hines know. He's co-ordinating things once we go in.'

Bert snarled. 'I won't need help from him, George.'

He tugged Bert's arm. 'Don't do anything stupid. I know you think you're a hard nut, Bert, but it's likely that Drake killed a police officer. If he's happy to do that, he won't think twice about you. He may be armed and no matter what sort of cosh you've got hidden in your jacket, it'll be no match for a bullet. You shouldn't even have a ruddy cosh. Think about Gladys.'

Bert reluctantly nodded but insisted he would try to do more than just watch. With everyone in position, they waited.

After what seemed an eternity, George heard the sound of a car engine and the crunch of gravel. Two headlights came into view and the Anglia came to a gentle stop twenty yards in front of him. He watched as Drake went to the passenger side and opened the door. James, in his tatty overcoat, emerged and allowed Drake to steer him into the derelict building. Drake pulled the wooden door to. George, with his back to the building, got out a torch and signalled with two flashes. Five minutes.

★　★　★

In the basement, James said a cheery hello to Agnes Drake. 'All right, missus? I'm fair set and raring to go.'

'That's pleasing to hear, Mr Woods.'

'I was telling Mr Drummond, I 'ad a sleep this afternoon so I reckon I could put in a good few hours tonight.'

She led him over to a table with a lamp on it. Under the light was a Piet Mondrian. James knew Mondrian simply because his work was so unique. In front of him was a collection of straight black lines and bold red, blue and yellow squares. It was all very abstract and, although James loved the modern, clean lines of Kandinsky, for some reason this particular style jarred. He leant in and studied the painting.

'Not my sort o' thing, that. Is it yours?'

'It doesn't really matter what you think, Mr Woods. Can you replicate it? We have a buyer for the original and need your replica hanging back on the wall.'

'Oh yes. You've started me off with quite a simple piece. The brushwork, see, it's quite basic.' To his relief, Agnes gave a confident nod, showing she assumed he knew what he was doing.

'What will you need?'

'An easel, paints and plenty of light. It's difficult to see colours under this light.' He held up a bag. 'I got me own brushes.'

Drake led him to the far end of the building. It was about the size of a double-garage, a little chilly and depressing. His fellow artists, four in total, had their backs to him and there were no nods of recognition or welcome. He noticed a camping gas stove with a dented kettle. The sound of the sea was louder here and James remembered that the reel-to-reel recorders were just beyond the partition. Drake gestured to the corner where an easel already stood.

'That'll be grand, guv'nor,' James said. 'Can I have another easel to put the Mondrian on?' His heart began beating a little faster and he subconsciously checked the time. He tapped his foot on the floor.

Drake studied him. 'You seem a bit nervous, Mr Woods.'

'Me! No, guv'nor, I'm fine. Well, I s'pose I am a bit on edge. I wanna make sure I live up to expectations. I mean, you're paying me a lot of dosh, aren't you?'

To his relief, Drake accepted his reasons. 'Just relax and enjoy it.'

'Right, guv'nor, I will.'

Drake went to go but stopped.

James caught movement to the side.

His heart leapt.

This was it.

Struggling to remain in character, he turned to Drake and jutted his chin at the kettle. 'A cup o' tea would be nice.' He spotted George. 'Oh, sorry, didn't know you 'ad visitors.'

George stood at the base of the stairs and flipped up his warrant card. As he stepped forward, three constables trotted down behind. Having been briefed on the layout of the basement earlier, George motioned for his men to spread out. One headed for the archway that led to the printing machine.

Meanwhile, George got down to business. 'Simon and Agnes Drake. I'm arresting you for the murder of police constable Bernard Potter and for art fraud.' The constable ducked back under the archway with a nod and two metal plates. 'I'm also arresting you for counterfeiting activities. You'll be sorry you started this little enterprise. Better get used to these sorts of surroundings.'

Simon brought out a knife and lunged at George who sidestepped the attack in the nick of time. He threw Simon to the floor and twisted his arm back. The knife skidded out of reach. George went to put handcuffs on him but Simon wriggled free. They grappled on the floor where Simon swung a fist and caught George in the stomach. They rolled back and forth exchanging kicks and punches.

The other artists scrambled to flee but more officers dashed down the steps to overwhelm them before they had a chance to bolt.

A groan from George prompted James

to act. He grabbed hold of a glass vase full of old brushes and smashed it over Simon's head. The man fell forward and George quickly snapped on the handcuffs.

He pulled Simon Drake to his feet and handed him over to Fulton. 'Keep an eye on this one. He's a slippery character.'

James' swung round. Where was Agnes? He dashed through the archway to see her standing on the top of the printing machine and reaching up to a wooden hatch which he presumed led to the ground floor. She spotted him.

'Get over here. Help me up.'

Keen not to expose his identity, he offered to go first with the excuse that he could help her better from above than below. He took his time, which only increased her anger.

'For pity's sake, what are you doing? Get up there and pull me up.'

James made the effort and eased on to the concrete floor. It was dark, the windows boarded up but, with several torches now aimed at him, he grinned. He reached down. 'Not sure that this'll make much difference, missus.'

'Just get me up,' she yelled.

He struggled to pull Agnes Drake through the opening. She was not a small woman and James almost laughed at the scene he was involved in. If Beth were here, no doubt she would liken it to another silent comedy, especially with Bert standing over the hatch wielding a cosh.

After so much effort clambering up, Agnes failed to see the number of policemen surrounding her as she emerged from the basement. It was only when she got to her feet that the truth hit home. She closed her eyes in resignation.

Sergeant Hines dashed forward and handcuffed her while Bert, to James amusement, remained poised and ready to pounce. They exchanged a grin.

James brushed the dust from his clothes as Agnes was led away. Outside the building, he heard her shout at George. 'Why aren't you arresting Freddie Woods?' Suddenly aware that he was undercover caused her to scream blue murder at anyone who would listen.

The doors to the police van were open to collect Simon, Agnes and the participating fraudsters. Confident that the coast was now clear, James sought out George who had asked for a forensic team to come in and do their job.

'James,' he said, 'are you looking to collect commendations? Because there's no doubt Superintendent Higgins will want to pin a medal on you.'

'If it wasn't for Bert, we'd still be none the wiser. He's the one that discovered it was all happening under our noses.'

'I don't want no bloody commendation. That wouldn't go down well with some of my mates,' said Bert. 'Present company excluded of course.'

George held out a hand. 'You push me to the limit sometimes, Bert, but occasionally you shine.'

'Like a diamond in the rough,' he responded.

They were interrupted by Father Sun, who had appeared in his dressing gown. 'What the hell's going on? And where's my wife?'

38

James buttoned his dress shirt and picked out a pair cuff-links. To his left, Beth was finishing her make-up and spraying herself with Je Reviens. It was a perfume that he found intoxicating. He smoothed his hair back and reached for his aftershave which he liberally applied.

'That smells nice,' said Beth. She replaced her make-up items in the drawer and stood up. 'Will you fasten my necklace?'

He stood back. 'Heavens, Beth, you look stunning. I can understand why you're so pleased with your dress.'

She did a twirl. The full-length gown was a beautiful dark mauve satin that shimmered according to the light and her pose.

'Yes,' she answered. 'When you went to the Wendover a few weeks ago. I popped to Liberty's but ended up in that little boutique on the corner.' She checked herself in the mirror. 'I must admit, it is quite flattering.'

James took the necklace and stood behind her. 'Flattering is an understatement,' he said as he fastened the diamond necklace. He kissed the nape of her neck. 'Shame we have to go out,' he added with a wink.

She turned to face him. 'We can pick up where we left off when we get back.'

James put his cuff-links on. 'I'll hold you to that.' He shrugged his dinner jacket on as Beth slipped her arms around his waist.

'You look very handsome.'

He turned to drape a bolero jacket over her shoulders. 'And you look very beautiful. Ready?'

She grabbed her clutch bag. 'I think so.'

The Midsummer Ball at Harrington's had become a much-anticipated addition to the calendar for many of their guests. This was the sixth one they'd held and many visitors had already booked their stay for the following year.

The format was a simple one: a buffet and dance that celebrated the long summer evenings. The weather had remained dry and warm so the doors from the dining room to the terrace were open wide, allowing residents to drift outside for some air and, if they wanted to, watch the sun set to the west around ten o'clock.

Paul, Adam, Julie and the rest of the staff scurried here and there to ensure the guests were catered for. Along the length of the interior wall ran tables dressed in crisp white linen and maroon napkins. Didier had provided a positive feast. Delicate vol-au-vents, flaky sausage rolls, dainty salmon and cucumber sandwiches, cheese and pineapple, pâté, egg mayonnaise, crusty bread, quiches, pickles and potato salad.

James watched as Didier, dressed in his whites, hovered at the entrance to make sure the food was set out exactly as he wished.

Anne and Beth had done a wonderful job with the floral arrangements, sticking to Didier's wish that they were not to have any perfume. The guests began making their selections and heading back to the many tables that surrounded the dance floor. Some had chosen to stay outside and enjoy the evening sunshine.

Anne, dressed in a midnight blue ball gown, gushed, 'This is lovely. And what a good idea to have a buffet instead of a sit-down dinner.'

Beth complimented her on her outfit. 'I can't believe you made this. You should be a professional seamstress.'

Embarrassed, Anne waved the comment away. 'Please don't try to compare this to your amazing purchase.'

'Y-you look like a film star,' said Stephen selecting items from the buffet. 'Are you going to have time to spill the beans about this c-case? Is that Father Sun man guilty of anything?'

'Patience, my friend,' said James popping a tiny sausage roll in his mouth. 'The band's about to start. We'll have a couple of dances, get people up on the floor and then ensconce ourselves outside.'

Two minutes later, the band launched into 'Happy Feet'. James slipped his hand into Beth's. 'May I have this dance?'

She didn't need asking twice. Beth adored dancing and James was pleased that he'd taken extra lessons all those years ago when he was still a young man. The pleasure of guiding Beth around the floor without tripping on her toes was delightful. They moved easily together and, for the next twenty minutes, waltzed, jived and foxtrotted. Alongside them, Harry had a lady in his arms, a guest about the same age as him. Fiona and William followed behind.

The band kept the pace going for a good half hour, then slowed the tempo down. The more relaxed 'In the Mood' was played and Beth decided they needed a drink. James caught Stephen's attention among the throng and signalled they would be outside.

They chose a table at the end of the terrace where they could enjoy the music but were able to chat without difficulty.

Adam brought over a jug of Pimms. 'Would you like some?'

'That would be lovely,' said Beth. 'Stephen and Anne will be joining us.'

The young man placed four glasses

alongside the jug.

James pulled him back. 'I say, Adam, how's your girlfriend?'

The young man beamed. 'She's very well, Lord Harrington. Thank you so much. I know you had a word with her.'

'She made her own choice, Adam, and I rather think you had something to do with it. She thinks a lot of you.'

Adam blushed and disappeared.

Beth admonished James. 'You shouldn't embarrass him like that.'

'I didn't. The man is always shy around you. If he wasn't such a gentleman I think I'd have to keep my eye on him.'

'He's the same age as Harry and Oliver!'

James winked. 'Men cannot help how they react if they are smitten.'

Anne sat down and demanded: 'Come on, James, we've been here an hour now and you've not said a word.'

With the drinks poured, James went over what had happened in the derelict building the previous evening; how the recording of the sea had fooled them; how the chirping of a pheasant had given him suspicions and how Stuart Drummond, aka Simon Drake, was a first cousin of Mother Moon's.

'Are y-you telling me that Father Sun had nothing to d-do with this?'

James couldn't help but laugh. 'Yes, that's exactly what I'm saying. He's a dreamer, Stephen. He lived his youth at the cinema dreaming. He read books that transported him to a world he wanted to live in. You saw the way he reacted when he heard Dulcie Faye lived in the village. You could tell he was star-struck. He lives in a fantasy world and wanted to create one for himself. Melanie told us he suffered with his nerves and started reading about ancient beliefs.

'When he read about some of these evangelical groups in America, he believed that sort of thing was for him. He truly thought he was doing something good. The religious aspect of it hindered things a little. He believed in something but not necessarily a particular deity. The Druids, the Celts, the American Indians — they were the sort of thing he could relate to, so he opened the commune. He was being completely honest with you about not having a problem with people worshipping their own god.'

'He had no i-idea that s-something was going on in that building?'

'None whatsoever. Beverley Kendall was, unfortunately, part of the gang. She married Johnny Norton because she loved him and indulged him in his fantasy. She wanted him to be happy. She organised everything there so he wouldn't suffer with stress. When Simon and Agnes Drake saw the set-up, they saw the opportunity and Beverley was enticed by the money involved. They were making thousands. Poor Johnny hadn't a clue what was going on. He was so besotted with his wife, he didn't realise she was part of anything untoward.

'Simon worked in the art world and that derelict building or, rather, the basement of it, was perfect for what he was working on. It was the ideal hidey-hole. They paid Johnny Norton five hundred a month to keep him ticking over. They're a rich family and poor

Johnny didn't question it.'

'That's an awful lot of money,' said Anne.

'Not to the Kendalls. Simon had quite a business going on. He was a fine-art student, owned a gallery in London. According to Herbie he is, was, well-respected in the art world.'

'What happened?' said Anne, adding that it sounded as if he had everything he needed in life.

James topped up their glasses as Beth carried on with the story.

'Money,' she said. 'He's one of those men who love money and what it can bring. He had the idea of creating the fake paintings.'

'Drake,' said James, 'knew of the private collections through his own contacts. He studied which of those contacts he could make use of. Take our Mrs Millerson. Simon Drake, it tran-spires, used to stay with her when he was at university. He's a friend of the family so she wouldn't suspect him. She didn't even mention him to George when he asked if anyone had taken an interest. It's a bit like the postman or milkman: they become invisible. She was thinking of strangers when, all of the time, it was a family friend.'

'Let m-me see if I have this right. Drake studies those people who have a specific painting or drawing in their collection. One that can be copied.'

'And one,' James elaborated, 'that isn't well-known. It's difficult to fake a recognisable piece of art to pass on.'

'He takes it, has it copied, and returns the copy to the owner.'

'Where Mrs Millerson was concerned, Drake had a soft spot for her. He copied it and returned the original. Sold the fake and the fraudulent provenance on to a buyer.'

Beth shook her head. 'How do people come up with these ideas?'

'And the work was b-being carried out in the ruins.'

'Mmm,' said James, 'there's a basement underneath the ruin. I must admit that was ingenious. Drake blindfolded the artists, took them on a trip in the car and brought them back to the same place. It only came to light because of Bert. If he hadn't been camping by the commune we would never have known.'

Beth reminded him of the reel-to-reel recorder.

'Yes, that jolted my memory. Both GJ and I heard the sea but, actually, that's exactly what it was, the sound. I couldn't put my finger on it at first. But now I recall getting out of the car and remembering how still everything was. But when I was in the basement, I heard a distance whooshing of the sea. When someone set that recorder going in the village hall, it slotted into place. And that young lad, Brother Neptune, said he heard engines. Well, that could have been the printing machine and, of course, Simon Drake coming and going.'

'And the pheasant,' Beth said.

'A more tenuous sound but, yes, I heard the distinctive cluck of a pheasant and, quite honestly, you don't often hear them near the coast. They're birds that prefer the countryside.'

'What h-happens to Drake?'

'Simon and Agnes Drake have been

charged and they'll receive their sentence sometime in the next few months. Beverley Kendall was found this morning trying to board a train to York so I'm sure that charges will follow there too. The police were unable to bring any charges against Johnny Barton. He appears to be in shock and completely demoralised. His world has collapsed and George thinks his nervous condition has returned.'

'What about all of those brothers and sisters at the commune?' asked Anne.

'Entirely innocent and joined the commune for the reasons they stated.'

Stephen shifted in his chair. 'I know it's s-selfish of me to ask but, what's h-happening with the commune?'

'You'll be pleased to hear that the Celestial Faith Commune has closed its doors. Without the contribution from the Kendalls, the place makes no money and Barton now thinks the house is tainted. I get the impression that he can't cope. George said he's moving back home, to his parents. Perhaps he'll think of something that'll work up there. My feeling is that he'll be forever searching.'

'And was it Drake who killed Bernard Potter?' asked Anne.

'On orders from his aunt. Agnes Drake was one Sister Andromeda, the elderly lady that I believe you met.' He registered the shock on their faces. 'She made the odd appearance as a doddery old lady just to keep an eye on things in the commune. She made sure the members didn't speak about Sister Bellatrix. She saw Potter poking his nose in and told Simon to do something. Draining the brake fluid was the first thing that sprang to mind. They worked well together. She did the organising, he had the contacts.'

'And Wendy Potter?'

Beth put her glass down. 'Back home with her mother. But what a shame that she didn't believe her father when he first voiced his suspicion.'

They reflected on how that would have been a life saved.

James swigged the rest of his Pimms. 'Come along, there's a wonderful band in there. We shouldn't be sitting out here.'

They danced until the band finished playing and Beth admitted that she didn't think she could dance anymore. James had had the occasional rest but Harry had insisted on stepping in to whisk his mother round the floor. The Merryweathers had departed a little earlier and Fiona and William, more used to farming than dancing, had retired at eleven. At one o'clock, a little later than scheduled, the band played the last tune.

It was two in the morning before the pair of them returned home. They made their way upstairs, footsore and exhausted. James turned the bedside lights on and, on Beth's request, unclasped her necklace.

He kissed the nape of her neck. 'Isn't this where we said we were going to pick up?'

She turned to him and smoothed his hair back. 'I think it was.'

He cupped her face and kissed her.

GRANDMA HARRINGTON'S CHICKEN PIE

Will make 3–4 servings

Half a dozen mushrooms sliced
1 leek sliced
1 small onion chopped and diced
2 chicken breasts cut into small pieces
1 tablespoon of plain flour
17 fl oz/500ml chicken stock (generally two or three stock cubes)
3.5 oz/100g broccoli florets
3.5 oz/100g peas
2 tablespoons of sour cream
Salt and pepper

1. Fry the mushrooms and the onion for a few minutes until they begin to brown
2. Add the leek and the chicken
3. Sprinkle in the flour
4. Add the stock a little at a time
5. Then add the broccoli and peas

6. Once the mixture begins to thicken, stir in your cream

We often have this mixture without any pastry. It makes a lovely summer dish with new potatoes. However, if you prefer it as a pie, simply place in a pie dish and cover with puff pastry.

Place in the oven on gas mark 5 until the pastry is cooked.

We do hope that you have enjoyed reading this large print book.

Did you know that all of our titles are available for purchase?

We publish a wide range of high quality large print books including:
Romances, Mysteries, Classics
General Fiction
Non Fiction and Westerns

Special interest titles available in large print are:
The Little Oxford Dictionary
Music Book, Song Book
Hymn Book, Service Book

Also available from us courtesy of Oxford University Press:
Young Readers' Dictionary
(large print edition)
Young Readers' Thesaurus
(large print edition)

For further information or a free brochure, please contact us at:
Ulverscroft Large Print Books Ltd.,
The Green, Bradgate Road, Anstey,
Leicester, LE7 7FU, England.
Tel: (00 44) **0116 236 4325**
Fax: (00 44) **0116 234 0205**

DECEPTION

V. J. Banis

Playboy Danton Rhodes preys on rich women, squandering their fortunes before the inevitable divorce. He never expected to fall in love with Lois Carter, a married woman with a watertight prenuptial agreement; but when he learns that Lois's stepdaughter Dee needs to marry before her next birthday in order to receive her inheritance, Danton smells an opportunity. As Dee's cousin Helen arrives at the family home, she finds chaos — Lois has been violently attacked, and the suspect is none other than the familiar face she picked up along the way . . .

THE MAN ALL AMERICA HATED

Gordon Landsborough

In the aftermath of World War Two, Alec McCrae is the most hated American anywhere: he acted as intelligence officer for the Japanese and tortured American prisoners, sending thousands to forced-labour gangs. McCrae has managed to elude his pursuers for six years — but when he and his associates are finally exposed and confronted on a flight bound for Australia, he causes the plane to crash-land on a deserted Pacific island. And if the fugitives are to remain free, they will have to murder all the surviving crew and passengers . . .